THE CRY

Helen FitzGerald is one of thirteen children and grew up in Victoria, Australia. She now lives in Glasgow with her husband and two children. Helen has worked as a social worker for over ten years. She has published three previous novels with Faber: *Dead Lovely* (2007), *My Last Confession* (2009) and *The Donor* (2011).

Also by Helen FitzGerald

DEAD LOVELY

MY LAST CONFESSION

THE DONOR

The Cry

HELEN FITZGERALD

faber and faber

First published in this edition in 2013
by Faber and Faber Limited
Bloomsbury House,
74–77 Great Russell Street,
London WC1B 3DA

Typeset by Faber and Faber Ltd
Printed and bound by CPI Group (UK) Ltd, Croydon CR0 4YY

A CIP record for this book
is available from the British Library

ISBN 978–0–571–28770–3

2 4 6 8 10 9 7 5 3 1

Part One

THE INCIDENT

I

JOANNA

13 February

It was the fault of airport security.

At airport security, Joanna's nine-week-old baby boy was screaming. Her partner was busy taking off his trainers. A stocky uniformed woman was saying: 'Can't take these.'

'What?' Joanna asked, her newborn gnawing at her T-shirt through his howls.

'These liquids. The bottles are more than a hundred millilitres. If you need more for the flight, you've got to have proof. Do you have something in writing?'

'No.'

'In that case, I'll have to dispose of them.'

'But you can't. It's Calpol – paracetamol – for the baby, and antibiotics. I've got an ear infection. And, look, they're not full.'

'Can I help?' a freshly scanned and shoeless Alistair offered.

'We'll have to throw these out,' the security woman repeated.

'I told you about the hundred-millilitre rule, Joanna.'

'Did you?' Probably. She couldn't remember.

Alistair turned from Joanna to security woman, from

problem to solution. 'Can one of us nip over to Boots and get some smaller bottles?'

'Well, yes, you can do that. But you'd need to go to the back of the queue and come through again.'

'You go on with Noah,' Joanna suggested. 'I'll go back and sort this.'

She handed over her baby and zig-zagged back the way she had come.

*

It was the fault of airport security.

If Joanna hadn't gone back, if she hadn't bought two small, clear hundred-millilitre bottles from Boots, if she hadn't poured liquids into each while kneeling on the floor in front of WH Smith, if she hadn't waited in the queue for another hour while her breasts ached: if she hadn't done any of these things, then she would still have her baby.

*

The flight to Melbourne took twenty-one hours. The first seven – Glasgow to Dubai – were the worst. Noah cried the entire time. She couldn't recall one minute when he didn't. For five of these hours, Joanna tried doing the things she was supposed to do, in the order she was supposed to do them.

Round One. One hour from Glasgow. Plane flying over the North Sea. Alistair watching a movie which made him laugh very loudly which made Joanna want to kick him.

4

Food? She pressed his head towards her breast – too hard perhaps? Was he biting and pinching at her deliberately? Was that a punch?

Nappy? She felt inside it with her finger. It was clean, thankfully, because if it hadn't been, her finger would now have poo on it.

Bored? The rattle and the Bananas in Pyjamas teddy bear made his eyes turn evil.

Tired? Are you kidding? At nine weeks, his determined angriness gave him so much energy that he almost wriggled himself out of the airline cot attached to the bulkhead in front of her. She caught him just in time.

Round Two. Three hours from Glasgow.

Plane flying over Germany. Alistair asleep.

Food? Wah.

Nappy? Wah.

Bored? WAH.

Tired? What sort of a mother are you?

*

She went through this routine, over and over. Round Three. Four. Five. And so on. Just as the mothers at the breastfeeding group had taught her.

'He's trying to communicate with his beautiful little voice,' one of them said. 'You just need to listen.'

'It's really not rocket science,' said another. 'Isn't he cute! Little petal.'

She hated the mothers at the breastfeeding group.

Did she hate Noah?

Is that why he's gone?

*

Alistair had walked Noah up and down the aisle twice in the second hour. He was glorious. People smiled at him, said: 'Oh, the wee soul, he's tired.' Offered to hold him for a while. Poor guy. New man. What a hero. Why had he chosen an unworthy and useless woman to be the mother of his child? He walked forty feet in the second hour, and then he handed Noah over, sat down, and ate his meal. Loved his meal. Enjoyed it. With red wine. He was so content that he fell asleep before the air hostess had cleared his plate.

Joanna hadn't managed any food or wine. Given the choice, she'd have opted for the wine, even though breastfeeding mothers get stared at with chisel eyes if they dare to drink.

Alistair was asleep. His very large head, which Noah had inherited (thanks for that, Alistair) was resting comfortably on a luminous green inflatable pillow. He looked pretty. He always looked pretty. When she first saw him at the polling booth, she was taken aback by his boy-band prettiness. You don't get men like that in Glasgow. His carefully messed dark brown hair never budged, and was perfectly in place as he slept. His hair helped him look younger than his forty-one years, standing erect to camouflage the thinning patch at the middle-back of his massive head.

How could he sleep through this? Noah's crying had drowned out the engine noise and the air conditioning. People were pressing earphones to their heads, turning the entertainment system's volume to maximum. They looked at Joanna occasionally, saying so much with their eyes. *What is wrong with your kid? Why, WHY, did they seat me near you?* These people would complain when they arrived at their destinations. *Some women should not be allowed to conceive.*

She gathered these looks and added them to her pool of bubbling rage. Her ear infection had taken hold of the back of her head and neck – a heavy, shuddering, all-consuming pain that made it almost impossible to think clearly. Noah would probably scream more loudly and the passengers judge her more harshly if she put him down to get two caplets of Anadin Extra and a dose of antibiotics from her hand luggage, so she wouldn't risk it, not yet.

'Emirates is child friendly,' she had read online. They weren't friendly at all. They were judgemental child-hating bitches, especially the one with the bright red bob. She was over forty, her hair dyed and groomed to perfection bar a few millimetres of grey roots; her size fourteen body bridled by magic knickers and padded bra. She'd plastered on so much foundation you could trace a wee set of boobs on her chin with a lengthy fingernail if you had the inclination and the fingernail. She was on the way out, Joanna assumed, clinging on to a young-girl's job for dear life, but not to the extent that she thought it necessary to be kind. This woman had cleared

Joanna's uneaten meal away while she was walking Noah up and down the aisle, rocking him back and forth in a pointless attempt to subdue him. This woman had said 'Yes, of course' when Joanna asked for an extra warm towel to wipe the puke from her shoulder, but hadn't delivered it. This woman hated Joanna, and Noah.

Everyone on this jumbo jet hated them. Probably even the pilots, who must have been able to hear him from the cockpit. They probably couldn't hear the radio because of him. They may well have considered crashing the plane to escape this noise.

Not like a cat on heat, the noise. Not as many pauses.

Not like a horror film scream. They're quite satisfying, those. Joanna did them sometimes, locked in the bathroom. It was her *time out*, as the mothers at the breastfeeding group had suggested. They probably didn't mean *time out* should be spent screaming horror-movie screams in a locked bathroom, but this is what she had taken to doing, since Noah.

Not pigs being slaughtered at the abattoir either. Joanna had heard this on a documentary on the Discovery Channel once. They sounded more content, the pigs.

She could not describe his cry. All she knew was that it never stopped and it had to stop.

Other people's babies didn't cry like Noah. There were two infants in her section of the plane. They hardly made a sound. Their mothers looked happy. Their mothers looked as if they were in love with them. Their mothers looked as

8

if they were in love with their fathers. Perhaps because their fathers were not sleeping.

Yep, Alistair was still sleeping.

STOP CRYING, NOAH!

She didn't want to wake Alistair. She would be a martyr instead.

Alistair had always managed to sleep. Every night, he went to bed around midnight, put his head on the pillow, and was dreaming happily within ten minutes. It surprised her that he had never once, ONCE, woken to deal with Noah's cry. Maybe he wasn't even asleep, clever fucker.

Right now, four hours into the seven-hour flight to Dubai, she looked at Alistair with his mouth half open, and wondered about smothering his pretty face with the pillow.

Oh, she wasn't really imagining that at all. No, no. She was just tired. She hadn't slept for more than three hours in a row for nine weeks. Plus, her neck was going to explode. She desperately needed her Anadin caplets and antibiotics. She stood up, with Noah over her right shoulder, and opened the luggage compartment above her. One of her bags fell out onto the lap of the elderly woman in the seat behind her.

'Oo!' The woman rubbed her thin leg, in pain.

'Oh shit; sorry,' Joanna said.

'I'm fine, really.' She stopped rubbing her leg and smiled.

Joanna felt terrible. And she should not have said 'shit'. 'Excuse the language. Here, let me put it back.'

'No, no, you have enough on your plate.' The elderly woman

stood and lifted the bag. It wobbled precariously as she attempted to get it back in the compartment. The passenger next to the old lady eyeballed Joanna as if to say *On top of everything, now you are letting a little old lady lift your bag!*

'Have you checked his nappy?' the injured woman asked.

'Erm. I did a while ago. I was just going to get—'

'Maybe you should try the nappy?' The woman made a sniffing noise.

Oh Lordy, she had forgotten the routine. She hadn't gone through the steps for a while now. Silly Joanna. She lifted Noah up and sniffed at his bum. The elderly woman and the passenger beside her winced. Oops, she shouldn't have sniffed at his bum like that, in full view of everyone. Joanna had forgotten how to behave in public.

He smelt. He was dirty. There was a reason for his cry!

'You're right!' Joanna grinned a crazy grin at the woman. Hallelujah!

Joanna put Noah in the cot and returned hand luggage Number One to the overhead compartment (black suitcase containing medicines, emergency toiletries, toothbrushes, and books for Alistair to read because Alistair would probably be able to read *three* books on this long-haul flight from Glasgow to Melbourne). She retrieved hand luggage Number Two (blue sausage bag containing nappies for Noah, wipes for Noah, Sudocrem for Noah, spare clothes for Noah, blankets for Noah, toys that Noah hated for Noah) and raced off to the toilet.

It was at the front of her section of the plane. The door proudly advertised baby changing facilities. It was occupied.

Her child stank.

And screamed.

People were tired now. They'd been flying for five hours. The cabin lights were off. It was nearly midnight in the UK. The four people in the queue in front of her had obviously decided to avoid eye contact altogether. If they looked her in the eye, they would have found it impossible not to throttle her.

At last, the toilet door was open. In a minute, she would have changed the nappy, and the world. The reason for the cry would be gone. Noah would fall asleep. Joanna would order a glass of wine without caring what the red-bobbed bitch thought, drink it in the dark, no eyes looking at her breast-feeding crime, and then fall asleep herself.

She had forgotten to put on her shoes. She forgot everything nowadays, Joanna. She forgot what she had just done and what she should do next. The toilet floor was covered in piss. As she stood over the smeared toilet, putting the lid down with her pinky and pulling down the tiny baby changing board, she could feel urine on the floor seeping through the thin airline socks from her disappointing Emirates goody bag.

She held his wriggling body still with her left forearm and fumbled to pull a wipe from the packet in the filthy sink. Nappy undone, she grimaced at his effort – four hard balls.

The petal was constipated. A breastfed baby should not be constipated. Maybe it was the cheese she had scoffed before driving to the airport. One third of a packet of strong Cheddar. On its own. She had no time to flourish it with bread or biscuits. Her greed and poor planning had made his tummy sore.

She couldn't wrap the nappy with one hand. As she was trying, the plane dipped suddenly and the seatbelt signs beeped on – turbulence. Noah wriggled. The four hard pieces of baby poo rolled onto the floor. Forearm still on his chest, she tugged a few sheets of toilet paper from the dispenser, reached down, and scrambled to grab the moving excrement. No big deal. Shit was part of the shit job. It was no more bothersome to her than picking up four Maltesers. She put the wrapped poo in the used nappy, managed to stick the bundle together with the Velcro, and shoved it into the overflowing bin.

Wipe, Sudocrem, nappy on. This was one of the many chants Joanna had taken to repeating. If she didn't say them to herself, she would forget. She would forget to put his nappy on.

When she walked out of the toilet door, the queue had grown, and she realised she was desperate for a pee. She had forgotten to go. Too late. She'd go some other time.

Joanna's ears were hurting. She hadn't managed to take her medication. Best laid plans. She'd probably missed two doses already. She walked past the steely queue and made her way to her seat.

Alistair was still asleep.

Despite the nappy change, Noah was still crying.

Just as she sat down, the air hostess with the red bob approached her with a kind smile.

'Excuse me,' she said.

Joanna looked up hopefully. She was going to help. At last.

The air hostess leant down and whispered, 'Some of the passengers are complaining.'

'Sorry?'

'The crying is upsetting the passengers.'

A film of angry blood travelled to her eyes. 'Oh really? Which ones?' She stood up, almost hitting the air hostess' leant-down head with her screaming infant.

'Just take your seat, madam,' the air hostess said.

'Hi everyone!' Joanna said, loudly enough for ten rows of five seats to hear, but not loudly enough to wake Alistair. 'This helpful lady has just informed me that some of you have been complaining about Noah.'

She was holding her baby like a mad Michael Jackson on the balcony. Realising this, she clenched Noah to her chest and continued: 'Who was it?' Not just ten rows now, the whole section could hear her. They hushed. There was a drama going down on flight EK028 to Dubai.

'Whoever you are, I know how you feel!' she said.

Joanna nudged past the air hostess – who looked a little frightened after making a weak attempt to stop her – and addressed the elderly woman who'd helped her earlier. 'Was it you?'

The elderly woman shook her head.

'You, then?' she said to a girl around eighteen years old sitting five seats back. 'Would you like to take him for a while? See if you can calm him down?'

'You?' Joanna had moved two rows further down and was holding the wailing infant in front of a thirty-year-oldish man in a suit. 'Would you like to complain personally? Well here he is!'

'Listen,' the businessman said. 'You need to calm down.'

'CALM DOWN?' she yelled.

'Joanna, honey, how 'bout you give him to me?' This came from Alistair. The air hostess had woken him and escorted him to the scene of the outburst.

'Sorry, everyone,' he said before thinning and cutie-pieing his voice as if bribing a dog with a biscuit. 'Come on . . . just hand him over to me, darling.'

Joanna almost threw the baby at him.

Or did she *actually* do this?

'She just needs some sleep,' Alistair said loudly, smiling. Almost everyone smiled back at him.

The glorious hero.

Joanna stomped back to her seat in her stinking socks, her pretty perfect man and slightly less distraught son trailing behind her.

*

'Hold him for a sec,' Alistair said, handing him back to

Joanna and getting the bag with the medicines from the over-head locker. He opened one of the clear bottles of medicine and tasted it. 'That's supposed to be strawberry? Yuk! Here, this'll settle him.' He spooned the clear liquid into Noah's protesting mouth, Joanna pushing what had escaped back in with her finger as gently as she could.

Alistair returned the bottle to the case and the case to the overhead locker. 'I think he's hungry. Look, he's having a go at your shoulder.' Noah's mouth was open, his head moving to the side, searching for food.

Joanna undid her shirt and pulled down her bra. Once upon a time, she would have taken care to cover her nipple in public. Now she didn't give a shit. Alistair placed the baby on her lap and he began to feed.

She felt the painful tingle in her breast ease and her nipple soften. The release of the milk felt like a class A drug might feel: ah, to be whisked away on a warm magic carpet. Maybe one day she'd try a class A drug.

Noah fell asleep as soon as the wheels hit the tarmac.

Of course he did.

2

MELBOURNE SUPREME COURT

27 July

'You were a passenger on Emirates Flight EK028 from Glasgow to Dubai on 13 February this year?' a female lawyer asked the sixty-something woman in the witness box.

'I'd been visiting an old colleague. He lives in Stirling.' The lady in the witness box, Ms Amery, did not seem nervous at all, quite the opposite.

'Do you recognise the accused?' The lawyer pointed to Joanna, who was sitting at the front of the courtroom beside her own lawyer. Joanna had been pointed to a lot these last hours. Each one stabbed harder at her chest.

'Yes.'

'Can you tell me how you met her?' The female lawyer spoke slowly, loudly.

'I may be old but my hearing and my comprehension are fine. No need to talk to me like I'm a brainless gnat heading for the hospice.' Ms Amery's comeback obliterated the supercilious look on the lawyer's face. 'I was seated behind her on the flight from Glasgow to Dubai and although the plane changed for the second leg from Dubai to Melbourne, we kept the same seat numbers, aisle seats they were. I was 18H,

Joanna was in the bulkheads with the baby cot – 17H.'

'She was travelling with her partner and her baby, yes?'

'That's right. She was . . . She . . . was . . .'

'Out of control?'

'Leading the witness!' Joanna's lawyer had taken to his feet.

The female lawyer smiled an apology. 'Can you describe Ms Lindsay's behaviour on the flight from Glasgow?'

'I was trying to find the exact word. It was a long flight and she was very stressed. Her baby wouldn't stop crying and no one was helping her.'

'Was she rough with the infant?'

'Objection! Ms Amery's definition of "rough" is subjective.' Joanna's lawyer didn't look up as he spoke, which somehow gave his words more power.

'Overruled.' The judge nodded to the witness. 'You can answer the question Ms Amery.'

'How was she with the baby? Gentle? Rough?' The female lawyer was aggressive now.

'Well . . . he wouldn't settle.'

'Was Ms Lindsay rough with her infant?'

'I wouldn't say—'

'Answer the question please. Yes or No. Was she rough with the infant?'

Ms Amery looked at Joanna again, and then at the lawyer, who moved in closer.

'Was she rough with Noah? Was. She. ROUGH?' The lawyer was no more than five inches from the witness's head.

'Yes.'

'You're saying Ms Lindsay was rough with baby Noah. She shook him.'

'Yes, yes, but—'

'No further questions.'

3

JOANNA

13 February

The fifteen-and-a-half-hour flight from Dubai to Melbourne was uneventful. They boarded the plane after a two-hour wait in transit. The airline had promised Joanna that her buggy would be available for them during this time. It wasn't. It was in the hold. There was no getting it out. And there were no spare buggies in the airport.

Despite this, it was a beautiful two hours. Joanna sat on a chair outside a café and gazed at the contented baby in her arms. She couldn't understand why she had been angry. How could she have been mad with this gorgeous child? Ah, she loved him. Little Noah.

Alistair looked sprightly after his long snooze and tapped away on his laptop. She adored his energy. From the moment Alistair woke, to the moment he put his head on the pillow, he was purposeful and happy. While Joanna could do nothing for long periods of time, often indulging in mini-depressions involving daytime talk shows and True Movies, Alistair was always busy, positive and uncomplicated. Her perfect antidote.

'I'm a nutjob,' she said, stroking his forearm.

'*My* nutjob!' Alistair smiled and kissed her on the lips.

So she was. Since his wife fled, she was all his: his to stroke on the forearm, to kiss on the lips, to get mad at when she wasn't coping, to ask for help, because he would always have the energy and the willingness to find solutions.

Need to believe we are for ever? *Have my baby.*

Need the tap fixed? *I fixed it!*

Need a mushy email? *Joanna, last night you looked more beautiful than any woman I have ever seen. Let's go to Amsterdam next weekend!*

Need to be told you're a wonderful mother and the cleverest and sexiest woman in the world?

'A nutjob who also happens to be a wonderful mother and the cleverest and sexiest woman in the world,' Alistair said, kissing her again then returning to his laptop.

In the first two years of their relationship, Alistair had been wildly romantic. After his wife Alexandra found out about their affair and left, he made big gestures. The beautiful love letters (well, emails), the trip to Amsterdam, the living room full of red roses when she turned twenty-seven, making love to her months later while saying: 'Remember this, can you feel it? We're making our child.'

She kissed Alistair on the shoulder: her administer of medicine, her fixer of things, her maker of happiness. Noah would sleep more soon, she would sleep more soon, and the roar and the tingle of those first two years would return.

Alistair was on the laptop typing an urgent press release involving the transport minister, a married fifty-two-year-old who'd claimed expenses for posh meals with a member of the Young Labour Society. The story wouldn't have been a story if the supporter in question wasn't blonde, the owner of a set of DD breasts, and only just sixteen. Joanna read the headline: 'Ross Johnstone defends "legitimate party meetings with promising young politician".'

'You quashing a shitstorm, hon?' Joanna asked.

He pressed Ctrl+S. 'Quashed.'

It wasn't long before Joanna fell asleep on Alistair's shoulder.

*

'It's time to board.' Alistair was smiling at her when she woke. 'Are you okay? What a nightmare that first leg was. He seems settled now, eh?'

'He does.' He had the longest eyelashes, this boy. And dark, dark hair, like his dad. He'd be a heart-throb one day.

'Here, you need your antibiotics.' Alistair opened the bottle, took a dab from the rim, taste-tested it, and spooned the medicine into Joanna's mouth. 'Is it still very sore?'

'It was, during the descent. It's a bit better now.' She put her hand on Alistair's cheek. 'I love you.'

'I love you too.' He kissed her on the forehead. 'I'm taking him for this flight, all right? You feed him when I say, but otherwise, you have nothing to do with him.'

'Really?' She looked at her sleeping baby again, lulled by his peacefulness, reluctant to give him up for so long. 'Oh, but . . .'

'But nothing. You need rest. And when we get to Point

Lonsdale, you're going to express some milk and Mum's going to take him to her house for twenty-four hours.'

'You organised it already?' Imagine – time off to sleep, eat, go to the toilet, eat cheese *with* biscuits, go for a walk, make love . . .

'I arranged it with Mum two weeks ago,' Alistair said.

Typical Alistair: thinking ahead, looking after her, getting things done. Sometimes, she had to pinch herself. Was he real? Was he really hers?

*

Joanna couldn't remember much of the first part of the flight from Dubai to Melbourne. For the first eight hours, she slept, waking twice when Alistair gently prompted her to feed the baby. It was the best sleep she'd had since his birth.

With five and a half hours to go, Joanna woke with a jolt. The cry. Her ear was throbbing with pain and Noah's noise was jabbing at it. Oh God, no, not this again. Every day seemed the same, every night, every minute, the same. It would never be different. This was her life now. Until she died.

The cry was coming from the back of the plane. Joanna looked behind her and saw that Alistair was holding Noah in the queue for the toilets, nappy and wipes in hand. She put her trainers on and walked towards Alistair and the baby.

'Let me take him,' she said.

'Absolutely not. He's fine. Just a dirty nappy.'

The toilet door opened and the businessman Joanna had accosted on the previous flight exited. When he saw Joanna, he glowered. He'd worn a suit the entire trip and it appeared unscathed. Lucky guy. Joanna's clothes were covered in all sorts of shite.

'Get back to your seat and rest!' Alistair said.

'Can I not have a pee first?'

'Well, okay.'

Locked in the cubicle, Joanna berated herself. Alistair had managed with the baby for eight hours, much longer than she'd managed on the first leg of the flight, and he was still cheerful, still willing and able to keep going. He was so much more capable than her. Why did she find a tiny baby so hard to deal with? The breastfeeding bitches were right: it wasn't rocket science.

Joanna did as Alistair kindly suggested after going to the loo, but couldn't rest. Her ear was killing her and Noah's crying was getting louder, more distressed. The nappy change hadn't worked.

'Have a kip, hon,' she eventually said to Alistair. 'You've done a marathon, you're a star. I've had enough sleep – I'll be fine, honest.'

'Are you sure?'

'Really, I'm fine.'

Alistair handed the baby over and was asleep within ten minutes.

For the next three hours, Joanna went through the routine

again and again. Nappy? Bored? Tired? Food? Nappy? Bored? Tired? Food? Nappy? Bored? Tired? Food?

She tried the emergency dummy she'd packed in case he might change his mind about it.

Nappy? Bored? Tired? Food?

She tried walking, rocking, singing, humming, tickling, massaging.

Nappy? Bored? Tired? Food?

The looks had started again. Passengers were getting annoyed. A young air hostess was scowling at her.

She wouldn't lose it this time. She would cope.

She might need a little assistance, though. There was nothing wrong with needing a little assistance.

It wasn't easy, getting the Calpol in. She lay Noah on her lap, his head resting on the crook of her left arm, opened the bottle, filled the spoon, leaned his head back, and gently prised his mouth open with her finger. Noah wriggled as she moved the spoon towards his mouth – some of the liquid dribbled down his chin and onto his bright red bib. He jerked his hand and a good dollop of it ended up joining the many stains on Joanna's once-white T-shirt too.

She put the medicine in the black case and the medicine-coated bib in one of its outside pockets, put the case back in the locker, and sat down.

Noah must have taken some of the medicine in because, within half an hour, he had fallen asleep on her lap. She felt her eyes closing within minutes of his.

When Joanna woke, Alistair was sitting beside her reading a book and Noah was wrapped up on his lap, baby-seatbelt on for landing. They were descending into Melbourne. The city sprawled on beneath her. In the distance, she could see smoke from the fires that were raging.

Joanna had travelled around Europe a lot after university, and every summer since she'd been teaching she went to Spain or Italy or France, but she'd never been to the southern hemisphere. She dreamed that one day she and Alistair would build a holiday house here with the money she inherited when her mum died. It'd have a veranda overlooking the sea. She'd researched the trees she'd have in her garden: a wattle tree, a lemon, and a *Syzygium*. She'd make Lilly Pilly jam from the pretty pink-red berries of the *Syzygium* while Noah jumped on the trampoline.

'Has he slept the whole time?' she asked Alistair.

'He woke and cried for a bit,' Alistair said, 'but I got him settled. You slept through it! Well done. See, it is possible.'

Joanna felt invigorated, happy. 'You, Mr Robertson, are the best thing that has ever happened to me.'

4

JOANNA

15 February

Alistair transferred Noah to the nifty buggy-cum-car-seat which was waiting for them just outside the plane. The baby was wrapped snugly in his blue blanket, his tiny face barely visible.

'Shh, no!' Alistair scolded Joanna when she leant down to check on him. 'Don't wake him!'

Alistair was right. Even looking at him might cause this blissful calm to erupt.

Wheeling Noah ahead of them in the buggy, they manoeuvred through the queues at immigration, collected their baggage, and exited the air-conditioned terminal building.

Joanna wheezed in a mouthful of boiling air and panicked – it felt like someone had put the nozzle of a hair dryer in her mouth.

They walked as fast as they could to the car rentals parking area, not wanting to disturb Noah by removing his blanket.

'Can you smell it?' Alistair's Australian accent was stronger already.

Joanna sucked thick air in through her nose. 'Eucalyptus?'

'Eucalyptus and . . .' Alistair clicked the doors open to the hire car, put his hand up and held it out '... bushfire.' A piece of ash from the fire that had been raging for three days floated down and landed on the palm of his hand. 'God it's good to be home.'

Alistair detached the buggy seat from its frame and strapped it into the car. He put the cases that were on the trolley Joanna had wheeled from the terminal in the boot, the smaller ones on top. A perfect fit. He'd probably asked the rental people to give the measurements of the boot to make sure the cases would fit before choosing this model. Joanna smiled at her organised manly man.

He sat in the driver's seat beside Joanna and checked his phone. 'Shit!' he whispered.

'What's wrong?' she asked quietly.

'That young labour girl with the tits has spoken to the *Daily Mail*. Says the dinners with Johnstone weren't just dinners. He liked to wear a dog collar. Shit shit shit. What's the time?'

Joanna looked at her watch, which she'd adjusted when they taxied in. 'It's 3 p.m. here.'

'So that's 6 a.m. in the UK. I'll call the office when we get to the house.'

*

Air conditioning now almost too chilly, they headed along the Tullamarine Freeway.

'Never thought I'd say this, but I am aching to be in Geelong,' Alistair said, looking at the smoggy Melbourne skyline ahead. Geelong, a one-hour drive from Melbourne, was a poor cousin to the money-dripping metropolis of Victoria's capital and Alistair had been scathing of it as a teenager and young man. He'd craved Melbourne or, better, London. But as he made his way to the Princes Highway which would take them west, he looked more and more excited. He told Joanna he was looking forward to eating burgers on the beachfront and mooching in the country-town-feel shopping centre and driving along the Great Ocean Road. But most of all, he was desperate to see his daughter, Chloe.

Joanna first met Chloe four years ago. It wasn't a good meeting. Joanna was in bed making love to her daddy. Chloe was standing in the bedroom door, next to her mummy.

'Who's that?' ten-year-old Chloe had asked, pointing to the naked woman on top of her father.

Joanna jumped off her lover, grabbed the sheet and attempted to wrap herself in it.

'That,' Alexandra said, 'is a fucking slut.'

Alistair sat up, completely naked. 'Alexandra, watch your language,' he said.

'Oh sorry, darling, of course,' his wife said to her already deflated husband. 'Swearing will traumatise our daughter.'

'Chloe, go to the kitchen,' Alistair ordered.

'But what are you doing with that woman?' Chloe asked.

'Kitchen! Now!'

Chloe obeyed her father and left the bedroom.

'Alexandra, will you please let us get dressed? We'll talk

about this calmly. Okay? And not in front of Chloe.'

They didn't talk calmly. Alexandra threw a lamp at Joanna, who dressed and left. Alexandra then hit Alistair, refused to discuss an amicable divorce, waited till Alistair left the following day for a conference, packed, and fled, taking Chloe with her.

Alistair phoned Chloe regularly in the months that followed, and would have flown to Australia to visit, if not for several emergencies in Westminster.

But his attempts to make contact dwindled in direct proportion to his growing desire to make a new family with Joanna. (*Need to believe we are for ever? Have my baby.*)

This new family might have been enough for him had the following story by feared Tory blogger James Moyer not popped up on his Google Alert shortly after Noah was born.

Aw, how sweet are these photos of Alistair Robertson and his family? Mum and Dad pushing their pride and joy through the Botanics. He's the right man to champion family values, the right man for Labour to prime for a safe seat in the next election.

But hang on, that woman's his mistress, not his wife.

And the baby's his second child, not his first. His first, fourteen-year-old Chloe, lives 12,000 miles away, and he hasn't bothered to see her for four years.

*And if you look even more closely, which I have, there's more ... The
ex-wife, Alexandra Donohue, was caught drink driving yesterday ...
on the way to collect her daughter from the animal sanctuary.*

The value of a Labour family?

Nada.

Alistair and Joanna had come to Australia to fight for custody
of Chloe. Alistair's lawyer was very confident. The mother
took the child from the UK without asking or even telling the
father: kidnapping, yes, they could call it that. The mother did
not reveal her whereabouts for over a month once she arrived
there: that'd be called non-cooperation or evasion of respon-
sibilities. The mother collected the child from her voluntary
work at the Healesville animal sanctuary under the influence
of alcohol, and was planning to drive the child home drunk:
that was neglect ... hell, that was criminal.

'It's not because of that idiotic blog,' Alistair said to Joanna
before they left. 'I don't care about work. Since Noah, since
our family, what matters is clearer than ever. That woman
was always a drinker, and now I know she's happy to endanger
the life of my little girl. Chloe should be safe. She should
be with her dad. She should be with an inspirational, kind,
caring, responsible woman – with you, Joanna – and with her
baby brother, she should be with her *family*.'

Joanna couldn't even cope with her own child. The thought

of looking after someone else's terrified her. But she loved making Alistair happy, and everything he said was fair and right.

As they drove along the freeway towards Geelong, Joanna turned to Alistair and said, 'Will she always hate me?'

'She doesn't hate you now,' he said, touching her thigh. 'She doesn't know you. Everything's going to be perfect. Everything's going to be just great.'

*

Alistair approached every situation, no matter how difficult, in the same way: Get the facts. Decide on a plan of attack. Get the job done.

According to Alistair, these were the facts of the affair:

He and his wife were strangers. When it ended they hadn't even had sex for a month.

Alexandra was, in fact, a mentally ill paranoid bitch with an addiction to alcohol.

He and Joanna were soul mates. She couldn't dispute this, could she? He had never felt this way before. She was his best friend. She was the love of his life.

Therefore there was nothing wrong with what they had done. They *had* to do it. They were *meant* to be together.

His initial plan of attack was simple: Explain the situation to Alexandra. Ask for a divorce. Remain friends in order to share the custody of an emotionally unscathed Chloe. Live happily ever after.

This plan hadn't worked well.

But Alistair maintained that he and Joanna had done the right thing, the only thing they *could* do, considering the strength of their love for one another. And it would all work out eventually if they were patient.

Alistair was a patient man.

And he'd been right in the end. Okay, so it had taken time, and it wasn't as simple as he'd hoped, but things are never simple.

It would work now. Everything would work now.

All they had to do was get the job done.

Get Chloe.

5

27 July

'State your name.'

'Chloe.'

'And your last name, Chloe?'

'Robertson.'

The girl, fourteen years old, appeared on a large television screen, set to the left of the judge and in front of the lawyer addressing her. She leaned her skinny upper body forward, as if she wanted to be inside the camera, and repeated in an innocent, childlike voice: 'Chloe Robertson.'

The ten-year-old girl Joanna had seen at the bedroom door four years earlier was now a tall adolescent. A line of light shone down the right side of the middle parting of her dark brown hair. She wore a T-shirt with 'Paolo Nutini' written on it. A Scottish singer. This was a dig, Joanna thought. She was sending the message that she loved Scotland, and that Joanna had made her leave. Joanna wondered if Chloe could see her. Was there a screen in her room which showed the courtroom?

'I'm just going to ask you a few questions, Chloe. Is that okay?' The lawyer, Amy Maddock, had two children of her own. Her voice sounded like one she had used many times to trick them – 'The needle won't hurt at all, I promise!'

'Yes.'

'Please stop me if I go too fast and ask me if you don't understand anything.'

'Okay.'

'Do you know this woman?' Ms Maddock's bony finger may as well have been a skewer in Joanna's chest. So the girl *could* see her. No matter how bad she felt since it happened, new things seemed to push her down further on a regular basis. The artist drew carefully with her pencil: eyes to sketchpad, eyes to Joanna. The scratching of pencil against paper overtook all other noises in the large courtroom.

'Yes,' Chloe said.

'How do you know her?'

'She had an affair with my dad.'

A teenager says it like it is, hey.

'When did you meet her?'

'I walked in on them in Edinburgh.'

'You "walked in on them". Who's "them"? What were they doing?'

'Objection. It's not in the best interests of a child to ask that.' Joanna's lawyer, Matthew Marks, came over as arrogant and posh. She wished she'd picked a lawyer with a child-friendly voice. This one sounded like the Child Snatcher in *Chitty Chitty Bang Bang.*

'Overruled. You can answer if you want to, Chloe, but I

think we understand what you mean.'

Joanna looked down at her lap and attempted to calm her breathing. *Don't answer, don't answer. No need to answer.*

'I'd like to answer please.'

The words jolted Joanna's head upright again. Chloe didn't sound childlike this time, but accusatory, almost sinister. She directed her eyes away from Joanna's and turned to the judge, a woman of around sixty. According to Joanna's lawyer, the judge's sons were both married with kids, and both doctors.

Judge, opposing lawyer: good mothers, both of them.

'They were doing it in my mum and dad's bed. I found out later she'd been after him for nine months.'

The courtroom artist was going for it now. A new reaction. A new page. Pencilling, rubbing, blowing, brushing the paper with her hand, pencilling again, eyes at Joanna, eyes at sketchpad. What was she seeing? The earth mother artist narrowed her eyes as she examined Joanna's face, answering her question: *A murdering slut, that's what.*

Joanna's nose was itchy and she'd been told she couldn't scratch it, not now. She couldn't scratch it and she couldn't fidget and she couldn't – *For God's sake, never!* – smile. She hadn't felt like smiling much *since*, but the daily coaching sessions Alistair had given her – about fidgeting and smiling and many other things – had firmly rooted that last idea in her head. *Don't smile, don't smile, remember Foxy Knoxy, remember Lindy.* She chanted it to herself, forgetting the original problem, which was a nose itch. *Why on earth would she smile? Don't, just don't.*

In the end, the urge to scratch subsided. She turned to the screen and focused: look sane, look responsible.

Chloe's eyes were right on hers. 'My mum's a good mum,' Chloe said. 'She and Dad were happy before her.'

6

JOANNA

15 February

Joanna turned to check on the baby. He was sound asleep, his face snuggled sideways into the blanket.

'He's going to be a lady-killer,' she said to Alistair, smiling. How she loved Noah when he slept.

'He's going to be prime minister,' Alistair said.

'Of Scotland!'

'Wash your mouth out!' Alistair scolded.

Alistair was a staunch Labour supporter. With a politics degree and MBA from Melbourne University, and a fierce determination to succeed, he had climbed from being a lowly council PR officer to political advisor to the Labour Party candidate of Victoria. He did such a good job that the British Labour Party poached him. As Alistair's father was Scottish, he was granted citizenship in the UK. He worked in London for two years until he was seconded to Scotland, where the Party was in need of a PR miracle. He was powerful and well respected, and – as reported in James Moyer's blog – was indeed being primed for a safe seat in the next election.

Joanna was socialist and pro independence. She voted for the Scottish National Party. From day one, they had enjoyed jibing at each other's political views.

They'd met on polling day. Joanna's school had been over-taken for voting. Alistair was supporting the local Labour candidate at the entrance and offered her an election leaflet as she walked in.

'No thanks, I'm not conservative.'

'Neither are we!' he said, watching her go inside. She had running gear on. She had good legs and an excellent bum. She knew he would notice.

'I can prove it to you,' Alistair said as she came out again.

'Prove what?'

'That we're nothing like the Tories.'

'Yeah?'

'Over dinner.'

He didn't tell her he was married until four weeks later.

*

The road to Geelong was famously dull. The only landmarks were the crosses at the side of the road, where people had died trying to get the journey over as quickly as possible.

A thick cloud of black smoke was visible ahead.

'Shit,' Alistair said. 'I thought it was up north, around Kilmore.'

He turned the radio on. The first channel was classical music. He pressed another button. A flat female voice was say-ing: 'If you live in Anglesea and Lorne and you are seeing flames, do not attempt to leave your house. It is too late . . . If you live in Torquay and you are seeing flames, do not attempt to leave your house. It is too late. If you live in . . .'

'Bloody hell,' Alistair said.

'What does it mean, too late? That you'll just die?'

'Probably means you'll have a better chance of protecting yourself staying put.'

'Will we get to Point Lonsdale okay?'

'Hang on . . .' Alistair listened to the rest of the broadcast. 'Sounds like it's further on, along the Great Ocean Road. I'm going to stop and ring Mum.'

*

Different couples make important decisions in different ways. Joanna had only been in one serious relationship before Alistair. His name was Mike. He was six months older than her. They were both English teachers who shared a love of Russian literature. They lived together for four years. And they made decisions by talking things through, calmly. They communicated well, Joanna and Mike. They averted crises. It was sad when they realised they'd met too young, and when Mike decided to go to Japan for a year. But they talked it through, and parted ways with a warm hug. Mike emailed her with his news from time to time. She replied with hers, from time to time.

With Joanna and Alistair, big decisions seemed to be made at the point of crisis, by Alistair.

'I'm glad she caught us,' he said over the telephone after his wife had slammed her fists into his naked chest. 'Now we can be together.'

'Chloe's gone,' he said the following day. 'I'll find a way to see her. It doesn't change things. We are meant to be together.'

Then, most recently: 'We're going to get her and bring her back with us. Our family will be complete.'

While packing for the trip, Joanna made a plan. As soon as they settled into their self-catering cottage at Point Lonsdale, she would suggest to Alistair that they set half-an-hour aside each day to talk things over. She didn't necessarily mean big things. In fact, it was the little things she worried about because you don't notice them growing. She liked her new plan and smiled as she zipped the last of the suitcases. Yes, she and Alistair would agree to this plan on the balcony of their cottage, clinking champagne glasses to seal the deal as they gazed at the bay. After that, all decisions would be made jointly and calmly. And there would be no more crises.

Unfortunately, in four minutes, this plan would go out the window.

Because in four minutes, she would face the biggest crisis of her life.

7

JOANNA

15 February

Minute One

Was there a lay-by? Or did they just park at the side of the road? A cross, wasn't there a cross about ten feet ahead? Were there really no towns or buildings in sight? Just the straight road behind them and the straight road ahead with black, ominous sky looming over its horizon?

Lorries, weren't there a lot of them? More than usual? What was usual? Passing lorries made the car shake, didn't they? Or was it just that one truck – Coles? – that rocked their four-wheel drive from side to side?

Did Alistair take the mobile phone out of his jeans pocket before he got out of the car, or after? Before? Was it already switched on? When did he notice there was no signal? Did he say: *Joanna, I can't get a signal so I'm going to walk over there*?

How long did it take him to walk from his side of the car to the fence? Ten seconds? Twenty? Did he say anything as he walked? Did he look at her?

What was she looking at? Him?

The cross ten feet ahead?

Her image in the mirror? Was she looking tired? Ugly? Was she really thinking about her looks?

She didn't turn and look at the back seat?

Why not?

Was it hard to hear Alistair when he yelled that he was going to climb the fence and walk further into the field? Was her window down? When had she opened her window? Why? To hear Alistair?

Minute Two

How did she know he still couldn't get a signal? Did he yell from the field?

Before she opened the car door to get out, did she turn around and look in the back seat? Why not?

Was it hot when she got out? Did she notice the wall of heat? Yes – Why? No – Why not?

Was it her suggestion that Alistair should try her phone?

When she walked towards the boot to show him where it was, what did she see on the way?

Did she divert her face from the back seat deliberately?

Did she open the boot? Or was it Alistair?

Did she unzip the small black suitcase?

From the back of the car, could they see into the back seat?

When Joanna closed the boot and walked along the side of the car, did she look in the back window?

Did she?

No?

Why not?

Minute Three

When Joanna opened the front door and sat sideways on her seat, legs out of the car, and stretched, was she feeling happy? Stretches are happy things, yeah?

Was it a lorry beeping its horn that made her wonder how on earth he was sleeping through this racket?

How long did it take for her to decide that she should maybe check on him?

Twenty seconds? Ten?

Why so long?

Where was she when Alistair asked her how to turn her bloody phone on? Standing at the side of the car?

When Joanna said: *Just hold down the button on the bottom right for three seconds*, had she looked in the back seat?

When Joanna asked Alistair: *How long has he been sleeping*, was she panicking?

When Alistair told her it must be five hours now, what went through her head?

Minute Four

Which one of them said this: *He's never slept so long in his life*?

Which one said: *It must be the Calpol*?

As Joanna knelt on the back seat and gently pushed the blanket away from her baby's face, was she trembling?

What was Alistair saying? That her phone was out of bloody juice? Was that it? Did another lorry beep? Was the car shaking?

What did his face feel like? Can she remember that? The feel of his face? How would she describe it now? Cold? How did her fingers feel? His flesh on her fingertips? Like ice? Ice cold? Is that how she'd describe it? Was Alistair aware of anything other than the phones? Was he still barking at her about the fucking phones? Was he at the back of the car, or at the side? Could he see her face? If he could, would her face have told him? Was he yelling at her, saying: *You should have charged the phone Joanna*?

Was the belt stuck? Jammed or something? Why did it take her so long to unbuckle? Or didn't it? Did it just seem long? Was it then that Alistair asked her if there was a charger in the car? When Joanna lifted him, how did she hold him exactly? Did she support his head? Or did she not bother? If she didn't bother, she must have known, yes? Is this when Alistair finally stopped the phone tantrum and asked if everything was okay? Why now? Had he seen her face?

Was she gentle when she put Noah on the ground?

Was the ground rocky?

Should she have put him on the ground?

What did she feel when she placed her cheek against his mouth?

Did she whisper this? *Noah! Noah!*

Shake him?

Yell this? *Alistair!*

How far away was Alistair when he dropped the phone and ran towards her? No more than four feet?

How long did she press her fingers against his neck?

How would she describe the feel of his neck?

How many times did Joanna say: *Oh God Oh God Oh God Oh God No?*

How many times did she say: *Please, please, Noah, cry?*

8

MELBOURNE SUPREME COURT

27 July

A heavily tattooed and goatee-bearded fifty-something fidgeted in the witness stand. 'Yes, I saw them.'

'You were driving from Frankston to Geelong?' Amy Maddock had turned on the female charm for the beefy truck driver. She changed posture and position according to the witness, Joanna noted. For this porn-hungry thug, she crossed one leg slightly in front of the other and lowered her head, all demure and girly.

'Yeah.'

'Could you describe what you saw?'

'I was goin' at a hundred k, so not much.'

'But you did see this woman?' She gestured towards Joanna with a soft voice and tiny smile.

'Yes, she was sittin' on the side of the road or somethin', kinda kneelin'. Looked like she was yelling and screamin' or something, her head up all angry.'

'Did you see anything else?'

'Just Alistair Robertson. He was standing over her. She looked aggro to me.'

'But you didn't see anything else? The baby?'

'No, just her, on the ground like I said, and him, standing over her. And her face angry, like she was yelling.'

'But you didn't see the baby?'

'No.'

'And you didn't stop.'

'Nah. They didn't wave me down, so I figured it wasn't car trouble. And she didn't look dangerous to me, like crazy violent or anythin', so I figured it was just a domestic, none of my business.'

9

JOANNA

15 February

There were no hills in this part of the world. Alistair jumped on the roof of the car and waved his phone at the sky, pleading with it for a signal, 'Come on, come on!'

It was just as pointless, what Joanna was doing, but she couldn't stop. 'One, two, three, four, five,' she counted, pressing two fingers crossed with two fingers onto Noah's tiny chest – 'One, two, three, four, five. One, two, three, four, five . . .'

Alistair was at the side of the road now, screaming when cars and trucks drove past: 'Stop you arseholes, stop!'

'One, two, three, four, five . . .'

'We'll drive to Geelong hospital.' He was standing over her.

'One, two, three, four, five.'

'Joanna.'

'One, two, three, four, five.'

'Joanna.'

'One, two, three, four, five.'

'That's enough.'

'One, two, three, four, five.'

'Joanna, stop now. Stop.'

'One, two, three, four, five.'

'FUCKING STOP!'

The next day, Joanna would notice two large bruises under each arm from where Alistair grabbed her and hauled her away from her son.

His voice came from a different place as he wrestled – from his teeth, it seemed: 'Stop it. Stop it. Stop.'

She kicked him in the shin, struggling to be released. He would show her his bruises the following day.

'He's gone. He's gone,' Alistair said.

She tried to push Alistair away. 'Let me go. Let me save him.'

'Our baby's gone. Noah's gone.' He managed to get both her arms behind her back, twisting them to restrain her. 'Get in the car.' He pushed her, forced her in, slammed the door and pressed the key to lock it. Face up against the window he said loudly: 'Don't move and don't look. I'm going to put him in his seat and then we're going to the hospital.'

She couldn't not look. How dare he ask her not to?

Alistair picked up Noah, put him in the car-seat without doing up the belt, and shut the door.

'Do up his belt! Do up his belt!'

He sighed, opened the back door again, lifted the left buckle, reached for the right, and struggled to press them together. 'I told you to look away!'

She would not look away.

Alistair slammed the back door shut, opened his, and fell

into the driver's seat. 'Turn your head to the front.'

She refused.

'Turn around now.'

She was on her knees, reaching to the back, her hand on Noah's little foot. 'It's so cold.'

She heard Alistair's head bash against the steering wheel, followed by a groan.

'His feet are so cold,' Joanna repeated.

'He died hours ago.'

This made Joanna turn around. 'What?'

'He's been dead for hours.' A thin line of spit connected Alistair's open mouth and his knee. She'd never seen him cry, so she wasn't sure if this was what he was doing. No noises, no tears, just dribble.

'Why would you say that? We'd have noticed.'

'We've been too terrified to look at him in case we woke him up. It's rigor mortis, Joanna.' His tone was worse than angry. Venomous. Accusatory.

'What?'

He pulled his head up and yelled. 'He's stiff, Goddam it!'

'Stiff?'

'You don't get stiff for hours.'

'You mean . . .'

'What I mean, Joanna, is he died on the plane.'

*

She was on her way to hell. That's why the sky ahead was

getting blacker. Joanna calmed herself with the idea. She died and went to hell, that's all – just as she knew she would, since the affair. Noah wasn't dead. She was. It wasn't real, just part of the hell she was going to, and deserved. 'I died. I'm just on my way to hell, that's all.'

'We're half an hour from Geelong.' Alistair's voice jolted her out of this wonderful alternative. 'Please try and be quiet so I can concentrate.'

They had been driving for ten minutes. Shock, and the sound of the air conditioning, had transported Joanna to a better place than this. Hell. But now she was back in the pas-senger seat of some rental car with Alistair driving, and . . .

She turned round.

'Noooo!' Joanna rocked her head back and forth, hoping dizziness might swirl this into nothingness. Rock faster, back and forward, rub it out, take it away.

'Cot death? Was it cot death?' The rocking hadn't worked.

'Maybe.' His voice was a little less venomous now, but only a little.

'Or was there something really wrong with him? Was he sick? Is that why he always cried?'

'Maybe.'

A rock and moan combination this time, before stopping suddenly: 'He was constipated.'

'Was he?' Alistair's 'was' was harsh, as if to say *I didn't know that. You should have told me. Maybe if you'd told me . . .*

'I stopped telling you things like that because you said

I should stop worrying about every little thing. Oh God, maybe he was crying because he was . . . because he was really sick and I missed it. I didn't notice.'

'Stop grabbing at me! We'll crash. Try not to think now. We'll talk at the hospital. Let's just get to the fucking hospital.'

She settled on a tiny head rock motion as she could think more clearly this way. 'Could he have been allergic to the Calpol I gave him?'

'You didn't give him Calpol.'

'I did. About three hours before we landed.'

Alistair swerved to the side of the road and stopped the car with a skid. He yanked at the handbrake hard then turned to her. 'What did you say?'

'Why? What?'

'When did you give him Calpol?'

'Why? That's not bad, is it? It was baby Calpol.'

'How much?'

'What?'

'How much did you give him?'

'The dose.'

Alistair opened his door and walked against the traffic to the back of the car. A lorry beeped and swerved, just missing him. He opened the boot. Joanna turned to see what he was doing, but all she saw was her baby. She stretched her hand out towards him, then retrieved it. She didn't want to feel the cold. But little Noah! From where she was, he just looked like he was sleeping. She turned back and put her head in her lap.

Alistair got back in the car and slammed the door. He held one of the unlabelled hundred-millilitre bottles of liquid before her.

'So you gave him a dose when I was asleep, yeah?'

'Yes.'

'Three hours before we landed.'

'Yes.'

Alistair snatched the bottle back and looked at it.

He opened the door, ran to the boot again, and came back with the second bottle of liquid.

'Oh no . . .' Joanna said as he sat back in his seat, bottle in hand.

'How many doses of antibiotics have you had since we left?'

'One. You gave it to me in Dubai.'

Alistair put his finger on the rim of the bottle he had just retrieved and tasted a drip of the medicine. It had about the same amount of fluid missing as the first bottle. 'This is the antibiotics.'

He opened the lid of the first bottle, touched the rim with his finger, and pressed his finger onto his tongue. 'Strawberry. This is the Calpol.'

Alistair put the Calpol on the dashboard – to his left.

And the antibiotics on the dashboard – right.

'I always taste it, Joanna.' He paused, looked at the bottles, then turned to her: 'Do you?'

*

In any relationship, the role of each partner is defined very quickly, Joanna's counsellor told her in the first of her sessions. She booked the counsellor five weeks after she met Alistair, a week after he told her he was married. Unable to extricate herself from him, she felt confused and upset by her behaviour. She'd never hurt anyone before. She'd never lied either, apart from the occasional white one (*Of course I came!*). She'd always done the things she set her mind to. And she'd never felt ashamed of herself. Now she was so ashamed that she hadn't told her best friend, and had paid thirty-five pounds to tell this overweight woman instead. Joanna listened to her counsellor, but she didn't want to hear about 'roles'. What she wanted was for the counsellor to say: 'Affairs are okay. It's society that's fucked. You go for it girl. And stop feeling so Goddam guilty. On the continent, you'd be mocked for not taking a lover.'

But, no, the counsellor did not say this. From her velour armchair, she looked at Joanna with concern and spent the entire session talking about roles. 'They are based on assumptions you make about each other's characteristics,' she said, 'assumptions which are made almost immediately, which may well be wrong, and which are very difficult to unmake.'

Joanna thought about this after the session. It was true. By the time she and Alistair had finished their first meal together – he ordered for her, the fillet of pollock – the following assumptions had been poured, levelled and set.

ALISTAIR	JOANNA
I'm a risk taker.	I'm a big fearty.
I'm ambitious.	I work to live.
I enjoy gathering facts.	I'm crap with details.
I remember things.	I'm forgetful.
I'm good under pressure.	I cave.
I'm a decision maker.	Am I?
I'm someone you should listen to.	I talk shite!

And there you had them. Joanna and Alistair. Alistair and Joanna. From day one till now. And she was okay with that. It wasn't bad, any of it. It worked. It would probably have worked for ever, if not for airport security.

She wasn't sure why, but she never told Alistair about the counsellor.

*

Alistair helped Joanna's limp, shaky body out of the car, and practically carried her to the small grass embankment at the side of the road. As she wobbled her way in a haze, she knew her plan to change the way they made decisions was just typical nonsense talk. She wasn't good under pressure. She wasn't a decision maker. Right now, she could barely breathe and walk, let alone think. The heat was choking her. She needed to vomit.

So, after Alistair held her hair while she was sick, after he lowered her down so her back was supported by the three-foot-high embankment; after he checked that passing cars could not see them and crouched down beside her; it was he who did the talking. And she who listened.

Because Alistair is someone you should listen to.

The Facts

He positioned himself a few inches away from her, his back against the dry yellow earth of the embankment, and stared ahead. 'I want you to focus,' he said. 'What we do next will change our lives for ever. Don't try and turn and look at the car. Look straight ahead and don't say anything. I'm going to list the facts.'

Her hands were shaking violently. She sat on them and stared ahead as he'd ordered. The field was flat and yellow and she couldn't see where it ended, if it did. Nothing was growing in it. No animals were grazing in it. The hot north wind that fuelled the fires in the distance carried eerie brown clouds of dust south, tussling with her hair on its way. A flake of ash danced at her nose, up down, up down, then settled on her right ankle. Now that she'd been placed in this spot, she couldn't move and didn't want to. She wanted to sit there till she died. Perhaps she could do that, die of thirst at the side of this road, never ever going back to that car. If she asked Alistair, maybe he would agree to leave her there. She would. She'd ask him, once he was done with the usual routine: listing the facts, deciding on a plan of attack, getting the job done.

Hang on, what job was there to do? How was any of this bullshit ever going to help?

His voice interrupted her thoughts. As ever, he listed the facts in point form. She didn't turn her head or move her eyes towards him, but she could see in her peripheral vision that he had stretched out his arm and lifted his thumb, ready to nail down the first.

'One: Noah is dead.'

His voice was steady, in control. His index finger came out to join the thumb that was heavy and pulsing with its fact.

'Two: It's our fault.'

His fingers were too short. And chubby.

'Three: One or both of us will be charged with neglect, or manslaughter, or murder, especially after your behaviour on the plane.'

Well she *had* murdered Noah. She *should* be charged with that. If she couldn't sit here till she died of thirst, her second choice would be to spend the rest of her life in prison. She almost broke the rules and said this out loud. She wanted the police to drag her away from this spot now. When they did, she'd cover her head with her T-shirt, so she wouldn't have to look at *that* car again.

57

'Four: One or both of us will go to prison. For a year, or maybe five, or for life.'

It'd be her who'd do the time, just her. Alistair would be okay.

'Five: A scandal of any kind will lose me my job. It'll harm the Party. And I might never get work again.'

He lifted his other hand to resume counting. His pace quickened, his tone hardened.

'Six: You will never teach again.'

Ah, the change in pace and tone was because he was talking about her now. He was angry at her. Quite right. It was his son she'd killed.

'Seven: You will never be allowed to work with children again in any capacity.'

So? She was going to die here on this embankment. Thinking about it, thirst would take too long. Two or three days maybe, she didn't know. If she prayed, perhaps the wind would change direction and bring the flames towards them. She closed her eyes and recited the only prayer she could remember.

I confess to almighty God

and to you, my brothers and sisters,

that I have greatly sinned,

in my thoughts and in my words,

in what I have done and in what I have failed to do,

through my fault, through my fault,

through my most grievous fault;

therefore I ask blessed Mary ever-Virgin,

all the Angels and Saints,

and you, my brothers and sisters,

to pray for me to the Lord our God.

She opened her eyes. The wind had not obeyed, the flames and smoke no closer. The fire wouldn't take her.

Instead, she'd get one of the duty-free bags out of the boot and put her head in it and tie it around her neck with the shoelaces from her trainers.

'Eight: You may never be allowed to go near children again.'

Quite right. She had murdered a baby. Her baby.

'Nine: You may not be allowed to have another child of your own.'

Another child. *Another child of her own.* Yes, he'd just said that out loud.

'Most importantly, Ten: We might not be permitted to see Chloe. We will definitely not get custody of her, which means she will be taken into care and made parentless. An orphan, at fourteen. My own daughter. My only child now. Little Chloe.'

Fact ten was actually three or four facts. Joanna supposed he hadn't wanted to go back to the first hand, which already had its fill. It was neater, this way. A lot of facts, though, for that small pinky of his.

Joanna stayed still, pretending that this stupid fucking demonstration mattered when Noah was dead in the back seat of their hire car.

He had a closing speech, and unfortunately he wanted her to change position while he delivered it, for maximum impact, she supposed. He took her hand from under her buttock and held it in his, which was cold. She wondered how it could be cold, in this situation, in this stifling heat. Perhaps because he wasn't human.

Using his other hand, he turned her face towards his. Her eyes were slow catching up, but eventually they landed where he wanted them.

He was dripping with sweat, she noticed. Beads on his forehead, huge patches under his armpits and above his stomach.

'Noah is dead. He must have been allergic to the penicillin.

It was an accident.'

This is as close as he would come to saying it wasn't her fault. It was an accident. Not quite not her fault.

'You're finished with the facts,' she said with confidence, on account of the long pause.

'I am.' He put his hands on her shoulders.

'I'd like to die here, if that's all right. I was thinking of using one of those duty-free bags, and I was wondering if you'd mind getting one from the boot for me.'

'Joanna, don't. We have Chloe to think about.'

Joanna leant down and tried to untie one of her laces. Her hands were either numb or just plain disobedient. She couldn't work out how to do it, but she persevered, and eventually managed to pull at the right piece. She pushed at the back of the loose trainer with her other foot.

'Stop that now.'

Ah, the shoe finally came off. Now, she just had to get the laces all the way out. She placed the shoe on her lap and began loosening and tugging. This was going to be easy, she thought. All she had to do was get Alistair to retrieve the plastic bag. He hadn't said no, but he wasn't budging. She wouldn't do it. She would never look at that car again. She'd persuade him, somehow. 'Got it!' she said, lifting the freed lace and turning towards Alistair with a triumphant smile.

You couldn't describe it as a slap, although she didn't actually see if his fist was clenched or not. Whatever, it landed on her left cheekbone, the force causing her head to do an

Exorcist-twist before falling down, down to the earth beside her ankles . . .

. . . Oh look, the flake of ash is gone.

*

When she woke, she was in the front seat of the car. The radio and the icy air conditioning were on.

'If you live in Anglesea and Lorne and you are seeing flames, do not attempt to leave your house. It is too late . . . If you live in Torquay and you are seeing flames, do not attempt to leave your house. It is too late. If you live in Aireys Inlet . . .'

Alistair switched it off when he realised she'd come to.

Her first impulse was to turn round to look in the back seat. She was thankful that the pain in her neck and head and ear (that's right, she had an ear infection. Shock and adrenaline had taken care of that till now) made it impossible to do so. She touched her sore cheek.

'I'm so sorry,' Alistair said. She moved her head as far to the right as her neck would allow her, and winced. Alistair's lips had changed in colour and halved in size. She looked down at his hands and wondered if the wheel might snap from the force of his clench.

As usual, he was driving too fast and hadn't bothered to put his seatbelt on. He was leaning in, his face a little too close to the windscreen.

Joanna was scared of him. He'd hit her. He'd never done that before.

She wondered if he was scared of her too. Perhaps that's why he wouldn't divert his eyes from the road to look at her.

They were both scared now, of everything.

'Joanna . . .' A whisper, this first word, rising deep from his throat. 'You can't abandon me.' His mouth fell open and stayed open, droplets of spit-tears gathering on his lower lip. His shoulders slumped and so began the chant: 'Don't leave me don't leave me don't leave me don't leave me don't leave me don't leave me don't leave me don't leave me . . .'

Forgetting the pain, Joanna undid her seatbelt, manoeuvred her face down under his arm and nuzzled it into his chest. She inhaled, searching for his fresh soap scent, but all she could smell was sweat and aeroplane. She breathed through her mouth. 'Hey, hey . . .' she said. 'I won't. I'm sorry. I won't. I promise. I promise. I won't leave you. I won't ever leave you.'

The Plan of Attack

Her breasts were rocks, volcanic ones with hot liquid beneath, bubbling and pushing to get out. She touched the left one, above her T-shirt. The heat radiated through the material and onto her hand. It must be seven hours or so since – this sentence was going in a direction she did not like. She caught the thought in time and refashioned its end – seven hours or so since. Just *since*.

Joanna realised she was going to have to catch and refashion almost all her thoughts from now on.

She knew what not leaving Alistair meant; the basics of the decision he'd made, to which she'd agreed. They'd fine-tune the plan at the cottage. Till then, they needed to remain calm, and drive.

The sky above was smoky now, like London fog only darker, thickening as they got closer to Geelong.

She pulled her T-shirt and bra forward and peeked inside. Her nipples had trebled in size but were not leaking. If a certain noise happened now, they would spray with the force of a power hose. This noise wasn't going to happen, ever, so what of her breasts? They'd probably continue to expand, painfully, until they exploded. Joanna would rather not die this way. Back at the embankment with the duty-free bag would have been preferable.

Or she could die here, now. Neither of them had their seat-belts on. Noah was dead already. A large, thick metal sign for Avalon airport was ahead of them. Alistair was driving at over a hundred and thirty kph. All she had to do was grab the wheel and swerve at the right moment. In five seconds, four, three . . .

No, she wasn't allowed to think like this, she'd promised. 'I need to express,' she said.

Alistair's knuckles were more relaxed now that Joanna was not leaving him; now that 'facts' three through ten had become fiction. 'Can you hold out twenty minutes?'

Alistair talked in Aussie time – twenty minutes equalled at

least forty. But 'Yes' she would wait.

Beep Beep!

Alistair's mobile made her jump, rock-breasts attempting to separate from her body on landing: Ow.

He lifted the handset. 'Reception's back. Five missed calls . . . Mum.'

Elizabeth was at home waiting for their call. She'd been tidying the garden and rearranging the furniture in her house in anticipation of their arrival. Her only child! The love of his life! ('I know she is, Alistair!') And her only grandson! She'd been crossing the days off the personalised calendar Alistair had sent her for Christmas, which was only three weeks after Noah was born. For each month of the calendar, there was a photograph. The one that would be on display now, February, was of Noah in his pram at the front of the flat in Edinburgh, the blue bunny blanket she'd sent wrapped around him as he slept.

'I'd better ring,' Alistair said.

'Not while you're driving!' Joanna would have insisted on this at any time but now it was more important than ever. The cops might see him. And if he stopped to make the call, she might be tempted to turn round and look in the back seat. 'Slow down and put your belt on. I'll do it,' she said, holding out her hand to take the phone.

He prepped her before handing it over and she was glad, because his last piece of advice ('Pretend you lose the signal if things get difficult') came in handy almost immediately.

'Elizabeth, it's Joanna.' She put as much enthusiasm into her voice as possible, but hadn't managed an exclamation mark's worth. 'We just passed Avalon.'

She held the phone away from her ear to soften Elizabeth's loud, over-excited voice – 'Oh, darlings! So close! I can hardly believe it? I'll put the kettle on. Was the flight okay? How's Noah?'

Joanna put the handset back to her ear and used Alistair's suggestion. 'Elizabeth! Elizabeth? You're breaking up. I can't . . . Elizabeth . . . Listen, if you can hear me . . .' (she knew she could) '. . . We're going to go to the cottage first. Noah needs a feed. We'll be at yours as soon as we can. We'll call you when we're on our way. Elizabeth? Sorry, you're . . .'

Joanna hung up, covered her face with her hands, and stayed in that position all the way to Point Lonsdale.

*

The small beachside town was deserted. There were no cars in the driveways of the large houses opposite the beach, no children in the play park, and no one sitting at the tables laid out in front of the town's three cafés. From the car, Joanna couldn't see all the way down to the beach, and wondered if that's where everyone had gone.

Despite Elizabeth's pleas to stay at her house, they'd wanted to be on the beach, and to have time to themselves. Their holiday cottage – a white Victorian weatherboard – was a hundred feet or so beyond the end of the small strip of shops. Alistair parked in the driveway and opened the car door. She stepped out of the car and into what felt like a fan oven. Alistair found the key under the mat, helped Joanna into the master bedroom, told her to lie down, and came back a few minutes later with the breast pump. She closed her eyes and tried to imagine Noah was at her breast, his tiny fingers toying with the soft flesh around her nipple, but this produced more tears than milk. After ten minutes or so she passed the apparatus to Alistair with two hands, as if she were giving him the baby.

'Doesn't look like as much as usual,' he said.

'It won't come,' Joanna replied.

He grabbed the pump and the near-empty bottle, took it away, and came back to the bedroom to go over the plan.

*

There was so much to remember and so much to forget.

She should remember turning the air conditioning on, having a shower – she could go first – and putting concealer over the mark where Alistair had slapped or punched or whatevered her.

She should forget Alistair emptying the Boots bottles down the sink and putting them in a plastic bag to dispose of elsewhere.

She should remember that she sat on the bed, pump at her breast, because she would have done that if he was alive. Remember? The milk was for Elizabeth, who was going to take

67

Noah for the next twenty-four hours and give them some time alone.

Forget that he added some water to the small amount she'd managed to express, and that he'd asked: 'Does this look right? Joanna? Joanna!'

Remember putting a load of washing on, including her vomit- and milk-stained T-shirt and the cloth covers for Noah's buggy-cum-car seat, and changing into shorts and flip-flops.

She should forget seeing Alistair put a small garden trowel in the packed-as-normal baby bag. (No shovel in the shed, damn!) Forget him searching for bin bags and placing a large black one on top of the car seat.

But remember unpacking things carefully. Babygros into drawers. Toothbrushes into bathroom.

Forget him tossing the dirty nappy he must have removed from Noah in the bin. 'No Joanna!' Alistair yelled. 'You remember I changed his nappy! Remember it!' He froze. 'Hang on, maybe they'll be able to tell from his nappy that he was dead. Could they tell that? Shit!' He raced to the bin, removed the dirty nappy, and put it in a plastic bag with the Boots bottles. So, this meant . . . she should forget all that . . . Yes, forget the stuff about the nappy.

She would never get this right.

*

'It's not too late,' she said, begged, as she walked behind him towards the car, careful not to look at what he was holding in his arms.

He didn't reply. Or he didn't reply in time, because a woman of around forty had arrived in the driveway with a huge smiley holiday 'Hello there!'

Alistair's hello was a little over-enthusiastic, Joanna thought. 'Hi!' One hand removed itself from the bundle of death in his arms, and extended as far out as it could to shake hers. 'Mrs Wilson?'

'You found the key, then. Ah, is he asleep?' She crooked her head to get a glimpse of the face Alistair had buried in his chest. The rest of him was wrapped in the blue blanket.

'Just.' Alistair turned to make sure she couldn't see. 'The house is gorgeous!'

'We like it. Quiet here, hey, with schools back; that and the heat. Blimey!' She fanned her face with her hand. 'You'll have the beach to yourselves.'

A glaring look from Alistair made Joanna realise it was her turn to say something. 'Are . . .' Her voice caught. She coughed. 'Are the fires near here?'

'Terrible thing. Ten dead that we know of. They're a way away. And there's a cool change coming in an hour or so. Lonnie will be fine.'

'We're just heading out,' Alistair said, opening the car door to hurry this along.

'The supermarket's open till eight. It's a bit more expensive than the big Coles in Ocean Grove, but it's nice to support

69

the locals. And there's a milk bar on its own at the other end of the town, just before the roundabout. I'd recommend Pasquini's for coffee and lemon cake. Lovely people.' With this, she patted the blue blanket. 'How old?'

'He's only sixty-four days old.' Joanna did not remember saying this, but apparently she did.

'The bloss. Well, I'll let you get on!' She turned and walked towards the end of the drive, pointing to the seventies brick house next door. 'Anything you need, just open the door and holler. Loudly! Jeff plays that horrible jazz all day long.'

10

MELBOURNE SUPREME COURT

27 July

Mrs Wilson didn't look happy in the witness box: her face bright red, forehead sweaty.

'Did they seem happy to you?' Amy Maddock asked.

'Well . . . I don't know.'

'Anything unusual about them?'

'No. I mean the baby was asleep and I didn't want to wake him.'

'Did you see the child?'

'Yes. Well, he was wrapped in the blanket. His dad was holding him.'

'What was *she* doing?' The lawyer managed to load the *she* with so much negativity. A skill, that.

'Nothing. Getting ready to get in the car.'

'Did she seem like a loving partner to you?'

Matthew Marks: 'Objection!'

Judge: 'Sustained.'

'Did she seem like a good mother to you?'

Matthew Marks: 'Objection!'

Judge: 'You can answer this question, Mrs Wilson.'

Why it was okay to ask this question and not the partner

one, Joanna would never understand.

'I remember she knew exactly how many days her baby had been in the world.'

'Did she seem like a good mother?'

'I have four children, do I seem like a good mother to you?'

Judge: 'Answer the question please, Mrs Wilson.'

She straightened her back, face even redder now, forehead dripping. 'I saw them for five minutes. He seemed hot and tired. She seemed hot. And tired. I have no idea what kind of mother she was.'

11

JOANNA

15 February

Getting the Job Done

'It's not too late,' Joanna said again as they drove out of town.

He didn't answer her. Later he would say it was because she hadn't asked him anything.

It took five minutes to get to the house, which was on the side of the swamp-like bay connecting Point Lonsdale with the historic seaside village of Queenscliff. A broken power line hissed and spluttered and arced at the side of the road. A single line of houses edged the bay. One of the houses belonged to Alistair's best friend's family. He'd been there on holidays as a student, and had emailed to ask about renting it. His best friend had replied the following day:

Sorry, mate. It's mine now, actually, but I've not quite finished the reno. No kitchen, water and power, I'm afraid. And yeah, let's catch up when you're here.

Phil

Joanna had booked the cottage on the beachfront instead.

Alistair got out of the car, knocked on the door to check no one was in, walked round the house to scour for signs of life and security cameras, then disappeared round the back.

Joanna sat, frozen, in her seat. Something had happened to her since they left the cottage. She had gone completely numb. She pinched her arm and couldn't feel anything. She slapped her face and didn't feel anything. She turned and looked in the back seat of the car – at the bundle of blue – and didn't feel anything. She got out of the car, opened the back door, unbuckled the baby seat, removed the blanket-covered bundle from the plastic-covered car seat, held it, didn't feel anything. When Alistair returned to the front garden and took the bundle from her, she felt nothing.

'Sit down, put your head between your legs,' he said. 'You're going to faint. The garden's just like I remember. It's pretty, Joanna. There's a beautiful Lilly Pilly tree, you know, like the one you want to plant. Sit down, don't move. Let me take care of it. You comfortable? Don't come round the back, you hear me? Stay there.'

'Let's not do this. It's not too late,' she said, but her legs had muffled the words and Alistair was gone anyway.

*

A cry.

She lifted her head from between her legs. As far as she knew, she could have been in that position for hours. There it was again. She'd never heard anything so beautiful in all her life.

The sound was not a cry. It was a siren.

Joanna got out of the car and looked up at the smoky sky. A helicopter, in the distance. The siren was a fire engine in all probability. She was about to yell for Alistair when he ran towards her, jumped in the car and started the engine. 'Get in! Quick!'

Alistair turned the radio on as they headed down the drive. 'If you live in Lorne and you are seeing flames, do not attempt to leave your house. It is too late.'

He turned right out of the driveway, skidding onto the empty road towards Point Lonsdale. He'd washed his hands – there must have been a garden hose – but she could see dirt in his fingernails.

The radio droned . . . 'If you live in Anglesea and you are seeing flames, do not leave your house . . .'

It was too late.

*

'Only one more thing to do,' Alistair said. He was looking after her. He always looked after her. She repeated his words in her head, over and over. *Only one more thing to do, only one more thing to do, only one more thing to do.*

Silly Joanna. She almost believed it at the time.

The black sky was a different black. When it cracked and let loose, she realised this was because clouds had joined the smoke.

The cool change.

Alistair often romanticised about them. 'Two to four days of crippling heat that make you want to move into the fridge on a permanent basis, and then the skies open and you dance in it!' She loved it when he talked about home. His face moved so much more.

Huge drops of rain, like stones, began to fall on the windscreen. Sparse at first, then more and more. They could barely see the shop when they parked across the road from it.

They looked around – no people, no cars – then looked at each other.

Only one more thing to do.

'Any questions?' Alistair asked.

She shook her head.

'You want to go over it again?' he asked.

She shook her head.

'You ready?'

She nodded.

'Good girl. Stay calm and remember the plan.' He kissed her on the forehead, got out of the car, and walked over the road and into the milk bar. She could see him taking baby wipes from the shelf as required by the script.

She counted her breaths all the way to 120, as required, then got out of the car and walked across the road and inside the small milk bar.

He hadn't specified what she should buy, so she grabbed

the first thing she spotted – a packet of Tampax – and put them on the counter.

The young shop assistant continued to thumb at his phone as he handed them the change, not looking up or replying when Alistair said thanks. He'd have to stop and take notice in a minute, Joanna thought, as Alistair held the door open for her to exit.

A vehicle drove past and splashed her legs.

But no, all clear, no one else in the street now.

They walked across the road together. Alistair opened the car door. Looked inside. Yelled something at Joanna. She didn't respond. He yelled it again. That's right, she was supposed to respond.

He yelled it a third time: 'He's gone!'

When she finally registered the words they were so welcome and wonderful that Joanna's mind decided to play a trick on her. She wouldn't have to remember what to remember and what to forget. She would believe it. It was a better truth. He was gone. Someone had taken him. She drank it down in a gulp.

'He's gone!' Alistair yelled. 'Gone!'

It entered her, filled her up, energised her. He was gone. Someone else had done a bad thing. Not her.

This was the Incident.

She looked at the baby seat, which was empty: no Noah, no blue rug.

She screamed. Her baby didn't exist any more. Someone

had taken him. She yelled. 'Where is he? Did you see any-one?' Alistair didn't hear because he was running to one end of the street, pretending to look for suspicious cars or people, yelling 'Noah!' then running across the road to do the same all over again.

Joanna raced back over to the milk bar, opened the door and said, 'Someone's stolen my baby!' thus handing the incident over: Here, world, this is yours, not mine. Take it.

12

MELBOURNE SUPREME COURT

28 July

'The court calls Joanna Lindsay to the stand.'

This was her moment. She stood and turned to look at the people gathered in the courtroom: the judge, the old lady from the plane, the woman who rented them the cottage in Point Lonsdale, the truck driver, the artist, the prissy female lawyer, the macho pretty-boy lawyer, the boy who worked at the milk bar, her best friend Kirsty, Alistair's mother, the journalists, the misery-voyeurs, Alexandra. She straightened the red dress she had chosen to wear against all advice. It was too big for her. She was under eight stone – pre-Alistair she'd been a happy nine and three-quarters. It was the dress Joanna wore the first time she and Alistair made love. *Made love!* The first time they fucked. She should have guessed he was married at the time. Why else did they do it in the back seat of his bright look-at-me wank-fest of a soft-top? It was so small she had to go on top and do all the moving, with Alistair pinned there like some extra gear stick clunking from fourth to fifth, yes baby, baby, yes.

She'd been preparing for this for a long time. Mad people always say they're not mad, so insisting on her sanity wouldn't work. Instead Joanna would have to convince the judge by looking, sounding and smelling sane. Was the red dress a sane decision? Maybe not. Shit. But the grey trousers and cream blouse Kirsty brought in for her felt wrong, all wrong. She was not looking for sympathy.

She'd practised her sane face in front of the mirror. If she smiled she looked evil. When she cried she looked like she was faking it. If she thought about Noah she looked broken, about Alistair, crazy. The best face, to her surprise, was the one Alistair had taught her to do after Noah died. Blank – no fidgeting, no smiling. 'Imagine someone will hurt me if you smile,' he'd said.

Oh dear, she was going to smile.

She'd practised her voice for days: calm, clear, no weirdness in it. 'My name is Joanna Lindsay,' she'd said to her reflection again and again. Her voice was always shaky – the drugs probably. She didn't even know what they were exactly, but there were a lot of them.

Before leaving for court, she sniffed under her arms. Did she smell sane?

Kirsty had arrived to prepare her for court mid-sniff. 'Do I smell mad?' Joanna had asked her friend, arm in air. Kirsty had taken a reluctant whiff. 'No. You shouldn't wear that dress. People will hate you.'

'Good,' Joanna had replied.

Joanna turned to the front of the court, and touched the small tear in the slit on the right of the dress from that first back-seat encounter. Yep, you could see it. And she was glad, because today she was going to break all the rules. She'd played her part long enough. Today was the second day of the court case, and she would make sure it would be the last. Today, everything would change.

'Ms Lindsay, can you please make your way to the stand?' The judge's tone was kind because she believed she was dealing with a mad woman.

'Of course,' Joanna said. The artist began scratching away at her sketch pad again. Something new to draw. A murderous woman in a slutty dress. Joanna turned and felt a smile spread on her face. Oops, a big cheesy against-the-rules grin. She then looked at the judge and said: 'I can do anything I set my mind to.'

Part Two

THE SEARCH

13

ALEXANDRA

15 February

I'm a mad bitch. I'm a mad alcoholic bitch. I'm a mad bad alcoholic bitch.

Let's break it down. I'll have to do that in court soon, break it down, so here goes. A solo role-play to pass the hours till they knock on the door and begin the process of trying to take my child, my life, away.

Are you mad, Mrs Robertson?

Alexandra <u>Donohue</u> is my name, and yes. Many times I have cried for more than two hours without stopping to wipe my nose. More than many times I've not been able to get out of bed. Once I wanted to take a holiday from my own head so much that I tweeted it: @alexa-d-donohue I want a holiday from my head!

And are you bad, Mrs Donohue?

My name is <u>Ms</u> Donohue, and definitely. I slapped my daughter twice when she was little. I don't know when exactly but I know why and it's because I'm bad and not because she was naughty. Also, I took Chloe away from her father for four years and I would have kept her away from him for ever if I could have, not all out of badness, but partly.

Let's talk about alcohol.

I drink it. Mostly in the house alone. I usually wait till after 5 p.m. I never drink less than half but rarely more than three-quarters of a bottle. The idea of not having a glass of wine – as in, if you said 'Alexandra, you are not allowed to have a glass of wine tonight' – would make me quite anxious. And okay, yes, there's the incident last month. Two glasses of red over lunch and the cops are random testing on Sydney Road and now it's official that I'm a bad mother and a felon and a complete idiot.

And you're a bitch?

Oh yes. Since I caught him with her especially, I've thought nothing but bitchy things. I've fantasised about hurting her, punching her in the face over and over till her lip splits and her nose bleeds and moves sideways. I've hoped that she won't lose the baby weight, that her stretch marks are grotesque, her boobs empty sacks like most women's are from feeding (but not mine!) and once, God forgive me, I prayed that their baby be born disabled, prayed that the child's problems be proof of their sins and their penance. I've wanted her to go through what I went through but worse: believing him, being crushed by him.

Mostly, I've dreamed *him* dead.

Imagining is as far as it goes, but that doesn't take away from the facts about my very serious flaws. Ask him, he'll say the same. He's good at facts.

Enough role-play. Chloe will wake at seven, she always does. It's past midnight. I need to sleep. I allow myself to check my fake Facebook profile three times a day, which takes some discipline, let me tell you. I have one check left, so that's what I'll do before going to bed.

The screen opens on my real account and there's a message from Phil, Alistair's childhood pal, and best man at our wedding. Phil came to Scotland a couple of years before Alistair and I split. Alistair was working in London during most of his visit. I was in the middle of doing up the bedroom in our flat. Phil insisted on stripping the walls and painting it with me. 'I've done Europe,' he said, 'but I've never done a feature wall.'

Alistair doesn't realise this, but I got custody of Phil after the split. I rang him in floods of tears after I caught Alistair screwing that woman. 'The arsehole,' Phil said. 'Self-obsessed dickhead. Leave him. Come home. I'll look after you.'

I open Phil's Facebook message. *Got a date for the hearing yet?* His profile pic makes me smile. He's in a scruffy blue T-shirt. His curly dark blonde hair is a mess, and it's impossible not to smile back at him.

Not yet. Nervous… I reply.

I look at other recent posts – nothing interesting – and, bang, Phil's back with a message already. *Dinner tomorrow?* I feel the butterfly in my tummy that I always feel with Phil, then I slap it away (as I always do) and type: *Got a PTA ladies night thing (help!). How about lunch?*

Maybe one day I'll say yes to dinner. Not yet, though. When I left Scotland, I promised myself I'd always, *always*, put Chloe first, and the last thing she's needed is some other man in her life. Anyway, Phil doesn't fancy me. We've been friends too long, we're too comfortable. And I'm a complete disaster area.

Nothing else on my Facebook, so I log out and back in under the one I invented for stalking purposes: Greta Xavier, a teacher, lives in Dundee. Greta made friends with four of Joanna's friends. None of them know my fictional or real self, but four years ago they all said yes to my friend request, and after that so did she, just after I left the country, and now I know her history and can track her movements. This in itself is evidence of madness, badness and bitchiness, and sometimes the posts I've read have sent me down past the three-quarters of a bottle mark to proper alcoholicness.

Joanna Lindsay changed her profile picture.
Joanna Lindsay changed her status to In a Relationship.
Alistair Robertson likes this.

I call it getting to know your enemy, keeping her close, waiting for Schadenfreude. She took my place and created a job vacancy. So I suppose she's not an enemy, really, she's me, only she doesn't realise it yet. She will one day, poor soul, fucking slut.

From my research, it appears she was happy and normal before him. One of many things we have in common.

She's an only child. If she has a father, she never talks about him. Her mother died six years ago last Easter and was loaded, by the sounds. Left her a five-bedroom house in Pol-lokshields, Glasgow, which she advertised to rent one week (seven days!) after I left Alistair.

Her best friend, Kirsty, is an events manager who lives in Highbury and looks good enough in a bikini to show her friends and her friends' friends. They get together in Lon-don or Glasgow once a month and go on holiday somewhere warm every year together. She's single. No kids. Her dad has bowel cancer and she's very close to him. She has blonde hair which she curls for big nights out. Kirsty doesn't use Face-book much and posts personal comments on Joanna's wall.

Kirsty McNicol posted on Joanna Lindsay's wall.
Babes! I've booked for next Sat. Get the bevy in!

Comment from Joanna Lindsay.
Yay! (You can send me private messages using the message button Kirst!)

When Joanna was seven she was very tomboyish and played football in an otherwise all-boys team.

She studied English Literature at Edinburgh University,

did her teaching diploma in Manchester, taught English to fifth- and sixth-year students at Hutchesons' Grammar in Glasgow, and commuted every day – from my flat in Edinburgh – till she took maternity leave. She goes running, enjoys gardening, likes bands I've never heard of, isn't very funny on Facebook, gets an uncalled for number of 'likes' for her dull comments about books and gardening, in my honest opinion.

She's twenty-nine, twelve years younger than me and Alistair.

I type in her name and wait for the page to appear, anger and fear swelling as it always does, me wondering why I do this to myself, why I don't just let it go, but I can't stop, I can't, I don't know who I'd be without the fear and the anger, I'd probably just *poof!* disappear, and there she is.

There *they* are. The profile picture, changed eight weeks ago. Man and Woman sit arm in arm on the red sofa I bought at Harvey Nichols in the living room I painted Pale Parisian Blue, smiling a smile which must be fake because the baby on her lap is crying and I know it's not possible to smile when your baby is crying. I wonder why they didn't wait and get one when his mouth wasn't wide open screaming. I wonder what happened to the floral cushions I bought to match the sofa.

Then I see the post on the wall, just an hour ago.

Kirsty McNicol posted on Joanna Lindsay's wall

Oh my God. I've just seen the news – NO! – Tell me it's not true. You're not answering your phone. Call me.

My first thought is plane crash and I'm surprised that I don't break out in a smile but go hot with panic instead. Maybe I don't want him dead.

Or the fires, I think, opening Google search and typing in their names. Maybe they were caught in it, in the car. My heart bangs. I'm afraid for them. I'm sick for Chloe.

A brief one-liner is all over the news already: *Baby Noah Robertson, 9 weeks old, is reported to have disappeared from his parents' car outside a milk bar in Point Lonsdale.* I can't find any other details, so I search 'Point Lonsdale' and 'Lonnie' on Twitter, my breathing fast and shallow as I make sense of the conversations.

HarryDean @hdean
Somethings goin down at milk bar in Point Lonsdale. Cops everywhere.

Fiona Mack @Fionamack
@hdean Fire close?

Harry Dean @hdean
@Fionamack Nah, raining like a bastard. Main street blocked off wtf

Bobblypops @bobblypops
Can see a dark haired woman across the road from mine yelling

Bobblypops @bobblypops
Shop keeper's being interviewed

Bobblypops @bobblypops
Man just knocked on my door asked if I'd seen a baby. #lonniebaby

Bobblypops @bobblypops
Baby gone missing in Point Lonsdale #lonniebaby

Jennifer Weston @jenniferwritesbooks
Oh God. Boy or girl? Terrible. #lonniebaby

Bobblypops @bobblypops
@jenniferwritesbooks Boy, nine weeks #lonniebaby

Fiona Mack @Fionamack
@jenniferwritesbooks @bobblypops He didn't just wander off then #lonniebaby

Bobblypops @bobblypops
Police fuckin lookin through my house and asking if I have a Japara #lonniebaby

Bobblypops @bobblypops
Coppers gone now. Taken from car outside milk bar #lonniebaby

Fiona Mack @Fionamack
@bobblypops Was he in the car alone? #lonniebaby

Bobblypops @bobblypops
@Fionamack cops say parents were in shop #lonniebaby

John Mitchell @johnnyonthepress
They left him in the car!? #lonniebaby

Bobblypops @bobblypops
Cops knocking on doors all along the main road #lonniebaby

Bobblypops @bobblypops
Poked head out door. The man won't stop yelling #lonniebaby

The Kiosk at the Beach @beachykiosk
What have I missed? R u serious? #lonniebaby

Patricia Coll @patsycoll
My prayers go out to them #lonniebaby

Susan Miller @susangmiller
I'm going to help FIND BABY NOAH! Are you? Please
retweet. #lonniebaby

Fiona Mack @Fionamack
What kind of person would leave a baby alone in a car #lon-
niebaby

Celesta Veste @celestaveste1
When will people learn? #lonniebaby

Bobblypops @bobblypops
Going out for a smoke. See if I can find out more #lonniebaby

The Kiosk at the Beach @beachykiosk
RT @susangmiller I'm going to help FIND BABY NOAH!
Are you? Please retweet. #lonniebaby

Susan Miller @susangmiller
RT @Fionamack What kind of person would leave a baby
alone in a car? #lonniebaby

What kind of person would leave a baby alone in a car? Almost immediately a terrible thought strikes me. They'll suspect me. I try to calm my breathing but all I'm doing is
breathing even faster and making myself aware of it. They'll
say he was going to take my baby, so I took his. I look at the

front door. The police will come here first, probably even before they knock on the doors of the local paedophiles. I check it's locked. I look out the window for headlights, listen for sirens. None yet.

Chloe. I should make arrangements. Warn her.

I should not have a drink.

I pour myself a glass of red wine and gulp it down. I know it'll cost a fortune, but I dial my lawyer's number anyway. She takes a while to answer then does so groggily. I tell her what I've read, wait as she types and reads the same, then recount my movements that evening. Collected Chloe from school at 3.15 p.m. Took her swimming. Came home. Had takeaway Roti Channai, watched TV, kissed her goodnight. Yes, I was with her all night, from 3.30 onwards, except when I ducked out to get the Roti Channai. Yes, I often nip out. I'm a single mother. She's fourteen. I ring Mum. She and Dad will be here in just over an hour.

I hope the police will take longer.

I open Chloe's bedroom door. She's clutching the small brown bear Alistair gave her for her sixth birthday. I sneak in at least once a night to watch my troubled near-woman sleeping like a little girl. It's incongruous and delicious, that she's hugging a teddy, just strings now, from eight years of being cried on and clung to. She's mad at her father for making little or no effort to see her, but she blames Joanna, not him. She misses her father. Like most children in this situation, she dreams that one day Joanna will disappear, and that her family will be a family again. I've lost count of the number of times she's asked me if I could at least try to get him back. 'That's not going to happen,' I say each time, suppressing the urge to tell her what I really think of him. It's hard, almost impossible sometimes, but she'll be a happier person if she loves and admires her dad. What if he takes her now? If Mum and Dad don't make it here from Diamond Creek before the police, they might just give her to him when they take me in. Even if he's shocked and grief-stricken, he's still the next of kin after me, so it's a possibility. I can't let that happen. I go back to the kitchen and pour another wine, drink it, then go and sit on the edge of Chloe's bed.

I stroke her fringe. I've worked out ways not to see him in her. Her dark lashes come from her grandmother, not from him. I always liked his mum and I've made sure Chloe's had contact since we came home. They meet in town, mostly – Chloe always comes back with Darrell Lea Coconut Ice and oodles of shopping bags.

She's frowning in her sleep. Another dream about her dad, she'll tell me when she wakes. 'He was eating dinner with me, nothing unusual, just sitting there eating,' she'll say, or something like that.

I whisper, 'Chloe.'

'Hmm?' She turns onto her other side, bear and all.

'Chlo. Wake up beautiful girl. I have to tell you something.'

'I had a dream,' she says, eyes still closed, but awake enough to hide the bear under the covers.

'Something bad has happened,' I say, taking her hand.

She opens her eyes and sits up. 'What?'

'Baby Noah has gone missing.'

'What do you mean?'

'Someone took Noah from your dad's car while he wasn't looking. Tonight, in Point Lonsdale.'

She's dressed in seconds, making plans about how to help. She wants to go and look for him now and wonders why I'm not ready myself. 'Maybe he crawled, maybe he got out of the car himself. Get a move on! We have to go there and look!'

I'm about to explain there's no way a nine-week-old baby can crawl but there's a knock on the door.

*

The police are wondering if Chloe is lying for me, assuming she's used to doing this since I grabbed her and left. The young female one with glasses keeps looking at her when I answer them. I follow her eyes and unfortunately Chloe does look like she's covering for me. 'Yes, we've been here all night,' she says. 'No, no one else has seen us.' She looks at me every now and then, as if asking: *Have I said the right thing?* I'm terrified she'll tell them I left her alone to pop out for the Roti Channai. It'd take me off the list of kidnapping suspects, but keep me on the unfit mother one. Chloe doesn't mention it. Good decision, Chlo, I think.

They won't tell me anything other than what I already know. The baby was last seen in the hire car in Point Lonsdale at around 6.50 p.m.

The male one with the sideburns wants to know about my relationship with Alistair now. I ask Chloe to go and watch television in the sitting room. She rolls her eyes, unhappy to be left out, annoyed that we're sitting in the kitchen talking when we should be out there searching, but she does as she's told, skulking off, shutting the door behind her.

I'm aware I have to be very careful. I've been preparing myself to tell this story to strangers for a long time, but I have to be even more careful not to sound like a crazy bitch now. I'm aware that my awareness that I have to be careful may make me sound like a crazy bitch.

'I left Scotland because I didn't want to lose my daughter,' I say, not finishing the sentence that's pounding in my head, which ended with 'to a narcissistic psychopath'.

'I have only ever wanted to protect my daughter,' I say, conscious that the aforementioned description wants to attach itself to every sentence and every thought that relates to him. It has wanted to since the first time I wondered whether it defined the man I had married, which was after I discovered the affair. I began to realise that our marriage was all lies, all just smoke and mirrors. In Edinburgh I thought our relationship had flattened because Alistair was working hard and I was homesick. I became paranoid that his lack of attention was due to me being no fun, or unattractive. He didn't ravish me the way he used to, but I thought the problems were small and normal, nothing we couldn't work through eventually.

We didn't fight. Things were dull, but comfortable. On reflection, I realise we didn't care enough to fight, and that things weren't comfortable at all. According to Phil, Alistair had indulged in other women before Joanna. He'd been deceiving me all along, and I had no clue. What an idiot I was. Is he a narcissistic psychopath? He ticks a lot of the boxes. Or is that just the scorned woman talking?

'What do you want to protect her from?' the female one with glasses and thin lips asks. And I find another way to explain. 'From losing me, her mother,' I say. 'When I found out he was leaving me for someone else, I asked if we could go home to Australia and share custody. He refused. I know him. He's stubborn, and his work's very important to him. He would never have compromised. I couldn't live there. My visa was based on him, y'see. If the case had gone to court in Scotland, there's a chance he would have won. I was unemployed and pretty depressed. I drank too much. He was successful and well respected. But I was a good mother to Chloe, I know I was. And he was never around for her anyway. That's why I took her. Here, look at this.' I take the scrapbook I started working on the day Alistair filed for custody and show them the first few pages – there's a photograph of me and Chloe baking cupcakes, smiling at the camera, flour on our aprons and clothes, one of us jogging together, one of me helping her with her maths homework. But they're not interested in my scrapbook.

'You were charged with drink driving last month?' the

female one asks.

'I had two glasses with lunch . . . I didn't think . . .'

'No.' She full-stops for me.

'How do you feel about his new partner?' the male one with sideburns and chin-dimple asks.

I swallow a snigger. *How do I feel about her?* I decide to be honest. 'I'm still angry at her, but I also feel for her.'

'You feel for her because of the situation?' the female one with the glasses and thin lips and French-polished nails asks.

'Yes.' This is true, but it's not just that. Beneath the thick layer of anger I feel for her lies a thin layer of guilt. I left a young woman with that man. I left her there to get pregnant to that man. I should have warned her. She wouldn't have listened, I told myself and still tell myself. It would have been impossible for her to listen, just as it was for me when Dad suggested I should play the field before settling down with Alistair. How can you listen to such negativity when a gorgeous sexy man has you on a pedestal, when he's telling you you're the most intriguing and beautiful woman he's ever known, when he's calling you his best friend and his soul mate, making mind-blowing love to you twice a day, smothering you with adoration, writing beautiful love letters, fixing things, organising things, making things happen? God, those early days were wonderful. No, she wouldn't have listened.

I'm not saying we are sisters in arms, definitely not. She's part of him. They are Team Enemy. Letting her in would be the same as letting him in, and I will never make the mistake of doing that. But sometimes the guilt nudges the anger from below and I worry for her, especially at night. I worry about the day she discovers him betraying her. I've imagined her coming to me, years hence. I might be ninety or so, in a home, and she'll come to say sorry, and to cry about the pack of lies her life turned out to be.

I have to admit, I find myself smiling when I imagine this meeting.

'That your car in the drive?' the female one asks.

'It is.'

'A Ute, yeah?'

'Yeah.'

'What colour would you say it is?'

The male cop has gone outside and is touching the bonnet as if he's taking its pulse.

'I'd say it's dark grey.'

'How much do you hate him?'

'Who?' Her change of tack is so abrupt it confuses me.

'Your husband.' She leans in. 'How much would you like him to suffer for what he did?'

'Ex-husband. We divorced a year ago. I don't want him to suffer . . .' I lean back, a liar.

'I bet the anger you feel for him is nothing compared to the anger you feel for her?' she says. 'I can tell you're filled with bad ugly shit-on-you hate.' She moves away, and points to the coat rack in the hall. My waterproof jacket. 'Is this your jacket?'

'It is.'

'Japara, yeah?'

'Yep.'

She touches it. Her colleague comes in from the driveway and stands to her left, nodding as if to say: she's touching that, just like I touched the bonnet of the Ute out in the drive, and that's 'cause we're the law, missy.

'It's not wet,' the female one concludes.

'What's that got to do with anything?'

'Your ex saw someone in a Japara – it was raining.' They're playing annoying-cop/annoying-cop. It's the male one who said that.

'You have a clothes dryer?' Female.

'Off the kitchen.'

The female cop heads to the laundry, leaving the male cop to cop a feel of my jacket, which he does, then gives me a look that says: *I am not telling you if it is hot or not!*

'Can we look around your house?' the male one with the sideburns, dimple and wedding ring says.

I don't object. I'd sound guilty.

As they search, I fidget on the couch and worry that they'll find him here, in the cupboard in the laundry or something, as I do when anyone accuses me of anything. Maybe I did do it. Maybe I did wear the Japara earlier tonight and get it wet stealing a child and then dry it in the dryer and hang it up on its hook in the hall. Maybe the baby's in the laundry cupboard. I blame Alistair for the paranoia. I was paranoid that he'd try and take Chloe from me, that he'd tell everyone

I was an unfit mother even though he used to say I was the most wonderful mother in the world. Alistair built me a solid foundation for paranoia.

He's not in the cupboard. Of course he's not. And the car engine's cold and the dryer's not been used and the jacket's not warm. I let them look on my computer and find out I have a fake account and that I stalk her. That's how I knew he'd gone missing, I explain. And they seem to understand. They seem to be getting nicer as time goes on. Or just disappointed. The latter, I'd say, because I'm sure they had straight backs when they arrived, both of them. They're slumping out the door now. They didn't solve an enormous mystery and won't be heroes on the telly. If I'm planning on going anywhere, I should talk to them first, the female one with the glasses, thin lips, incongruous nails and flat chest says. They will need to speak to me again. If I skip town, it will be very suspicious.

As they begin to head out, my parents arrive, about-facing and reinvigorating the cops. Maybe the old fogies did it. Maybe they *will* be on the telly. They take Mum and Dad into the living room and question them. Chloe and I both eavesdrop, ears against door.

'Pat Donohue,' my dad is telling them . . . 'Unit 2/18 Yoker Street, Diamond Creek. No siblings. She's our only child.'

'We prayed for another one,' my mum is saying, 'but it never happened. My name? Annie Donohue. Same address.' Her voice is shaky. She's scared for me. 'The separation was difficult but my daughter is not spiteful. Okay, yes, she did take

Chloe away from him but he didn't make much of an effort and she did try...'

My dad's interjecting: 'Al only had Chloe's best interests at heart. She had no one over there. It would have been an impossible life for both of them. She'd never hurt anyone.'

The female cop's asking them where they were tonight.

'Having fish pie at Dennis and Molly Ewan's,' my mum's saying.

'From six till ten-thirty,' my dad's confirming.

*

Chloe's been understandably torn about Noah. Since she found out Joanna was pregnant, she's referred to him as 'The Replacement'. But she's distraught now, suddenly feeling a sister's love. Mum hugs Chloe, and they sob together. She hugs me next but I'm not tearful. I'm waiting for Alistair to call. I know he will, as soon as they let him.

Dad pours the rest of my bottle of wine down the sink and clears the rubbish and dishes from our takeaway. No one wants to ask what this will mean for the custody hearing. 'What should we be doing?' he says instead. Always practical and proactive, just like Chloe. He's the one paying for the top-notch lawyer to make sure his daughter isn't slaughtered in court, and that he doesn't lose his granddaughter.

'He'll want to see Chloe,' I say, turning on the news.

I shudder: Joanna Lindsay is on screen. She's not what I remember: naked in bed, rosy cheeked from fucking my husband. She's not how she is on Facebook either, smiley public face saying everything is great, I am great, my baby is great, my life is great(er than yours). She's standing on the street where it happened, surrounded by police and onlookers. She has wet tangled hair, a grey expressionless face, milk stains on her T-shirt, and is thinner than I remember. I feel a heavy tingle all over but especially in my stomach, a heavy tingle like I'm filled with leaden sherbet. The tingle fuels thoughts so shallow I don't want to admit to them. Fuck up! Yes, that's the first. Do something SO idiotic, Joanna Lindsay, that the whole of Australia will see what a numbskull you are. She has a tiny pot belly! That's the other thought. I want her to turn sideways so I can see just how much bigger her stomach is than mine. I am not a good person.

A police officer hugs her. She looks devastated. I'm surprised at what my heart does, it gains weight and heads south, thump. Joanna Lindsay is a sad, lost, poor girl.

Chloe answers when her dad rings and it's decided. We'll call the police to let them know where we're going, and take her to see her father now.

*

The house is just the same as it ever was, except the weatherboard needs a paint and the grass has turned to dust. It feels weird not to go in – Elizabeth and I got on well – but I won't, I tell them. I'll stay in the car. There are three police cars parked on the street in front and two journalists taking photos and waiting for interviews, microphones in hand. Mrs Robertson's black Golf is in the driveway – I recognise it. I watch Chloe walk up the front path and along the veranda, my mum and dad behind her. When the door opens, it's him. He looks even younger than he did four years ago but his head seems to have grown and his body shrunk. He's short. I never took much notice, but he's stumpy. I don't find him attractive at all. How wondrous. I don't find him attractive! He's kind of puky, with his thinning over-worked hair and his under-worked body. (That's a bit of a spare tyre, I think. Just a bit, but it's there.) He's oddly proportioned, short and balding and fat. Phil runs 5k every night. Phil looks good for his age, not like some old guy trying to look young. Phil has all his hair. Why am I thinking this? We're just friends. As if Phil'd ever go for me.

I am one shallow piece of work to be thinking these things, but he's still at the door and I can't help it.

What strikes me more than how he looks is that he is a stranger. I scan him one more time and wonder who he is and why I allowed him to kidnap my self-worth. He's just some guy. Some guy who makes me burn with anger. I can feel it now. He hugs Chloe. I hear someone crying, or more than one person. Hard to tell. They all go in, shut the door.

I wonder if Alistair thinks I'd be capable of something like this, really. He knows I have a Japara – he gave it to me in the early days, when he still bought me thoughtful presents. He bought his and hers, in fact, so we could hike together 'in any weather, at least once a month'! He wouldn't know for sure that I still have it, but he does know I loved it, and that I never throw things out. I berate myself for caring what he thinks. It's always annoyed me, that I care what he thinks of me.

I'll be here a long time, I suppose. I wonder about heading to the pub. I wonder about texting Mum to tell her I've gone for a walk and to text back when they're done.

There's a knock at the window. A woman. I press the button to wind down the window and she pokes a microphone at my face. 'Excuse me, are you related to the Robertsons? Would you answer—'

I press the button and the window goes up, not fast enough. 'Go away,' I say pushing her microphone out so it doesn't get caught.

As uncomfortable as it is, I will not go away. I won't risk losing Chloe to him, no matter what. I don't trust him.

Another knock, a woman squealing: 'We just want to ask you a few questions.' I wave her away, and turn the radio on to drown her out.

She knocks, bangs on the window. Another journalist bangs on the other one. The car feels like it's shaking. I put my hand on the horn and leave it there till they back off a little, only a little. I open the window and tell them I'll get the police to move them on if they don't leave me alone. I notice Joanna looking out the window to see what's going on.

I close the window, sigh, and shut my eyes, wondering what they're doing and saying in there. He'll be hugging my daughter and telling her he loves her. My mum and dad will be nice to both of them, my issues superseded by theirs. It angers me. It shouldn't I know. See, I really am bad.

I need a drink.

Gone for a walk, I text Mum. *Txt when you're leaving and I'll meet you at the car.*

She texts me back: *ok.*

Two journalists follow me. 'Who are you?' 'Are you related?' 'Do you know the parents?' 'Just a few questions.' I run, and they're not desperate enough to keep up with me.

The pub is closed. It's 4 a.m., after all.

I run back to the car, elbow some hacks out of the way, get in, and lock the doors. The curtain in the house twitches. Joanna.

I will not feel sorry for her. I will not lose focus. No matter what has happened, I will not lose Chloe.

I can't help but turn round and when I do I see she is still at the window. If there is a bond between us – two mothers fearing they will never see their child again – I refuse to welcome it.

I've thought about her so much over the last four years she's become as important and as mystical as the Holy Ghost. But there she is, and even from this distance I can see she's just a shaky little girl. On her first day of school, I was seventeen, form six, smoking, pashing, doing exams. I wonder if the terror and sadness in her eyes has only just arrived, because of the baby, or has it been there for a while, because of him. After all, she's known what a good liar he is from the start. I didn't know till it was over.

I turn on the radio and stare at it instead of her. It's weird that she's looking at me for so long. Uncomfortable. I'm not looking but I can sense her.

It's the first story on the news. They're looking for someone dressed in a Japara, and for someone who drives a white Ute. They're also questioning a paedophile, some guy who lives nearby and was released recently. He's forty-seven. I feel ill.

I look to the window again. Yep, she's still there. I wish she'd go away. It's creepy. Why is she staring at me? Shouldn't she be doing something to find her child instead? Her nine-week-old baby is gone, for God's sake, and they're questioning a paedophile.

*

Chloe comes out an hour later and slams the car door after her. She won't talk to me.

'Are you okay?' I ask Chloe again after we've driven a few blocks, but she doesn't answer. The little girl who still clings to a teddy bear in bed has morphed into the teenager that's been taking over these last two years. Loving eyes have turned angry. Admiring smile now suspicious, disdainful. I know better than to press her when she's like this. I wait till she's asleep to find out what happened.

'Tell me everything,' I say to Dad when she dozes off half an hour later.

Dad, like me, is good at recounting events and conversations. He does it in order, and doesn't leave anything out. Chloe hugged her father, he tells me. He told her he loved her, that she hadn't changed a bit. He told her she was like a bright light, that when she came into the room everything changed for the better. He told her he could cope with anything with his beautiful girl by his side. She might have found this gushing a bit much, because she stopped him short, asking him and the police question after question about exactly what happened and where and what Noah was wearing etc. She asked for a printed photograph of him and took notes in a small notebook, which is now in her jeans pocket. She completely ignored Joanna, who didn't even try to talk to her. There were three police officers in the house, tapping phones and whispering to each other but otherwise not doing very much at all. Alistair was 'as much of an arsehole as ever'.

'Why?'

'Mega efficient,' he says, 'brushing Chloe off when she began repeating her questions, ordering the police about.' Dad puts on a deep authoritative Alistair voice: 'Question the shop assistant... Search the houses again... Japaras! Look for Japaras! And Utes! White Utes! What other sex offenders live in the area?'

The voice is spookily accurate. It's so weird that I once found Alistair's voice a turn-on.

'He didn't say a word to me or your mum,' Dad continues, 'although we didn't push it after saying how sorry we were. And once Chloe sidled away he just ignored her too.'

Same old same old, I think to myself. 'And what about Joanna?' I ask.

'Oddball, if you ask me,' he says. 'Not crying. You'd cry, wouldn't you? She just stared out the window. Chloe?' Dad turns round to make sure she's still out for the count. 'She really sound asleep?' he asks Mum.

'Yeah, the blossom,' Mum whispers, kissing the top of her head.

'When we stood to leave,' Dad continues in a hushed voice, 'Chloe said to the police, "Maybe she did it," pointing to Joanna.

'Alistair was furious with her: "What a thing to say!" He told her to apologise.

'She refused and he yelled: "Apologise this minute, young lady!"

'"Why should I?" she said. "I'm not the one who keeps losing you your children." Then she stormed out.'

'Shit, what did Joanna do when she said that?'

'Just stared at her. Weird woman. Maybe Chloe's right.'

'No, you think?'

'Ninety per cent of cases like this it's the parents.'

14

ALEXANDRA

16 February

I don't wake Chloe for school and she's furious when she realises it's 10.30.

'Of course I'm going in! I need to tell people to look for him. They might let me talk at assembly,' she says, throwing on her uniform.

'Hang on!' I yell, chasing after her with the first packed lunch I've prepared in years. 'Stand at the door with this.' The lunch box is new, blue, and impressive, with containers inside for fruit, and a clip on the side for a non-sugary drink. 'Smile!' I say, holding the camera.

'I really don't feel like smiling,' she says, and shuts the door behind her.

I print the smileless photo and stick it in the scrapbook – proof that I am the kind of mother who makes lunch from scratch and packs it neatly into a nifty blue box.

Phil's already texted me twice. I ring him on his mobile. 'Yeah, we're okay. In shock.'

'I've not gone in yet. I'll take the day off.'

'No, no need. I've got things to do. I'll see you for lunch – The Lemon Tree?'

'Okay, twelve thirty. Let me know if you want me to come over before then.'

I go for a run to clear my head then meet Phil at the café round the corner from Melbourne University in Carlton, where he works as a physics lecturer. He's sitting at the window and it strikes me that we have a regular table. The television is on in the corner and Phil's watching the same report I saw last night. He's wearing the kind of mismatched gear a prospective girlfriend would need to change immediately: brown shoes, blue jeans, black T-shirt and grey zip up cardigan. I think he looks ace.

He stands to hug me. 'Is Chloe okay?'

'In shock, I think. She asked if she could use your scanner to get posters done after school?'

'Course, tell her to ride over. We could take Ziggy out for a walk after.' Ziggy is Phil's ten-year-old Australian terrier, Chloe's favourite creature in the world.

I usually wait at least ten minutes before seeking counselling from Phil. I can't wait so long today.

'I thought if I saw him I might feel nothing.'

He must be so sick of saying the same things: *No, Al, you did nothing wrong. He's the bastard, not you, him. You just have to get your head around the fact that he's not who you thought he was.* If he is fed up, he never lets on. 'To feel nothing, you need to forgive him,' he says.

'Forgiving him seems as appropriate as forgiving cancer.' I was pleased when I came up with this line in my head, and excited to finally say it out loud. When Phil doesn't respond or look impressed by my insight, I turn to wave for the bill and knock over the vase on the table, spilling water all over his jeans.

'My clumsiest dear, whose hands shipwreck vases,' he says, patting his trousers with a napkin.

'What?'

'It's from a poem I like. Makes me think of you.'

'Shit, I know that woman!' the guy at the table next to us says, looking at the television.

We prick our ears to listen. Both men at the table are in suits: business lunch, I suppose.

'Really?' The older man opposite him says.

'Yeah . . . well, she was on the same flight. Her baby wouldn't stop screaming and she went nuts – held her wee boy at me, kinda dangled . . . like this . . .' The man holds his hands before him as if strangling something. '. . . and yelled: *Why don't you complain to him personally?* or something like that, can't recall exactly. I suggested she calm down and she practically threw the baby at her husband. That's her! I can't believe it. God, that's terrible.'

The news report is live outside the Point Lonsdale Milk Bar, and is intercut with pictures of Noah, and the Facebook one of the three of them on the sofa in Edinburgh. The young guy in the suit tut-tuts then says very loudly, 'He seemed like a good guy on the plane. But she's fucking nuts. A hundred bucks says she did it.'

*

Chloe chucks her school bag on the floor when she gets in at four, feeds her budgies and hamsters and cat, and makes to rush out.

'Hey!' I yell. 'Why don't you take Blake with you?'

'No,' she says, putting her helmet on in the hall.

That's a shame. She and Blake Henderson have been best mates since we moved here. He's a serious boy, with a gorgeous Corgi and a love of books and photography. Then, a few weeks ago, it just stopped. It's been weird not having him around the house, even weirder that neither of them will say what happened.

'What about a kiss, then?' I say to Chloe.

She makes a noise by my cheek, wheels her bike out of the hall, and rides off towards Phil's.

A few minutes later, Gene Henderson arrives at the front door. Blake's mother is the only school mum I've connected with. Happily married, and running her own business as an interior designer, she's down to earth and uncomplicated. She asks about Noah and gives me a hug of support, knowing how difficult this will be for my daughter. After I've told her everything I know, she changes the subject. 'I finally got it out of Blake,' she says.

'And?'

'And . . . I quote . . . "It became awkward between us when Chloe began straightening her hair. At our age, it's difficult for boys and girls to be friends. I'm sure we will again one day."'

'He's like forty!' I say.

'He's weird right enough,' Gene says.

How sad, but Blake's right – they're kindred spirits, they'll be mates again one day.

'I've been roped into a ladies' night,' I tell Gene.

'You idiot! I'm eating an entire chocolate cake, opening a bottle and watching *Offspring* – again. Which reminds me I need to go for a swim to earn it. Check ya later.' With that, Gene's out the door.

*

I don't get to the phone in time when Alistair calls – thank God. He leaves a message. 'Chloe, it's Dad. No news yet, I'm afraid. I hope you're okay. I'm really sorry about last night. Can I see you this week? I'll call again tomorrow. Bye darlin'.'

She plays the message over and over when she gets home from Phil's. 'He's got an accent,' she says. 'I didn't notice last night.'

'You going to call him back?'

'Nah,' she says, heading to her room.

Mum and Dad arrive to babysit at seven and I go to the school with a cake from the coffee shop. I've put the cake on one of my plates and messed up the icing a bit so it looks like I baked it. The hall is filled with tables selling soaps and make-up and stuff considered to be of interest to ladies.

I'm not comfortable with all these girly things, and hate the word lady, but I decide to try and overcome this, placing my cake on the baking-goods table and smiling at the two women behind it. They don't know who I am and my presence does not interrupt their conversation.

'She seems aloof, know what I mean?' Woman One says.

Woman Two: 'Apparently there's like two dozen paedoes in a thirty k radius.'

Woman Three (who has overheard from the Nails table): 'You talking about the Robertson baby? My aunty Mary's from the next town, Queenscliff . . .' The eyes of the other two light up. '. . . and she heard they've already taken someone in for questioning. Check this . . .' Woman Three scrolls on her iPhone till she finds the relevant item, then passes the handset to One and Two.

I'm hovering and they don't find this odd – in fact, they tilt the iPhone so I can see the screen, which has a photo of a man who's around fifty. The caption reads: 'Convicted sex offender Henry Kelly released from prison to address in Wallington.'

Woman Three: 'Got out a week ago. Living just down the road from Point Lonsdale.'

Woman One: 'What an ugly man.'

Two: 'Sick bastard.'

Three: 'Should tell people when someone like that moves round the corner.'

One: 'Look at his eyes.'

Two/Three: 'God'/'Evil.'

Three: 'I can't look at them.'

One: 'Take it away. He's making that fudge turn in my tummy.'

Three: 'Hey, I made that!'

One /Two: 'I can't stop eating it'/'It's delicious!'

The phone is returned to its owner.

Pause.

'I have never once left Frederick in the car.' Woman One.

'Crazy thing to do.' Woman Two.

'Wouldn't leave Dante even for a minute.' Three.

As for me, I've had enough. I've almost escaped when Chloe's English teacher accosts me at the door. 'I'm so sorry about what happened. How's Chloe?'

'She's holding up.'

'If she needs more time off, we understand. I can get her the homework sheets.'

'More time off?'

'We can't imagine how she must be feeling.'

'She didn't come in today?'

The English teacher blushes. 'We assumed . . .'

'I'll have a word with her,' I say, doubling her blush.

*

I admit I part-ruined my daughter by reacting the way I did four years ago. A good mother would have slapped her adulterous husband, yes, but then she would have cried into his arms, which he would have opened – what man wouldn't open his arms to the crying wife he was just caught wronging? – and spoken softly of 'our child'. 'We should stay together for her,' a good mother would have said. 'She's only ten. This will ruin her life! We have to get through this as a family.'

I know he'd have agreed. No matter how filthy and frequent the sex she was giving him, he would have said, 'You're right, Lex. I'm sorry. Can you forgive me?' He probably would've kept screwing his mistress, but a good mother would have minded this less than destroying her child.

Instead I didn't even give Chloe the chance to say goodbye to her father, I plonked her in an unfamiliar school and house to be badly fed by a mother who cried each evening into a wine glass.

If I had my time again, perhaps I would cry into Alistair's chest instead, ignoring the stench of sex on the hairs there.

No, I could never ignore past betrayal and live with the worry that it would continue. I had to leave. The world changed when I found out Alistair had been lying to me. I changed. I wasn't a best friend any more. I wasn't the love of someone's life any more. I wasn't a wife. I wasn't attractive or clever or witty or fun.

He changed, too: disappeared more like, up in smoke with all my happy memories. Who was this man I thought I couldn't live without, the one I loved so hard in the early years, and more softly in the latter as is the way with love?

Who was this man who had seemed to care about me and obviously didn't?

But I had Chloe. And that, I told myself when I arrived in Australia with three suitcases and the £3,000 I'd withdrawn from our joint account, was all that mattered, and would never change.

I knock on her bedroom door and wait till she opens it.

'You didn't go to school today,' I say, walking towards her bed and sitting on it. 'Where were you?'

If I was a better mother, she'd be afraid of me, at least a little. She sits at her desk and types away on her laptop, not even looking at me.

'Did you go to see your father?'

'No.'

'Where, then?'

'Library.'

'Why? Stop typing and look at me.' She doesn't. 'Why?' I almost yell.

'I can leave home soon and look after myself so it's none of your business what I do and where I go.'

Rage takes hold as I grab the laptop from her, yanking the plug out.

'That's my property!' she screams. 'I'm calling the police.'

She's written a list of facts about Noah's disappearance on a Word document: timeline, places, people, evidence, tweets, links to articles, quotes from news reports, Facebook posts.

'I'm going to find out what happened to him,' she explains,

shaking in anger. 'You watch.'

I shut the laptop lid and move towards her, guiding her trembling hand into mine. 'It's a good idea, writing things down,' I say. 'And I'll support you with anything you think you can do to find Noah. But you have to tell me what you're doing and if you want time off school, you have to ask me. Can that be a deal?' Before I finish the sentence I scold myself. *Can that be a deal?* What a wimp of a mother I am. 'That *is* the deal,' I correct myself, turning our healing hand-hold into a sealing handshake.

15

ALEXANDRA

17 February

I take Chloe to the school gates and watch her walk up the steps. When I get home, I glue myself to the news. They're about to make an appeal. Must be about a hundred journos at his mother's house now. I pour myself a coffee and take my seat, almost excited, almost as if I'm at the movies and it's gone dark and I'm about to be entertained.

The front door of his mother's house opens. Joanna and Alistair walk out and stand on the veranda. She doesn't know what to do with her hands. They dangle heavily at her sides, then anchor themselves in the pockets of her jeans. Her face is white. Her eyes are not red. She's not crying. She should. It looks wrong that she's not. In fact, she looks cold and hard and not very likeable. She doesn't usually look like this. She usually looks pretty and approachable, the type of girl I would have wanted to be mates with had she not fucked my husband and my life.

'Our baby, Noah,' Alistair says, using all the skills years in PR and politics taught him, 'was taken from our car two days ago, 6.50 p.m., fifteenth of February. He was wearing a white Babygro. He has dark brown hair and brown eyes.' I can tell

Alistair is upset that his son has no other features that might help identify him. No birthmarks, like the star-shaped one on the right side of Alistair's neck. Nothing. This baby looks like every other baby. And is wearing what every other baby wears. A white Babygro.

'The police are continuing to look into the sightings of a white Ute and a man or woman dressed in a dark coloured Japara. Please, if anyone has any information that might help, contact the police immediately.'

He holds the microphone for Joanna to take. She takes a while to get her hand out of her pocket and it shakes as she holds it.

'Please, if you have seen our baby, or if you have our baby...' She breaks off and glances at Alistair, who I notice is squeezing her elbow. 'I mean Noah. If you know anything – about Noah – could you please contact the police. We just want...' She again looks at Alistair, who is now sobbing like I've never seen him sob in his life. 'I'm sorry,' Joanna says, 'I'm too distressed to talk.' She almost jabs Alistair in the chest with the microphone then walks inside and slams the door. Alistair is visibly annoyed that she has done this. 'My partner and I are in shock,' he says to explain her behaviour. 'Devastated.' A tear falls down his cheek. 'Please help us find Noah. Someone has taken him. Do not be distracted by ludicrous rumours that waste precious time. If you know anything, be brave, and come forward. If you have him, please bring him back to us.' He gives the reporter to his left the microphone and walks inside, closing the door behind him.

*

My shift at the café starts at eleven. Two regulars from the hairdresser's next door order coffees and yap loudly at the counter. I listen as I froth the milk.

'Nah but it's the dirt under his nails,' the heavily made-up colourist called Tania says. 'My friend Jan says her mate Gabe, Gabriel but they call him Gabe, which is a cool name I reckon, was one of the cops who first got there like, and Jan says Gabe says his partner totally saw dirt under that Alistair Robertson's nails and they were just off the plane and why would there be dirt, there just wouldn't be, and it's not like he has a dirty fingernail kinda job, is it, and anyway he would have washed them before the flight.'

How this girl doesn't need to take a very deep breath after this I will never know. I pour the milk into the coffee cups and sprinkle chocolate on top.

'You reckon he did it?' the (probably) gay hairdresser called Johan asks Tania.

'Nah, but well I'm just sayin', why would he have dirt under his nails unless he was like burying a kid in the ground or something? He says he fell over but I think it's a crock of shit.'

'That's eight dollars forty, thanks,' I say, putting the lids on the takeaway cups.

'And also on the news she looked so out of it . . .' She hands me ten dollars without pausing. 'Like on drugs I reckon, and it

124

wouldn't surprise me if she was a junkie and maybe forgot . . . thanks . . .' I've given her the change and they're walking towards the door, coffees in hand. '. . . to feed him and so he goes and buries him and that's why he's got dirt under . . .'

My mobile rings as the door closes behind them. It's Chloe's school. She didn't make it further than the top step. The café owner, Giuseppe, is a kind man, and he lets me go straight home.

She's not there. I leave text and voice messages on her mobile then start phoning everyone I know who she knows. I'm about to scour the streets when she comes in and makes straight for her room.

'Where were you? Chloe, come back here! I've been worried sick. Where have you been?'

'At an internet café in Brunswick.' She tries to shut her door but I grab it in time.

'What did I tell you last night?'

She turns and looks at me. 'Nothing useful. No one's saying or doing anything useful. Tomorrow it'll be too late. It'll be too fucking late.'

It's not the time to pick her up on the swearing. 'What were you doing at the internet café?'

'I set up a Twitter account and a Facebook page and put his photo and all the facts I know on them. A few people have already done blogs and pages and Twitter hashtags but they're all idiots, their details are all wrong, full of bullshit. Someone who knows the facts should be doing it, someone who cares. So that's what I did at the café this morning and you wouldn't believe how many people have messaged me already. Point Lonsdale residents, the guy from the milk bar, and a cop, I reckon, although he or she would never admit it to me. After that I phoned the police in Geelong and spoke to Detective Phan who's working on the case and I asked him exactly what they were doing.'

'What did he say?'

'He wouldn't tell me anything so I insisted on speaking to his boss, who's called Elaine Larson, and she spoke all softly softly to me as if I was a five-year-old with learning difficulties. She said they were doing everything they could but she wouldn't tell me exactly what and accused me of being rude. I asked if I could do an appeal on television and she said she'd have to ask you and Dad so I phoned Channel 10 and David Papadopoulos will be here with a cameraman any minute.'

It's hard to be mad when you're impressed. I need time to think this through, but a van's parking in the drive already. 'What are you going to say?' I ask her as she changes into the T-shirt she somehow managed to get printed on the way home. FIND NOAH is in thick black lettering at the top. Underneath is a photo of her nondescript baby brother.

'I'm just going to ask for help,' she says, then heads back into the living room where David Papadopoulos and his cameraman are ready to go.

'My name is Chloe Robertson,' she says calmly into the

camera. 'My little brother Noah Robertson was last seen two days ago – at 6.50 p.m. on the fifteenth of February. He was in a baby car seat in the right-hand side of the back seat of a black 2010 Range Rover, Vogue model. It had a Victorian licence plate with blue characters on a white background, number VHA 538. The car was parked opposite the milk bar on Point Lonsdale Road on the outskirts of Point Lonsdale, twenty metres from the roundabout that joins the road with the Bellarine Highway. My father Alistair Robertson and Noah's mother Joanna Lindsay were in the milk bar at 6.50 p.m., when they say he was taken from the unattended car. Please, if you have my brother, bring him home to his family. He's just nine weeks old. He looks like this.' She points to her T-shirt. 'Like any other nine-week-old baby, you might think, but look how dark and thick his hair is. And he has beautiful long dark eyelashes. And big brown eyes. He was wearing a Marks & Spencer's white Babygro, and he was wrapped in a square blue cotton blanket one metre by one metre, with a beige embroidered bunny in the middle about four inches long and two inches wide. He was wearing a Huggies newborn disposable nappy which has a picture of a teddy on the front and a light olive green border. I am begging you,' she finishes, not tearful or even shaky, 'if anyone saw anything that night, or knows anything, do the right thing and tell the police, or tell someone you know, or tell me on the Facebook page 'Find Noah' or DM me on Twitter @findnoah.'

I whisk her away after that last sentence and shut her bedroom door, my back against it as I make sure the two men leave. They pack and go quietly with a polite thank you.

'You feel a lot for little Noah,' I venture, surprised at her determination.

'Of course I do.'

'You want to talk about it?'

'We have the same blood,' she says. 'We might have become really close one day. We might have done brother–sister stuff like holidays, I dunno. And someone stole him.'

Just like I stole you, I think.

'Someone could be hurting him right now, killing him. Someone already could have. Of course I feel a lot. It's natural, and my duty.'

'You must be wanting time with your dad, no?'

She shrugs. 'What does he see in that woman?'

'I don't know Chlo. I don't know her.' I don't want to talk about Joanna, so I change the subject. 'I'm proud of you. But from now on, there are rules. Anything you do, you have to do with me.'

'Okay,' she says.

*

After watching her plea on the 2 p.m. news bulletin, we sit down at the computer to go over the work she did online that morning. The Twitter account – @findnoah – already has 708 followers and her tweets look professional and clear. The Facebook page – also Find Noah – is similarly impressive with 1,278 likes and 76 shares. Messages are flooding in already, some of them with details that have not been shown on the news: from a friend of the local police officer, the girlfriend of the shop assistant, the owner of Pasquini's café.

I'm feeling full of pride when Alistair phones.

He's yelling at me. What kind of mother am I, letting a fourteen-year-old go on television? Why didn't I speak to him first? How could I have let her use the words 'when they say he was taken from the unattended car' as if . . . Can't I see I am putting her in danger! Jeopardising the organised, careful and faultless work of the Victorian police force? How could I have let her set up Facebook and Twitter accounts? And phone the police! How—

I hang up on him.

Arsehole.

Arsehole with a point, damn it. Once again I have shown the world that I'm a shit shit shit mother. Another strike against me.

'What was he yelling about?' Chloe asks, sitting on the kitchen bench. I can sense she's nervous, that she's hoping her father is proud of her, like I was before he phoned.

'You need to leave all this up to the police. I'm sorry, but I was wrong to let you do the broadcast. If you have any ideas, talk to me about it but you have to leave this to the grown-ups.'

'That's what he said?'

'And he's right.'

When she stands I notice she's taller than me. Has she grown two inches in two days?

'Fuck him,' she says. 'Fuck the police. And fuck you.'

When the front door slams, I don't waste time pouring wine into a glass before drinking it.

*

I have to tread a fine line: being firm enough to keep Chloe safe – and the kind of mother who'd win a custody battle – but not so firm that she'd rather live with anyone than me. I devise an action plan and explain it when she comes home at 10 p.m., a little drunk maybe, don't know for sure. I'll need to tackle that later. I explain that together we will close her Twitter and Facebook accounts. I tell her I'll ring the police every two days and report back to her about what's happening. She can ring or visit her dad whenever she wants. And each evening – after school – we will plaster posters together. I print out the 'Find Noah Plan' I typed earlier, and we both sign it. I stick a copy in the scrapbook.

'That scrapbook's nuts, Mum,' she mumbles.

'Is it?'

She doesn't answer. Instead, she gives me a hug and tells me she loves me.

My firmness level might just have hit the mark.

But when we withdraw from the hug I get a whiff of her breath and it's confirmed – she's been drinking.

It's 1 a.m. The incidents which preceded my decision to be here are as follows:

Alistair's phone call brought on the rage that turns me into an online stalker. I checked Joanna's Facebook account. Deleted. I Googled them and zoomed in on the walk-in-the-Botanics shot the press have latched on to. I printed it out. I fizzed with fury as I stared at it, wondering why I let him yell at me on the phone like that, why I just took it, why I can't get the fucking arsehole out of my head.

I checked Chloe was sound asleep, left her a note in case she woke before morning, got in the car, then got back out. I couldn't leave Chloe for over two hours now, not with the hearing coming up. I paced the hall for a while, angrier with each step.

Fuck it. Fuck him.

I drove to Geelong.

And that's why I'm sitting in a treehouse in the small park behind Elizabeth's. I had planned to go in and give him a piece of my mind, but there was a security guard at the door, and at least three journalists on the nature strip. I chickened out, drove to the street behind, and climbed the tree.

Alistair and I used to smoke joints here when we visited during breaks from uni. I was fun back then. Now I'm nuts. And the ladder's wobbly, and the boards are rotten. And I am a woman in a tree spying on her ex.

The window to Alistair's bathroom is open. He's sitting on the loo. I shouldn't look.

I look. He's crying. Howling. Groaning.

I drove here hoping another real-life viewing of him might cure me, but no, despite his despair, I feel rage.

She comes into the bathroom. I can only see her hand, on his shoulder. I need to move to the left to see her face. I lose my balance and reach for the top of the ladder . . .

And it falls. I try to grab it, my first thought being: Shit, they'll hear me.

Not only do I fail to stop the ladder falling into the park with a loud first thud and a quieter second one, but I fail to realise that noise is not the big issue here.

I am a woman stuck in a tree.

*

Ninety minutes later I'm in Phil's car, embarrassed.

He drives for a while before saying anything. 'Y'know, it doesn't make sense to forgive cancer, but it makes sense to try and avoid it.'

'How?'

'By not smoking, for example.'

'You're either being very clever or very dumb.'

'By not seeking him out, Al. You seek him out. The Facebook, the Googling . . . Do you realise we haven't had one conversation that he doesn't enter into? Ever since you got back, you haven't been able to stop yourself.'

I take this in for a minute, then open the glove box. He knows I'm a lolly addict, and usually has some for me if we're driving somewhere together. Sure enough, there's a huge packet of Allens Strawberries and Cream inside. When I rip open the wrapper, half of them fall on the floor.

'Whose palms are bulls in china, burs in linen,' he says.

'What?'

'It's from the poem I was talking about the other day. I think of it as my Ode to Al.'

'Who wrote it?'

'John Frederick Nims.'

'Hmm . . . my poem, eh? About a clumsy idiot.' I hand him a lolly.

'It's not about that really,' he says.

'Oh yeah, what's it about?'

He hesitates. 'Give me another one of those before I slap you.'

I hand him a second. 'I'm still not sure which one you are,' I say, chewing on mine.

'What?'

'Clever or dumb.'

He grabs another and smiles. 'I bought Strawberries and Creams!'

16

JOANNA

15 February

Police Interview with Joanna Lindsay
Conducted by Detective Binh Phan
Geelong Police Station, 110 Mercer Street, Geelong,
VIC, 3220
9.16 p.m., 15 February 2011

Phan: What I'd like to do is start at the beginning.

Joanna: When was that?

Phan: When you left the holiday cottage. Tell me everything you remember after shutting the door.

Joanna: Alistair was carrying Noah , and the owner, Mrs Wilson, came to the drive and said hello. It was so hot. He was wearing a white Babygro and he was wrapped in a blue bunny blanket. Then he put him in the car.

Phan: Was he awake?

Joanna: No. We stopped at the milk bar on the edge of the town because we'd run out of wipes.

Phan: Just to go back a bit. When you were at the drive talking to the owner and when you got in the car and drove away, did you notice anyone hanging around your cottage? See anyone?

Joanna: No. The place was quiet, 'cause of the heat and fires. Just Mrs Wilson.

Phan: Noone else?

Joanna: Noone else.

Phan: And what time was it when you stopped at the milk bar?

Joanna: Um, I don't remember... six-something? We parked, then Alistair went in. A couple of minutes later I remembered I needed to get something.

Phan: What?

Joanna: Tampons. When I came back out, he wasn't in the car.

Phan: You had your period? Weren't you breastfeeding?

Joanna: Um ... They were for ... um, discharge.

Phan: And before you went in, did you check on Noah?

Joanna: No. Um ... I just jumped out.

Phan: Was he sleeping?

Joanna: He was silent.

Phan: And when you came back out, was the car door next to his seat open?

Joanna: No.

Phan: Any other doors open? Any sign of forced entry?

Joanna: No. No.

Phan: Had you left the doors open?

Joanna: Um, I must have.

Phan: Would you usually do that?

Joanna: No. I wasn't thinking.

Phan: But you had the keys.

Joanna: No. Maybe Alistair had them.

Phan: When you came back out, did you notice anyone in the area, any cars?

Joanna: No.

Phan: Did you have a good look around?

Joanna: When I realised he was gone, I ran into the milk bar to get the guy to call the police then came back out and Alistair was looking. He was yelling Noah, No . . .

Phan: Are you okay? Would you like a glass of water?

Joanna: I'm okay.

Phan: When you were in the shop the first time, did you hear anything? A car? Voices? Noah crying?

Joanna: No.

Phan: Do you have any enemies Joanna? Anyone who might want to hurt you?

Joanna: No.

Phan: The exwife?

Joanna: Oh... No, I don't think she'd hurt anyone.

Phan: Chloe?

Joanna: No!

Phan: Does Alistair have any enemies – political rivals, say?

Joanna: Not that I know of. He's not important enough, is he?

Phan: How much money do you have?

Joanna: In my wallet?

Phan: No, altogether: bank accounts, property.

Joanna: Oh. I own a house in Glasgow worth about half a million. Alistair owns the flat in Edinburgh: it's worth a bit more, I think, but he has a mortgage, not sure how much. It's with Halifax, seven-fifty a month. Pounds. We have a joint account with around two thousand in it at the moment. And savings of twenty thousand. And I have a bank account of my own with another forty. That and the house was my inheritance – Mum had a business head.

Phan: We've tapped your phones, Joanna. We've taken your laptops and need your passwords: Facebook, email etc.

Joanna: Okay.

Phan: We'll need access to your houses in Scotland – can you arrange that?

Joanna: Of course. My friend Kirsty can let you in.

Phan: Good, just in case we find something there that might help. If you think of anything else, please let me know straight away. I'll be at the house tonight and to-morrow. We'll have someone there while this is going on, security. You're going to be hounded. I suggest you stay inside unless you're with one of us. And we'll set up a search base at the hall across from the primary school in Point Lonsdale. We'll do everything we can.

Joanna: Thanks. Thank you , Detective. Is that it?

END INTERVIEW

Joanna read her statement through, as requested, and signed it at the bottom. The police escorted them back to Elizabeth's.

She managed to trick herself into believing her story, but only for a few hours, hours that passed in a frenzied blur of snapshots.

Screaming at the shop assistant to phone the police.

Alistair running around the street, yelling, searching, doing all the things parents have been criticised for not doing in the past.

A female officer with red hair arriving a few minutes later and giving her an unexpected and painfully kind hug.

Journalists, filming.

More police cars arriving. Two officers knocking on doors in the street.

Neighbours gathering around the shop, peering at her, at Alistair, at the car.

Alistair mentioning something about a *Yoot* and a *Japa*-something, whatever they were.

Giving her statement in a small square interview room, Alistair's words coming out with surprising ease. The thirty-something Vietnamese detective firm, but sympathetic.

Arriving at Elizabeth Robertson's home to find her grey

with shock, but active to the point of manic, making tea for the police, going over what had happened, going over the possibilities, banging her fist on the table about what they should be doing.

Being grabbed by Alistair in the bathroom and told what to say to her best friend, Kirsty – 'No, don't come over. Your dad's ill, he needs you. Please, for me, don't come.'

Police tapping phones and eating the banana cake a neighbour dropped over.

Chloe arriving with her dark hair and deep eyes, like her dad, like Noah.

Alistair hugging Chloe. Chloe awkward with her dad.

Chloe ignoring Joanna. Joanna avoiding Chloe.

Chloe accusing Joanna. Joanna welcoming it.

Opening the curtain and peering outside to see Alexandra waiting in her car, fresh and pretty, her blonde hair now hippy-short.

Aching to go outside and talk to her, tell her what had happened, ask for her help.

Catching each other's eyes for a moment.

Staring and staring at Alexandra. Beautiful, lucky Alexandra.

The frenzy blurred Joanna's reality for a few hours, but once everyone left, and she was alone in the house with Alistair and his mother, it jerked back into focus. She lay on the double bed in Alistair's old room and thought about the moment that she killed her son, replaying it in her head. She was sitting on her seat, she was opening a bottle, she was giving him medicine that he was allergic to with a little white spoon. She was killing him.

She wanted to confess. She wanted to die. In that order.

Elizabeth Robertson was in her bedroom praying. A dark chant hissed through the house. Joanna covered her ears with a pillow.

When Alistair came in, he handed Joanna a glass of water and two tablets, which she took without asking what they were. There was a long silence before she said: 'This is wrong. I'm not going to do it.'

Alistair sat on the bed beside her and held her hand. 'We lost our son. We don't deserve to lose everything else as well. It's not wrong. We're not hurting anyone.'

'Are you sure?'

'One hundred per cent. What we're doing is making sure there's no more suffering – for Chloe, but for us too. We're not bad. We're not evil.'

She nuzzled into his chest. 'I'm not evil?'

'You're good, my darling. You're good. And it'll be over soon.'

17

JOANNA

16 February

It woke her an hour or so later, the cry. She felt her breasts harden as the noise grew louder. She held them, they were burning, bursting. She got out of bed, and followed the sound. She walked into the hall, towards the front door, and opened it. The sun was up. It was cold, at least twenty-five degrees cooler than when they arrived. She stood on the veranda and listened. It was faint now, but definitely coming from somewhere across the road. Barefoot, she followed the sound, the pain in her breasts easing and the cry softening with every step. A bright red rosella, with blue and yellow wings, was pecking at a tree in the garden opposite. She hadn't noticed this tree before but it was a Lilly Pilly, the same tree that Alistair had buried Noah under. There was no fruit this time of year, but she recognised the lush green foliage and the soft comfortable shape of it. At least twenty feet high and almost as wide, it was the kind of tree you want to picnic under. Her body warmed, breasts melting, some milk releasing at this communication, this sign. The rosella made a noise like a squeaky toy, not the one she'd heard, and flew off. Noah had spoken to her. They were connected, by the Lilly Pilly tree.

She snuck back into bed beside Alistair and lay awake imagining the actual tree. If she could hear him through a relative of the tree, imagine how wonderfully clear his presence would be if she was at the actual one. When Alistair woke, it was the first thing she asked him. 'Tell me about the tree.'

'What?'

'His spot. Describe it to me.'

Alistair rubbed his eyes and turned onto his side to look at her. 'Okay. It's at the far back of the garden. And the garden's huge, two acres at least. It's pretty and green and the leaves are so glossy and thick the sun doesn't get through so there's no grass under it.'

'How tall is it?'

'Um, about the same as the one across the street from here.'

'Does it harvest berries every year?'

'I think so.'

'I'm going to find some in the shops and make jam.'

'Joanna . . .'

'Yeah.'

'You can never go there, you know that, right?'

She stared at him.

'Before we get up, I need to go over some things with you.'

This would become a morning ritual, one she dreaded, often pretending to be asleep to avoid. It always started with pills.

'Take these.'

'What are they?'

'Valium. To calm you down, help you cope.'

She took the tablets with a sip of water, hoping they'd make her feel calm to the point of nothing.

'I put the Boots bottles and the nappy and the trowel and his blanket and the bin bag in one plastic bag and buried it. I filled his grave by hand, patted it down. There was dirt on my hands and in my nails and the cops noticed when I was in the station. I told them I fell in mud when I was running along the streets, searching. Did they ask you?'

'No. I told them you searched the area, though.'

'Good, so that's why there was dirt, okay? Oh no, if they found any in the car last night. Shit. Did they? I don't think so, they didn't say anything, but maybe they did and want to test it before asking us. Thank God those cadaver dogs didn't detect anything. The plastic bin bag was genius. Glad I thought of that. But there wouldn't be any dirt in the car. If they find any in the car we can say . . . Shh, right, let me think. Something simple. Did I look inside the car again after we raised the alarm?'

'I don't know.'

'I think I did. Yeah. I did. Of course I would have done that to double check, and look for evidence. So we can say the dirt in the car must have been from when I looked through the front and back seats before the police arrived. But listen, if they say something that means they don't buy that – for whatever reason, dunno if the soil's different at the milk bar from Swan Bay, say – I could also explain that I jumped the fence on the Geelong Road looking for a signal earlier in the day and dropped my phone. Yeah, that's it. That's fine. A backup plan. We stopped at the side of the road twice on the way to Geelong because we wanted to ring Mum about the fires. I can say we couldn't get a signal and I walked around a bit to get one and jumped the fence, dropping the phone in dirt. That works in case any drivers saw us too. So my hands and the car might have been dirty from that too. Okay?'

'Okay.'

'Shit, I nearly forgot. Why did you buy tampons? You don't need them when you're breastfeeding, do you?'

'I know. I didn't think. I told Phan they were for discharge.'

'Right, good girl.'

'So my discharge is now on file.'

'Can you think of anything else?'

'What were you saying about a Japa-something?'

'Japara. It's a raincoat. Like a Barbour.'

'You saw someone?'

'I'm surprised you didn't too. You sure you didn't, about a hundred metres down the road?'

'I don't remember,' Joanna said. 'And a Yoot? You mean a boy or something?'

'A utility vehicle, like a pick-up. U-T-E. I saw one just before. So did you.'

'I did?'

'Yes. There'll be a press conference soon. We need to ask the public for help. Can you do that?'

'I don't want to.'

A set of instructions followed.

'I know honey, but you have to. If you feel confused or cornered you say: 'No comment.' If they push you, say: 'I'm sorry, I'm too distressed to talk.' Don't smile, ever. Don't fidget, that looks like you're hiding something. Cry, don't hold it back, the more the better. Try not to be alone with Mum. If her hope and pain's upsetting you, go to the toilet, lock yourself in. Don't get into conversations with her. Only call your friends when I'm with you, especially Kirsty. Forget the situation with Chloe for now. I'll deal with that. Stay off the internet. No emails. Don't watch the news. Don't feel guilty about people helping. It makes them feel good about themselves. Tell everyone the same thing, over and over. You know it by heart. No new words. None. If it gets too difficult, cry, or say 'I'm sorry—''

She finished it for him: 'I'm too distressed to talk.'

'Right. We made this decision for good reasons, remember that. What we're doing is right. If you ever need to talk, talk to me. I'll always be here for you. Always. But please, try and forget where I put him. You can never go there.'

'Are you finished?' she asked.

'Have you got it all?'

'Yes.'

'Do you have any questions?'

'Can I go to the toilet now?'

Elizabeth was sobbing over breakfast. A paedophile had been released after questioning and Elizabeth was upset. *Yes, what a shame*, Joanna felt like saying: *What a shame a paedophile didn't take him. That would have been excellent.* Joanna went to the toilet, as instructed, and stayed there for an hour.

For the rest of the day she sat on the sofa and looked out the window at the tree across the road. She wasn't expected to be competent or articulate, so no one intervened. Activity hummed around her: a website was created, posters designed, printed, copied and distributed to the volunteers based at the hall in Point Lonsdale, police came and went, talking about possible sightings that made Elizabeth ecstatic with optimism. Detective Phan hovered over the tapped phones, waiting for a kidnapper to call, she supposed. Their hire car, which had been cordoned off and examined at the scene, had been taken away for further examination, and Alistair set about hiring another. A request for holiday photos went viral on the internet, and 260 photos taken in Point Lonsdale on the 15th had already flooded in. Horrifying, but two convicted sex offenders had been identified by police – accidentally snapped in the background by unsuspecting beachgoers. Neighbours and community voyeurs brought flowers and food. A police officer stood guard at the front of the house. Someone tried to shut the blinds because reporters were taking photos from the pavement. 'Please leave it open,' Joanna said.

Alistair was busy, decisive and convincing. He hired a PR guru as soon as they'd given their statements. Bethany McDonald had done the MBA with him and was 'a driven, power-hungry bitch'. Ergo, perfect. She'd been involved in the Sydney Olympics and had major celebrities tweeting about the disappearance within an hour. 'Jacie Malbo's offering a reward!' Alistair announced after one of many energetic telephone conversations with Bethany. 'Twenty thousand bucks. And he'll mention it at his gig tomorrow if we've not found him by then; put his photo on a huge screen on stage.'

He spent ages tweaking the MISSING poster on his laptop. 'His face should be bigger . . . The contact details should stand out . . . The colour's all wrong.'

He took call after call from journalists, repeating the story over and over, unflinching. He went outside every hour to update the media on the pavement. Impressive.

The only moment he lost his cool was when he phoned a colleague in London, MP Richard Davis.

'Richard, Alistair Robertson here,' his voice wasn't even shaky. Kept his cool always, that's why they hired him. 'Fine. Well, not fine at all, but, you know . . .' Joanna could hear the even voice on the other line.

'Well,' Alistair answered, 'we need as much coverage as we can get – get his face and what he was wearing out there. But nothing financial, obviously. Speaking of which . . . I've been mulling over Johnstone-gate.'

Long pause.

'There's no need. I can deal with it,' Alistair said, visibly annoyed.

Longer pause.

'I understand we need to be careful but . . .' Alistair breathed fast through his nose as he listened, increasingly unhappy with what he was hearing. 'Aha. Right you are.' Alistair hung up, then hung up again, harder, almost breaking the phone.

'What is it?' his mother asked.

'Nothing.'

'Everything all right?' one of the male police officers asked, clocking the semi-violence he'd just witnessed and making Alistair nervous.

Alistair calmed himself to answer. 'They're getting someone else to take over for me for a while. Sorry about that. I thought a bit of work might help keep me sane.'

'Good idea not to be worrying about work now, I'd have thought,' the officer said.

'That is a good idea,' Elizabeth ventured.

The look he gave his mother made her recoil a little.

When Alistair shut the living room curtains again at dusk, Joanna went to bed. The breast pump was on the bedside table. Alistair must have put it there. She tossed it under the bed and soaked up the pain.

She woke to the cry again that night. It faded when she got to the tree, and the rosella wasn't there this time, but it soothed her and she slept an hour or two afterwards.

148

18

JOANNA

17 February

When she woke, Alistair and his mother had left a note saying they were at the police station. Against Alistair's advice, she went to Elizabeth's computer and tried to log on to her Facebook and email accounts, but her passwords didn't work. Alistair – or the police – must have changed passwords or cancelled her accounts. Probably for the best, she supposed, but she felt so bereft and lonely and longed for something familiar. If only her mum was alive. What she'd do to talk to her, to hold her, to tell her everything, to ask her what to do, how to get through this. Kirsty was the closest she had to family now.

Her mobile wasn't in her handbag. In case the police hadn't taken it, she rang the number several times from the landline, following the old fashioned brrrring brrrring until she found the handset on a dusty hard-to-reach shelf in the boiler cupboard. Alistair had hidden it. But he'd forgotten to switch it off. Ha! She checked Elizabeth's car was still gone, and dialled Kirsty's number.

In the past, Kirsty always knew exactly what to say. When her father ran off, Kirsty told her to take action; she phoned his production company office and forced Joanna to talk to him. Her dad said sorry, that he loved her, that sometimes parents grow apart, that he'd write to her, that he'd come and visit as soon as the next shoot was over, and that he'd bring her over to his new home in Canada. This conversation made Joanna feel better for a while, till she realised he wasn't going to do any of those things. But Kirsty nursed her through. And when her mother was dying, Kirsty brought takeaway curries and books into the hospital for her and held her when she needed to cry.

This time, Kirsty said all the wrong things.

'It was the fifteenth of February here when it happened,' Joanna said when she called. 'But it was the fourteenth of February for you, for the whole of the United Kingdom, where I belong. So I lost that day, the fourteenth. It went, just like he did. So you see somewhere on that plane a whole day disappeared and took him with it.'

Joanna's weird ramblings made Kirsty cry more loudly. 'Oh poor Jo. My poor Jo. I wish I could hold you. You mustn't give up hope. Is Alistair looking after you? Is someone good there to look after you?'

'Just talk, let me hear your voice.' Joanna said, her only hope being that she'd stop with these words of misguided kindness, but Kirsty could only cry. She was so worried for Noah, so devastated for her wonderful friend, so guilty that she couldn't be there for her. After the conversation, Joanna hung up feeling worse than she had before. She decided not to call her again and felt thankful that Kirsty couldn't come over – her dad was having chemo – then she berated herself for feeling thankful. She'd become a monster.

*

Alistair returned to say there would be a televised appeal in an hour. He set to, preparing her for the ordeal.

'One more time!' he said, pacing the bedroom as Joanna stood, exhausted, in the corner, a hair brush acting as microphone in her hand.

'I just want him to come home,' she said flatly.

'Say his name!' A yell-whisper. He was getting good at those.

'Okay! Noah. Noah. Noah. I want Noah to come home.'

'Don't stop the tears. Let 'em flow.'

The doorbell rang. It was time to go out there and face the world.

She'd felt like this before. Words on the tip of her tongue, itching to jump off. *I fucked a married man. I am in love with your husband.* There were cameras, journalists, neighbours and volunteers everywhere. A police officer stood either side of them. *I killed my baby.* She could just say it, right here, right now, and that would be that.

Alistair had stopped talking. He was handing her a microphone. She bit the tip of her tongue and the words there turned to blood.

'Please,' she said, 'if you have seen our baby, or if you have our baby…'

Alistair squeezed her elbow.

'I mean Noah. If you know anything – about Noah – could you please contact the police. We just want . . .'

She turned and looked at Alistair. He was letting 'em flow. 'I'm sorry,' she said, 'I'm too distressed to talk.'

Joanna was too distressed to talk for several hours, and was only jolted from her private torture when she heard Alistair yelling in the living room. He was screaming down the phone: 'What kind of mother are you, letting a fourteen-year-old go on television? Why didn't you speak to me first? How could you have let her use the words "when *they say* he was taken from the unattended car" as if . . . Can't you see you are putting her in danger!'

Joanna rewound the news bulletin and listened to Chloe's impressive plea. 'My God, she is amazing,' she said.

Alistair had hung up on his ex-wife, and turned his fury on Joanna. 'She's accusing us. *When they say he was taken . . .* She's fucking accusing us.'

He stomped out the door, leaving Joanna smiling at the teenager on screen. 'She's amazing,' she repeated to herself.

*

Joanna eventually fell asleep for an hour or so, waking to find that Alistair was not in bed beside her, but in the bathroom. He was sitting on top of the closed toilet seat, crying. She went in and put her hand on his shoulder.

'I should have known,' he said.

She knelt beside him.

'I had him on my lap on the plane. I put him in the buggy, then in the car. How could I not have known?'

A bang outside interrupted them. Joanna looked out – couldn't see anything – and shut the frosted window.

Alistair wiped his eyes and leaned into Joanna's shoulder. 'I should have noticed. I might have saved him.'

They cried together for a long time. Joanna believed she could never feel closer to him.

19

ALEXANDRA

18–28 February

Day one of the action plan and Chloe's been to school and seems calmer. I've printed 300 posters and bought a bucket, paste and two brushes. We've decided to start where it happened and work our way out. On the ninety-minute drive to Point Lonsdale, Chloe says she doesn't want to ring her dad. After his reaction to her television appearance, she doesn't ever want to talk to him, or see him, again. Once this might have made me smile inside. It doesn't. It makes my stomach ache.

Noah has been missing three days but there's no sign in the town that anything ever happened. The area outside the milk bar is no longer cordoned off. A couple of people are chatting outside the hall across the road from the primary school. A smattering of locals are walking happily along the beach. Everything but the supermarket has closed for the day. We loop posters around the few light poles on the main street but the poles are too thin and it's hard to make out what the poster says once we've pasted them on. We put one on the public toilet in the play park, one each on the front windows of the closed coffee shops, the bakery and the gift shop, and the lady in the supermarket puts two up for us. 'We're all praying for his safe return,' she says sadly.

I'm surprised at how much Chloe knows as we wander along the quiet main street. That's the house they rented. That's where the person in a Japara was spotted. That's where they were parked when he disappeared.

We don't talk on the way home and I think that's because the whole episode was so desperately depressing. On the road from Point Lonsdale to Geelong I see burnt land in the distance and dark half-trees like claws. This post-bushfire view matches our mood.

Day two of the action plan is even worse. When I phone the police they refuse to tell me anything. I'm tired after my shift at the shop and we don't talk all the way to Geelong. We start putting up posters in the main shopping drag and in the streets leading towards Alistair's mother's house. But it feels pointless. Chloe sleeps on the way home.

Day three and the action plan officially fails. We're back in Geelong and many of the posters we put up yesterday have fallen off. One has been covered with a missing cat poster. Herman, is the cat's name.

On the way home Chloe says: 'He's dead. I don't want to do this any more.'

*

For a week now, Chloe's come home from school and shut herself away in her room to study. She's grieving. I'm no longer worried about her doing anything dangerous or inappropriate. Alistair phoned twice more in the first week, leaving a message each time saying there's no news and that he hopes she's okay. He's made no effort to see her beyond that and hasn't called for seven days. I'll never forgive him for it, no matter what he's going through.

Chloe's right: Noah probably is dead. Everyone's thinking it. And as time goes on, people are becoming more suspicious of Alistair and Joanna.

The political blogger who always had it in for Alistair, James Moyer, has posted today that Labour is about to sack him. He writes:

Suspicions rise over Labour guru and mistress . . . How can this rotten party keep Alistair Robertson as its advisor, spokesperson and spin doctor? A reliable source states that they might soon be official suspects. He'll get the heave-ho any day. And who can blame Labour when there are so many unanswered questions about the disappearance of baby Noah (the best site is www.lonniebabytheevidence.com – check it out) and so much to dislike and distrust about the poor child's parents?

'Lonniebaby: The Evidence' is indeed damning. Whoever's writing it seems to know everything. It's comprehensive and impressive, feeding new information each day, and posing questions that no one else seems to be posing. I scan the 'Unanswered questions' page, which gets longer day by day.

How could Alistair Robertson have known exactly what someone was wearing (a Japara) when he was a hundred metres away and it was pouring with rain?

When they got to their holiday house, they put a load of washing on – including the cloth covers to the car seat and Noah's buggy seat. Why?

I can understand them popping into the shop for a few minutes, but wouldn't they have locked the car door? It was open. There was no sign of forced entry.

Why were there no other fingerprints on the back door of the car? Only Joanna Lindsay's and Alistair Robertson's?

If Alistair Robertson's explanation about the dirt under his fingernails is to be believed – that he fell in the mud when he was searching for Noah – wouldn't he have had mud all over him? A source says he only had mud in his nails and some on his knees. Why? Do people ever fall so neatly? Aren't these more like the mud marks you'd get from kneeling down and clawing at the earth?

If Joanna's capable of lying and cheating and home-wrecking, then what else is she capable of?

Why hasn't she ever cried?

One of my anonymous sources gave details of Joanna's first interview with the police. When she was asked if her baby was asleep when she went into the shop, she answered: 'He was silent.' Silent? I don't know about you, but I think this is a strange answer.

Is she mentally ill? Neighbours were seen carrying her across the street to her mother-in-law's house one week after he disappeared. Anonymous1 says she was having hallucinations, talking to a tree. And a doctor was seen visiting the house shortly after.

Joanna Lindsay's father abandoned her when she was thirteen. What effect did this have on her?

What kind of teacher is Joanna Lindsay? Even her pupils are starting to doubt her. One has told me she was 'flaky'; another 'volatile' and another says she was 'obsessed with books about suicide'.

Why have none of Joanna Lindsay's family or friends come over to Australia to help with the search and to support her?

Is she on drugs? Have the police tested her?

If Joanna Lindsay was breastfeeding, why was she buying tampons? Breastfeeding mothers do not get their periods.

The questions posted today are frantic and angry:

Why didn't the police search the mother-in-law's house?

Is there a crucial piece of evidence in the mother-in-law's house? Anonymous1 says there is.

Why did cadaver dogs only check the hire car?

Were the dogs accurate? In many cases they are not.

The more I read the more I realise that the finger is being pointed at her, not at him. I find the barrage of hatred towards her very unpleasant reading, to my surprise, and decide to stop looking online.

*

My lawyer just phoned to say the custody hearing is still going ahead and she wants to meet me this afternoon to make sure we're prepared. I wonder if they really think they should go ahead now, considering. It seems crazy, but typical of Alistair not to request a postponement. He won't lose a battle, even if it's because he's fighting a much harder one.

The office is on the twenty-third floor of the Rialto Building in Melbourne. The lift is so fast and smooth it feels like magic. When I get out, I have to stand still for a few seconds till I'm certain there's floor beneath me. I don't like heights, so I walk along the centre of the corridor and stare at my feet all the way to reception, careful not to catch any expensive views. The carpet's soft and unmarked. The background music's annoyingly serene. I'm two minutes late, which Dad'll have to pay for, bringing the total spend so far to $2,270. The receptionist is young and gorgeous. You can hear the meeting when they hired staff for this place: *Cute chicks with cleavages entice male clients.* If women had the money, they'd have Brad Pitt at reception.

'Latte, Ms Donohue?' It must be noted on her computer that latte is my hot beverage of choice. I don't take it because they ended up billing me nine bucks for one the first time I came. The biscotto I didn't ask for was three.

A minute later, my lawyer sits me down and asks me how I am but I've learned to avoid expensive small talk. 'Fine. Is the hearing really going to happen?' I have a list of questions on a notepad and I intend to demand direct answers to all of them.

'I've not heard otherwise so we need to prepare as if it will take place. There's no date yet, though.'

I move on to question two on my pad. 'How will what's happened to them affect my chances?'

'Good question.' She rocks her plush leather chair back and forth.

'I know. Could you answer it please?'

She's not shocked at my bluntness. I was a human rights lawyer, before Alistair dragged me to the motherland. A lawyer and a friend and a happy person. I couldn't practise over there and haven't been able to get back into it since coming home. The job isn't exactly single-parent-friendly and my head isn't exactly working again yet.

'I can't imagine anyone would think it's a sensible time for them to take over the care of Chloe. There are a lot of rumours about them. She doesn't come over well at all: the affair, leaving him alone in the car. A website has been set up which is devoted to the alleged evidence against them. Lonniebaby: The Evidence. It's getting over ten thousand hits a day. But on the other hand, it may increase their sympathy vote. And of course it depends if things are still okay at home for you and Chloe?'

'Things are fine,' I say, deciding that two days off school after a tragic event is nothing to be concerned about. 'This is a reference from my boss.' I pass her my reference, which is the third piece of information I need to convey. It's from Giuseppe at the 'Burg Café saying I have worked there fifteen hours a week for twelve months now and that I'm honest and reliable.

'Nice place to work?'

'It is.' I move on. 'I'm making this scrapbook.' I put it on the desk in front of her. 'There are photos of us doing things together, tickets to events we've attended, birthday cards, pictures and little notes she's done for me, things like that.'

The lawyer takes it and begins leafing through. She's going to take too long. I grab it back from her. 'I thought you could use this in court.'

'Right,' she says. 'Sure, give it to me when you're finished and I'll take a look.' I'm not sure she's as impressed with this book as I am. I move on again.

'Alistair rang Chloe on the sixteenth of February and left a message saying he would phone her again and arrange to take her out somewhere. He left two messages after that in the first week but hasn't been in touch since. Chloe doesn't want to talk to him or see him. Make a note of that. Is there anything else I need to do?'

She explains that a social worker will visit me in the next day or so to assess my home situation. They won't give a time: surprise is key to the assessment. She hands me a consent form to sign, which will allow the social worker to contact Chloe's school and my GP. I'd normally ask more questions about this, but Mum and Dad can't afford it, and I have nothing to hide.

'What are my chances?' I ask.

'Eighty per cent your way, unless something happens to change that.'

'Like what?' I ask.

'Like if Chloe changes her mind and doesn't want to live with you. She's still firm about that?'

'More so than ever.' I think I'm telling the truth.

'Or like they become official suspects, which is possible. It's hotting up against them out there. I know a police officer in Geelong who said there's talk of searching the mother-in-law's house, which was never done.'

'Why would they do that?'

'No idea. But there must be a reason. And if the police officially suspect them, you're home and hosed. So unless something happens that makes you seem like an even worse mother than Joanna – which would be damn hard – you have nothing to worry about.'

I sign the consent form, say thanks, tell her that was five minutes total without latte or biscuits and leave before she can ask me where I got my shoes.

*

By the time I get home, something has happened that makes me look like a worse mother than Joanna. Two police officers are at the door and my drunk fourteen-year-old is projectile vomiting onto the driveway. Instead of going to school, they inform me, she hitch-hiked to Geelong, drank a half a bottle of vodka on the beach, and was caught trying to break into her grandmother's house. The officers are from Geelong and they're very understanding about it, driving her all the way home (with the window open). One of the officers is a fairly young Vietnamese guy in plain clothes. I've seen him on the news in the background. His name's Phan, and he seems kind. Chloe told them she thought the house was empty and 'just wanted to have a look inside'. Joanna was home, asleep. She didn't want to press charges.

Before I manage to get the door open, I hear a man's voice say: 'Mrs Robertson?' I turn around and a third professional is on my porch. He flashes his ID: 'I'm Tim Shaw . . . from Social Services.'

I can imagine the report he'll write for the custody hearing, this twenty-two-year-old who's never been alone with a child for more than an hour, let alone tried caring for one full time. (Yes, the first thing that came out of my mouth was: 'But . . . Really! How old are you?' and yes, I should not have done this because, you're right, it was insulting and judgemental and will result in an even worse assessment than the one my puking daughter and the two police officers were already ensuring.) It was probably his youth that gave him the energy to do so much in the hour it took me to get home from town, mind you. He'd phoned the lawyer and asked her to fax the letter of consent I just signed allowing him to get information about me and Chloe from relevant professionals. He'd phoned Chloe's school, and knew she'd missed three days without permission, and that she had been behaving so badly in five out of eight classes (which I didn't know) that a special inter-departmental meeting was being held about her tomorrow. He'd also phoned my GP, and would like to talk to me about that once the police are gone and Chloe has been cleaned up and put to bed.

'If she runs away again, phone us straight away,' Phan says as he leaves.

Oh God.

On the tram home I'd planned to change into a floral dress and bake an earth-mothery cake in case the social worker visited. I'd imagined Chloe coming in from school and feeding her animals and giving me a hug and generally demonstrating a most excellent home life.

Instead Chloe's kneeling at the foot of the loo with the door open. Social Work Boy, whose suit does not have the desired effect of making him seem older and cleverer, is holding her hair back while she makes such terrible heaving noises that I fear the contents of her feet might come out her mouth.

Once she's emptied, I put her to bed like he ordered me to, as if I wouldn't have done this without being prompted in an irritatingly right-on way. (Would I have? Maybe not. Maybe I'd have put her on the couch.) 'Have some sleep,' I say, tucking her in. 'And we'll talk about this after.'

'Mum?' she garbles.

I stop at the bedroom door. 'Yeah?'

She holds out her hand but I'm too angry to walk back over to the bed and take it.

'Mum, come here!' she says loudly enough for Social Work Boy to hear from his position in the kitchen.

I go over, hold her left biceps with my thumb and fingers more tightly than I mean to, and whisper: 'You know I could lose you? Do you know that? I'm so fucking mad with you, Chloe Robertson.'

When I release my grip she starts crying in a way that I've never seen her do before. A drunk, twisted, loud, scary cry. 'Ow!' she screeches. 'Mum, I love you, don't be mad at me! Mum!'

Social Work Boy has come to the bedroom door and is looking at us.

'I'm not mad at you,' I say to Chloe.

'You said, "I'm so fucking mad with you, Chloe Robertson," and you pinched me!'

I grab her hand. 'Shhh, shh honey. No, no. You've had so much to drink, and you're not used to the feeling, are you? It's horrible. I'm not mad with you. This is a terrible time. You're going through an awful, awful time. You need to cry it out, cry it out. I'm not mad. You're my baby girl. I love you.'

'You're my baby girl too, I love you too,' she says.

Social Work Boy is now standing beside me, raising his eyebrows as he gazes down at Chloe's left forearm, which has a red thumb mark on it from what must indeed have turned into a pinch.

She conks out ten minutes later. The social worker stays put the whole time, watching as the thumb mark fades to a very light pink, but does not disappear.

When we go back into the kitchen, I notice him noticing the half-full bottle of wine beside the unwashed dishes. By now, I've almost resigned myself to the fact that this toddler in a suit will hand my daughter over to Alistair or some children's home as soon as she wakes up and I want to empty said wine into my mouth and then bash myself over the head with the bottle till I die. I resist, take a deep breath, and offer him tea or coffee. He'd prefer tea, thanks, white no sugar. The kettle seems to take about an hour to boil.

He has a sip, places the mug on the kitchen bench and leans forward. 'How's the depression?'

He's obviously got all the information he needs about Chloe's neglect and abuse, and has moved on to the causes. I'd been to the surgery twice for anti-anxiety medication – two years ago and six months ago, I explain. Both times I went because I was sick of arguing with Alistair in my head, sick of thinking about what he'd done to me, all day, all night. I wanted something to take the hate away. I wanted something to make me indifferent. 'It wasn't depression.' I can tell I sound defensive. 'I was anxious, after the separation. Neither prescription agreed with me so I just worked through it myself.' In fact, I'd only taken one pill each time. In both cases, they'd made me feel crazier than I had ever felt in my life.

'What about alcohol?' He nods towards the wine on the bench.

'I try to keep it within the fourteen units a week limit.'

He raises an eyebrow.

'Often I don't succeed, but I rarely have more than three glasses a night. I used to drink a bit more in Scotland. I was lonely over there.' I tell him this because it will come out in the hearing anyway. Better to be up front. 'That's twenty-one, still too much. I know it's not great for my health, but I never drink to the point of getting drunk, not since I've been on my own with Chloe.' I wrack my brain – did I tell the doctor the same thing? It's the truth, so I assume I did.

'You were charged with drink driving in January.'

'I'd had two glasses of wine with lunch. It's no excuse, but I was only just over the limit. I thought I'd be all right. What I think happened is I didn't eat enough.' Could I sound like more of an alcoholic?

He's not taking notes but I can almost hear the marks against me going *ker-ching* in his head.

He asks about Mum and Dad and I tell him we see them at least three times a week and that Chloe's their only grandchild. They're in a small retirement flat now, older and a little less active, but they dote on her. He says he might give them a call if that's okay. He looks around the house next, nodding disapprovingly at things like the two DVDs on the coffee table, which are rated eighteen, and the vodka and gin bottles on the dining-room shelf.

Thinking on my feet, I grab the scrapbook from my bag and hand it to him. 'Chloe and I have been making this together for years,' I say, 'a kind of mum–daughter journal.'

I watch his face as he leafs through the pages, moving on from birthday cards with sweet messages to the pages with photographs of us doing various activities together. There's

167

one of us roller skating, one of us with shopping bags on a tram, one of us baking cupcakes, one of us playing basketball in the park, one of us walking Phil's dog, one of us getting our nails done. I can hardly breathe I'm so pleased at my creation.

'I like the silver zig-zag on the black,' he says, pointing to a close up of Chloe's nails.

I look at the nail photo. We both had the same – only Chloe's were black and silver, mine white and silver.

He flicks through the other photos. 'Funny how your nail polish didn't wear or chip through all these activities.' He goes through each one, pointing at our nails, all identical and perfect.

'And how Chloe had the same stain – is that chocolate cake mixture? – on the same white T-shirt every time?'

I'm mortified to have been caught out. All those activities were done the day after Alistair's lawyer rang to say he was filing for custody. I dragged Chloe around the city, snapping like mad while she complained that this was the stupidest idea I had ever had in my life.

'Ah, that stain just won't come out!' My attempted cover-up is feeble. We both know it. I shut the book and put it back in my bag.

'Yoohoo!' Mum and Dad are here! 'You here, honey bunch?' With all the commotion, I've left the front door open and they've let themselves in. Please God, let my mum and dad salvage this.

Social Work Boy talks to them in the living room for over

half an hour and I can hardly stand it. I check on Chloe, who's snoring like an old alcoholic. The thumb mark is gone. I do the dishes, I look in the fridge so I can cook something a good mother would cook. There are some ready-made meatballs. I take them out of the packet, toss the wrapper in the bin, then realise he might see it there, and turn it upside down. I grab icing sugar (damn, no flour) and sprinkle it on the bench, then scrunch the preformed balls into one meaty heap, add some dried rosemary, and begin rolling them again and coating them with icing sugar. When they surface, the kitchen is satisfactorily messy, and I've re-made half the meatballs. Mum, Dad and the boy are all smiling. I have no idea yet if this is a good thing.

He holds his hand out to shake mine.

'Sorry, she'll need to eat when she wakes. I'm covered in mince!'

He glances at the meat on my hands: 'Your mum says Chloe's a vegetarian.'

'Oh . . .' I eyeball Mum, who's turned as pink as her cardigan. 'These, um, they're for me.'

Fuck!

20

JOANNA

18–28 February

On the third day, Joanna went to the desk in Elizabeth's bedroom. Elizabeth and/or Alistair had compiled a file of letters and printed out emails. Most were from strangers, sending prayers and money, but one was from her school.

> *Dear Ms Lindsay,*
>
> *We can't believe what's happened and want you to know we are thinking of you and praying for Noah. We have already raised £427 to help with the search and we're raising more every day. Can you let us know where to send it?*
>
> *With love,*
>
> *Year 5c and 6b and all the students at Hutchesons' Grammar School.*
>
> *Xxxx*

And one was from her ex-boyfriend, Mike.

> *Joanna and Alistair,*
>
> *All my thoughts and prayers for the safe return of Noah.*
>
> *Love Mike*

Lovely Mike. If only they'd stayed together. She could have gone with him to Japan, or she could have waited for him. They could have made good decisions together for the rest of their long, happy lives.

She couldn't stand hurting the people she cared about like this. She sat down at the desk and began writing a letter of confession. She'd only written: 'Everyone, do not pray for me, please . . .' when she heard the back door opening. She ripped the note she was writing into small pieces, took a handful of papers to read later, raced to her bedroom, and hid them under the mattress.

*

On the fourth day, Joanna took her phone into the toilet and went online. When she read blogs or news reports from people who were compassionate, she smashed the wall with her fist, making it bleed on more than one occasion and cracking some of the plaster a little more each time. When people were being mean or suspicious, she smiled. Please, people, be suspicious, she prayed. Wonder about the dirt under his nails. Wonder about what kind of parents we are. Suspect me of being the murderer that I am.

She couldn't follow Alistair's instruction to forget the Chloe situation either. She hadn't asked about it, but Alistair hadn't mentioned postponing the hearing. If anything, he'd probably use the situation to his advantage and go ahead. She would talk to him about it soon. She would tell him to cancel it. It was ridiculous to pursue this now. How ludicrous to imagine she'd be capable of looking after someone else's child.

Most of all, Joanna couldn't stop thinking about Noah's grave. She longed to go there. She knew she couldn't, so instead she went across the road in the early hours of the morning and touched the leaves of the neighbour's tree with her fingertips. 'Hello, baby,' she'd whisper. 'Hello, little boy. I can hear you. I can hear you, Noah.'

*

On the fifth day, she and Alistair spent several hours at the police station. As she repeated her statement again and again, the fictional events became like a prayer to her, a chant. She fed him at the cottage, she expressed milk, she forgot she needed tampons, she ran into the shop, etcetera etcetera, Holy Mary, Amen.

After they were both interviewed separately, she watched Alistair look at pictures of Japaras and Utes on the internet, two officers over his shoulder as he said *No, no, yes, yes, that's the one, just like that.*

She watched as Alistair looked at photographs of sex offenders. Did the person in the Japara look at all like him from the back? The shape? Big? Small? Thin? Like him?

No, um, can't be sure, maybe.

God this man was good.

She watched Alistair scrutinise a photograph taken on

CCTV of a man holding a baby in a service station in Ararat. The baby was crying.

'You must know that's not him,' Joanna said. 'Noah was smaller, and more beautiful than that. He had dark, dark lashes!'

The police asked about enemies again. Did they have any? Political opponents, for example?

No.

'Are you sure Alexandra wouldn't do something like this? For revenge?'

'I couldn't imagine it,' Alistair said, with a worried look on his face that made the female officer raise her eyebrows and ask again.

'Are you sure?'

'I'm sure,' Joanna said for him. 'She's not a bad person. And she has an alibi, doesn't she? She was home in Melbourne with Chloe.'

Her answer made Alistair raise his eyebrows. Which made the female police officer raise hers again.

'What the hell are you doing?' Joanna snapped in the car. 'Trying to frame her for it? Leave the poor woman alone. As soon as we get home, I need to talk to you alone.'

*

Joanna was furious and took him straight into the bedroom. 'Sit down,' she said.

'What? What is it?'

'The police were asking me about enemies again when I was in on my own. They showed me a photo of you and a red-haired woman, smoking out the front of the hotel in Harrogate where that conference was last November. Your arms were almost touching.'

She could tell he felt worried, something about the shape of his mouth. He came back with this: 'And they asked me about a secret bank account of yours, with forty thousand pounds in it. Forty thousand pounds, Joanna. You saving for something you don't want me to know about?'

The account wasn't a secret exactly, but she liked knowing it was there, all hers, just in case. She didn't want to talk about this. 'Who the fuck is she, Alistair? A bit on the side, or are you in love with her? Is she the next me?'

He put his hands over his face. 'Oh my God, we have to stop this. We're going crazy.'

'Who is she? And when did you start smoking?'

'It's tearing us apart. You're doubting me? You don't trust me? I have the occasional cigarette at boring conferences. I don't remember some redhead having a fag nearby last November! After everything we've been through together, knowing how much I love you, how I'd give up everything for you, again and again, you doubt me? I can handle anything. I can even learn to cope with losing Noah. But I can't handle that.'

He cried easily these days. She softened as the tears came. 'Okay, okay. I don't doubt you.'

Alistair dried the tears with his hands, and embraced her, waiting a moment before saying: 'To get through this, we have to stick together. And we have to remain calm.'

*

She kept her fever a secret for a couple of days, welcoming the distraction of shivers and heat, relieved that nothing but head pain seemed real. But a week after Noah had died, she woke at 8 a.m., drenched in sweat. 'I didn't hear his cry,' she said to a frightened looking Alistair.

By the time Alistair caught up with her, she was already across the road, clawing at the trunk of the Lilly Pilly tree. 'Noah!' she sobbed. 'Mummy's here! Your mummy wants to talk to you!'

Alistair scooped her up and carried her home. 'Darling, darling, you're burning up. Shh ... Let's get you back to bed. Let's get the doctor out.'

'Here, take these,' the GP said later. She heard the word fever, the word shock, the word delirious, and a disjointed discussion about post-traumatic stress disorder. Her temperature had soared to 104. She was sweating and shaking.

They thought she was asleep, and left her alone for several hours after the neighbours carried her home. Hiding under the mattress like some ten-year-old who's scared of the dark, she searched Google on her phone, drinking in the speculation. There was a new blog post since she'd checked last time.

All over Twitter, people are wondering: What kind of woman would leave her child alone in the car? Well I'll tell you what I think. I think the kind of woman who would do this is also the kind of woman who is comfortable lying to the world. The kind of woman who cheats, who sneaks around, who steals a good woman's husband, who wrecks a child's life.

At the moment, this is just what I think. It's my opinion. I believe Joanna Lindsay is morally repugnant. I believe she has always been a liar. I believe she is guilty of the murder of her son.

I am determined to prove that my opinion is fact and this blog is dedicated to that. This blog seeks Justice for Noah.

It has been one week since Noah disappeared. Here are just two of the comments posted by readers so far:

Why hasn't she searched for her baby? Since he disappeared, she's locked herself inside her mother-in-law's house. What kind of woman doesn't even try to find him?

On television she was so aloof. She didn't cry. What kind of woman wouldn't cry?

Comments welcome here

Or, if anyone has any information or thoughts they'd like to convey privately, please email me at justicefornoah@hotmail.com. Discretion guaranteed.

Perhaps if she hadn't been feverish, Joanna would not have set up another email account and contacted the blogger immediately.

To: justicefornoah@hotmail.com
From: anonymoussympathiser@gmail.com
Dear Blogger

Her thumb was sweaty and shaky. It took a long time to write the message.

You're right. This woman is a bad woman. I have inside information but I am not ready to disclose my identity. Can you assure me that it is safe to talk to you?

An email popped back three minutes later, during which time Joanna curled herself into a ball under the duvet and moaned into her knees.

If your information is useful to the search, it will be published under Anonymous1. Your identity is safe.

Joanna thumbed back:

Thank you. This morning, Joanna Lindsay was seen being carried across the road by neighbours. She had been talking to a tree. Crazy! She has been sedated.

'What you doing under there, honey?' Alistair was standing beside the bed, and moving the duvet down.

When had he come in? She put the phone under her bottom and answered, 'Nothing.'

'Everything's going to get better, I promise.' He kissed her boiling forehead. 'Oh honey, you're burning up. Rest darlin', rest. Everything will get better. You know I adore you?'

*

The fever was worse the following day and she had no idea what was going on outside the bedroom. Alistair and Elizabeth took turns to give her water and spoonfuls of soup. They passed on messages from Kirsty and colleagues and estranged relatives.

Alistair gave her medicine. 'No, it's not penicillin, honey – shh, stay still, stay still – this is Valium and this is an antidepressant and this is co-codamol,' he said, putting pills on her tongue, spooning liquid into her mouth.

She had no energy to argue, but she knew the liquid was antibiotics. Every time he administered it, the memory of what she had done made her gag and convulse.

Alistair ran her a bath in the en-suite that evening, helping her into it, sponging her, helping her out, towelling her dry.

When he left her alone to sleep for the night, the fever made her hallucinate. Whenever she opened her eyes, she saw lines connecting objects – from door to box to window; from chin to pillow to chest; from table to bookshelf to lamp. Even when she closed her eyes, the imprint remained. She was too weak to wonder why, but she was seeing triangles, everywhere.

Flashbacks, too. Vivid, colourful, and with texture she could feel: Noah's Babygro soft against the crook of her arm in seat 17H, his lips soft too as she prised them open to kill him with the poison on her spoon.

Perhaps she *was* suffering from post-traumatic stress disorder. She certainly felt unhinged. In the middle of the night, she emailed the blogger again.

I have word she's in bed, she messaged. *There is talk that she is hallucinating. She is seeing things!*

Thank you for your message, the blogger replied. *Please let me know anything else. I promise I will not disclose your email address to anyone.*

*

Joanna still wasn't strong enough to get out of bed two days later. She lay there, noticing things, examining the room. It was painted royal blue, with a large window overlooking the back garden and neat white blinds that had been closed since she collapsed. It was Alistair's childhood room, still filled with his things. Cricket and football trophies were arranged with perfect symmetry on the chest of drawers. Books on politics and history and a collection of Stephen King novels filled the shelves. The Robertson clan crest was framed in thick brown oak – VIRTUTIS GLORIA MERCES – whatever that meant. Alistair's father emigrated to Australia from Stirling at the age of twenty-three – hence the family crest and Alistair's permanent UK residency and the red, blue and green kilt he wore to posh events in Edinburgh. They had lots in common, she'd thought when they met – the Scottish thing, the interest in politics, being only children, their family background.

What else? His grade-seven school shirt was pinned to the door, covered in the signatures of his classmates. There was a framed school photo on the wall behind the bed – Alistair must have been about fourteen years old, the same age as Chloe. He was identical to her, in fact: brown eyes with the same fierce intensity. Beside that was a shot of his father on a tennis court: a stern, traditional looking man – light brown hair and dark eyes. He was a GP; died of skin cancer when Alistair was thirteen. There was a lot of father-memorabilia – his medical qualifications, framed; photos of him giving a speech somewhere important; shaking hands with someone important. Based on the information in this room, a detective would surmise that Alistair's father was significant and masculine, and that his son revered him.

Joanna and Alistair had bonded over their fatherlessness, because Joanna's also disappeared off the face of the earth when she was a teenager. She came home from Kirsty's one evening to find his bags and his guitar gone, her mother crying in the bathroom, and a note that read *Joanna, I'm sorry. I'll be in touch, Daddy, xxx.* Being in touch turned out to mean three birthday cards: *You're thirteen! Happy fourteenth! I can't believe you're fifteen already!* He never phoned her back after that one call she made with Kirsty's encouragement. And she didn't even have his address, somewhere in Canada with 'that young cinematographer from the Iceland shoot and her two brats', her mother said. She blamed her mother at first, as daughters do. Her mother took it on the chin, as mothers do. When Joanna's mum died of lung cancer – six years ago now – her dying words were: 'Find your father. Forgive him.' She held her mother's hand as she groaned her way through an un-peaceful death and thought, screw that, he can go to hell.

'Do you think we have attachment issues?' she joked to Alistair in a hotel one afternoon.

'I think I'm attached to you,' he responded.

When Joanna looked back on these cute moments, she couldn't find the cute in them any more. When she pictured that hotel room, for example, she could hear Alistair's phone buzzing in the background and him not answering it. She could see the near-empty bottle of wine on the bedside table that she drank too much of in order to feel okay about what she was doing, she could hear the workmen outside because it was daytime, feel the cheap nylon sheets of the grotty Laterooms hotel they'd snuck into, remember saying 'Answer it' and Alistair saying 'Nah, fuck her.'

Nothing cute in that memory at all, then. Lying there on

the hotel bed, she thought she was in love, but perhaps she'd have loved anyone who made her come three times in four hours.

And another time: driving to the country, and Joanna asking Alistair to tell her about his father.

'He was always at work,' Alistair said. 'I remember wanting to go fishing with him, but he put it off again and again. "Next weekend!" he'd grunt. "Stop pestering me boy!"'

Joanna reached over and stroked his leg. This was a special moment she told herself she'd always cherish: vulnerable Alistair, revealing himself. Looking back on it now, she remembered that she had to reach from the back seat of the car, where she was lying so no one could see her. As Alistair drove out of the city, she could only see the tops of things: trees, houses, street lights. She was on her back thinking that this was her world now: everything was decapitated, nothing was on the ground, nothing had roots. She remembered the car stopping in a country lane and thinking to herself: Limber up, Joanna, you have to shag him, on this seat, and you only have an hour. Quick, where's that wine?

Of course, they both had daddy issues. Alistair had turned into his and Joanna had fallen in love with hers.

From her bed Joanna could see a box with ASCOT VALE written in thick black pen on the side. Alistair and Alexandra lived in this Melbourne suburb before moving to the UK. They must have stored the box here.

She was meeting past-Alistair, in-context-Alistair, for the

182

first time. The room oozed him – competitive, driven, fatherless. She didn't like the room, she didn't like him.

Joanna swung her legs out of the bed to get up, but felt something sharp against her leg. The edge of a card. That's right, she'd stashed some there days earlier. She reached under and began reading them.

One was from someone who'd gone through something similar. She recognised the grieving woman's name immediately – who wouldn't?

I know how you feel. People will say you're not a real woman. They'll say you're a bad mother. They'll say you're a liar. They'll dig into any mistakes you made in the past, point the finger at you. And all the while you're dying inside because your child is gone, and all you need is to know. All you need is to find out what happened to him, to know where he is. I understand the terrible purgatory – no, hell – you're in. If you ever need to talk…

Joanna couldn't read it all: this poor, innocent woman, assuming that Joanna was in the same situation. She put it back in the envelope and slid it under the mattress.

There were several cards from strangers – prayers, thoughts, two cheques, one for a hundred dollars, one for twenty pounds.

There was a letter from a Ms Amery. 'You probably don't remember me,' she wrote, 'but I sat behind you on the plane from Glasgow. You dropped your case on my leg and felt bad about it. I can't get the image of your baby boy out of my head. You had such a terrible flight. I wish I could have helped you more. If there's ever anything I can do for you, here's my telephone number – 555 78345. My address is 12 North Ambrose Street, Parkville, VIC. Anything.'

Joanna wished the old lady had helped more too. Perhaps if the arseholes on that flight had helped her more, Noah would still be alive.

She threw the card under the mattress with the rest, stood up, and almost fainted with dizziness. Steadying herself against the wall, she walked slowly towards the box under the window, opened it and took out two expensive heavy orange saucepans. Alistair said he liked cooking, although he always seemed grumpy when he was doing it. (Out of my kitchen! Turn that music off!) To be a good cook, he needed the best equipment, so he'd bought the same saucepans in Scotland. Underneath the saucepans were two photo albums.

The wedding photos were painful to look at. The invitation at the front stated that Alexandra and Alistair were to be married on the old steam train that goes from Queenscliff to Drysdale, passing Swan Bay on its way. 'Als Unite!' was printed in gold leaf at the top. In the photos, Alistair and Alexandra were waving and smiling from the window, looking as optimistic and as in love as a young couple can be. Alexandra's hair was shoulder length. Her dress strapless. Her figure perfect. Joanna didn't like what she was feeling as she looked at the shots – Alexandra and Alistair saying vows inside the train, dancing to jazz on the platform at Drysdale, clinking glasses on the balcony of a grand Victorian Queenscliff hotel afterwards. Even the geeky looking best man seemed to be wildly in love with Alexandra – in almost all the photos, he was in the background, smiling and staring at her with puppy-dog affection. She wasn't sure if it was jealousy, but it made her queasy. Als Unite! She put the album and the saucepans back in the box and took the other photo album back to bed with her.

This one was even harder to look at. The captions underneath were not in Alistair's handwriting, must have been Alexandra's.

The Als go hiking in Freycinet!
Look what we did! Chloe Elizabeth Robertson, 7'4"
Chloe's first tooth!
Chloe's first day of school.
Dad and Chloe building the best sandcastle in the southern hemisphere!
Mum, Dad and Chloe at her fourth birthday!
Chloe, 9, Queen of Stirling Castle!

Joanna mustered all the energy she had and walked over to put the album back in the box.

As she knelt beside the box, she noticed the small black suitcase she'd brought with her from Glasgow. She crawled over to the bed, hauled it out, and held it at her chest. She kissed it, opened the zip and inhaled the smell of the empty case. Could she smell Noah? No. But as she gently zipped it up again, she felt a small bulge in the inner front pocket. Alistair had emptied it, but he must have missed something.

Noah's red bib, the one he was wearing on the plane. She held it to her face, feeling the crustiness scratch at her cheek. She knew what the crustiness was. The lethal medicine had spilled onto the bib when she gave it to him.

She could hardly breathe. She threw up on the floor.

'Are you okay?' Elizabeth had heard her and was standing at the door.

Joanna stuffed the bib into her pyjama bottoms. 'I'm so sorry.'

'Oh darling, no need. Let me take care of that.' Elizabeth noticed the album on the floor. She smiled, came back to clean the mess, put the album in the box, then sat at the edge of the bed. She had a bowl of warm water and began wiping Joanna's face with a wet flannel.

'It upset you, the album?'

Elizabeth would have been a great nurse, Joanna thought. One with soft hands and a soothing voice. She nodded, her lip quivering with a suppressed sob.

'Don't give up hope. We'll find him.'

The brittle bib was proof of what had happened: hardened, framed evidence. It was falling down the leg of her pyjama bottoms.

She stopped herself from saying the words that were pounding in her head: *We won't! Not alive, anyway.* Instead, she said, 'Were you surprised when he told you about me?'

'I wasn't . . . It wasn't a surprise. He's always been . . . is *passionate* the right word? Drama follows him, always has. Marriage, parenthood, I always worried he might struggle with it.'

'Are you angry at me, for being a home wrecker?'

'No, Joanna. If there's one thing I know, it's that we women need to stick together.'

'He didn't tell me he was married for a month.'

Elizabeth tutted.

'Was Alexandra a good mum?'

'Yes.'

'I wasn't.'

'Of course you're a good mum,' she said, wringing the wet flannel and dipping it in the warm water again. 'It was all he talked about when he phoned me. How beautiful you were with Noah.'

'No!'

'Yes!'

'What do you think about Alistair trying to get custody?'

'I think a child should have a father and a mother. And she shouldn't lose her other grandparents either, the little darling. She's very close to them.'

Joanna looked around the room. 'I'm not sure I really know your son.'

Elizabeth put the flannel in the bowl and the bowl on the floor. Joanna wished she could take back what she just said. She didn't want to antagonise Elizabeth, but God it felt good to talk to someone.

Elizabeth took her hand. Thank God, she wasn't annoyed. 'Can women really know their men?'

'I want to.'

Elizabeth took in the images Joanna had been examining these last days. 'As a toddler he'd run off without warning, climb on rooftops and jump off, that kind of thing. I don't know how many times I lost sight of him when out shopping. Had to call the police when I lost him on the foreshore once. He was impulsive, always getting up to mischief. But lovable, you know what I mean? Poor Alistair,' she said, 'losing his dad at thirteen. It changed him. Or, how should I put it? It brought some of his less admirable qualities to the fore. And you know what boys are like – I did my best, but they never take much notice of their mothers.'

Did the same happen to me? Joanna wondered. Did my dad ruin me by leaving? She didn't dwell on this, never had. 'I don't want to take Chloe away from her mum.' There, she'd said it.

'You can't always work together in the traditional way, like I did with Alistair's father. We met on Ward 2-South in Geelong Private. I dropped a clipboard and he picked it up! Afterwards, I was the homemaker and hostess, he the well-respected GP. The old-fashioned way worked for us but it can work in all sorts of different conditions. I just hope there's some way for Chloe to keep both her parents.'

'But Alistair doesn't want that,' Joanna said.

'He's angry, that she ran off. He might come round.'

'You think he's the kind of man to come round?'

Elizabeth shrugged. They both knew Alistair was not this kind of man.

'Where is he?' Joanna asked.

'At the police station. We didn't want to excite you, but there's been another sighting.'

'Has there?'

'Yeah, this one sounds ... look, sorry, I won't raise your hopes.'

'You haven't.'

'Oh, dear Joanna.' Elizabeth took a hairbrush from the bedside table and began brushing Joanna's hair.

'Elizabeth, the calendar we made for you. Can I look at it? I don't have any photos here. I need to see his face.'

She brought it in straight away, placing it gently on Joanna's lap. 'Do you want me to stay?'

Joanna shook her head and waited till the door was closed. She retrieved the bib from her pyjama leg, placed it under the mattress with the letters, and touched the first picture. January – Noah wrapped in a white sheet in Joanna's arms in the hospital. Joanna's smile was genuine. She was happy. Noah wasn't crying. She stroked his face with her trembling finger and turned to February – Noah in his pram at the front of their flat, sleeping, wrapped in the blue bunny blanket he died in. She kissed the photo and her mouth distorted into a howl that lasted hours, and only stopped because Alistair came into the room and tore the calendar from her.

She heard him yell at his mother in the kitchen. 'What were you thinking of? Didn't I make it clear what she needs right now?'

She heard Elizabeth defend herself. 'The girl needs to cry.'

'She needs rest! And to not be reminded!' He banged something, probably a door.

Joanna curled herself into a ball, moaning as she kneaded her soft breasts in an attempt to will back the painful tingle and the hardness. She pinched at them, squeezed, but they were nothing now: useless, soft, nothing.

Scared she'd be caught, Joanna typed a hurried message without correcting the mistakes.

To: justicefornoah@hotmail.com
From: anonymoussympathiser@gmail.com

Why would a bresstfeeding mothert need tampons?
Why did they wash the buggy and car seat covers?
The police never searced the mother-inlaw's housew. They shld.
Anonmyous1

*

Alistair woke her for the morning briefing session by shaking both arms quite roughly.

'What? What is it?'

Pale and angry, he placed two Valium in her mouth, then calmed himself by fluffing pillows and helping her sit up so she could listen comfortably. 'Are you feeling okay?' he asked.

'You're scaring me. What's happened?'

'All plans change,' he said, offering her the cup of tea he'd placed on the bedside table before waking her. 'I just need a backup.'

'Talk sense, Alistair.'

'I've been suspended. That fucking James Moyer is all over the internet again: "Suspicions rise over Labour guru and mistress." The arsehole! He goes on to mention this blog. Whoever's writing it is on to us.'

Alistair was pulling at his fringe. Be careful, Joanna thought, or that'll fall out too. 'How can they suspend you?'

'Richard Davis phoned from London an hour ago. He has inside info that the police were tipped off by an anonymous source who says there's something in this house to incriminate us. Add that to the shit this Lonniebaby blog's been printing and we're suspects. Not officially yet, but soon. Maybe someone else knows. Someone close. What could be in this house? What would the police think might be here? I've been searching everywhere. I can't find anything. Can you think of anything?'

'Um . . .'

'Please, think!'

'I am thinking.' Very hard in fact. She could end it all now, leave the bib where it was, and end it all.

'This will ruin our lives, Jo! As if they're not already ruined. Help me look. Please get out of bed and help. Mum's out. We're together in this, in everything. You have to think! I'm going mad. I'm scared. I need you!'

Joanna reached under her mattress and felt for the bib. She held it up to him, terrified at his reaction.

'What . . . ? Where . . . ?'

'He had it on when I gave him medicine. I found it in the suitcase last night. We forgot to deal with it.'

Alistair felt the crustiness. 'But how would anyone know about it?'

The sight of the bib made her cry.

'How would anyone know?! Have you been speaking to someone?' he yelled.

She found lying to him easier than she expected. Nine months of lying to everyone during the affair had taught her a thing or two. 'I've been here, in bed. No one could know. Unless someone found it there before I did. The police were all over the house that first night. More likely it's not the bib, just they're suspicious and want to look around.'

'You're fucking crazy! What do you think you're doing, holding on to it? Not telling me!'

'I'm sorry,' she sobbed.

She watched from her bedroom window as Alistair lit the barbecue in the back garden and burnt what she had left of her son in the gas flames. He then cooked several sausages, deep in thought as he turned them till they were ready.

He'd calmed down when he came back in with a plate of sausages wrapped in bread. 'I'm sorry. I'm so sorry for talking to you like that. This is awful. I'm trying to hold it together but I'm cracking. I'm so scared someone knows something, saw something. And I can't believe they suspended me.'

Joanna pushed the plate away. 'I'm not eating those.'

'Oh God, of course, I'm sorry. I just had to use the barbie after, you know . . . in case they notice it's been on.' He put the plate on the floor out of her sight.

She put her hand on his shoulder. She loved him when he allowed himself to be vulnerable. That's right – she loved him. Of course she loved him.

He lay down beside her. 'Hold me Joanna. Hold on to me.'

*

Phan and his crew arrived an hour later. Alistair knew them well. Up till now they'd been allies but there was no tea and banana cake this time. Journalists gathered outside as the police lifted cushions and rummaged through drawers. Elizabeth arrived home, joining Joanna and Alistair on the sofa. 'What a terrible waste of time and effort,' she sobbed.

Detective Phan apologised when he left, having found nothing, and telling them so. 'We have to follow up every lead, you understand,' Alistair's ex-ally said.

'Of course. Anything that helps find him. I just hope no more time's wasted.' Alistair shut the door and exhaled loudly.

Joanna heard something in the back garden at around midnight and got out of bed to see what it was. Alistair, putting something in the tool shed. What was that? She heard him come back in, and the shower in the hall bathroom turning on and staying on for a long time. Another door. The hum of the washing machine. She pretended she was asleep when he got in bed beside her. He wrapped his arm around her and kissed the back of her neck.

'Hi.' She used her best just-woken-up voice.

'Hey, there you are. You've been so unwell. I hate it when I feel you're somewhere else. Do you hate me, Jo? Have you stopped loving me?'

She turned and embraced him. 'Of course not.'

His eyes were so close to hers that she couldn't focus on them. She moved back a bit. 'What were you saying about a backup plan?'

'Oh, nothing. We'll be okay now. We're going to be okay.'

*

The following morning Alistair woke her to say: 'It's time to get out of this room.' He took off her pyjamas and put bubbles in the bath. 'Everything's over. Everything's going to be fine. One step at a time. Today, just move as far as the lounge.'

When she'd finished washing and dressing, he escorted her to the sofa, put a blanket on top of her, put on a DVD of *The*

Sound of Music, placed a glass of water, some pills, and two other DVDs (*Grease* and *Strictly Ballroom*) on the table in front of her, kissed her on the forehead and said: 'I'm going to the city. I'll be back for dinner.'

He was almost out the door when she noticed it was raining outside and that Alistair was wearing his raincoat. He didn't have this raincoat in Scotland, but she recognised it from one of the photographs in the albums in the box. It made her feel uneasy but she couldn't pinpoint why. 'Who you going to see?' she asked.

'My lawyer. Then Bethany. There's lots going on. The reward's up to seven hundred k now. She thinks she can get us a slot on *60 Minutes* and Del Rio Editions have made an offer for an autobiography.'

'Jesus!' she said under her breath.

He shut the door before she could have a go at him. There was excitement in his voice as he rattled off the PR plans. He was excited by *60 Minutes* and by a possible book deal.

Jesus!

Elizabeth made Joanna some buttered toast for breakfast and asked her about a hundred times if she was okay, and if there was anything she needed, before heading out to distribute leaflets.

Alone at last, Joanna went to the bedroom and took a photo album from the box, flicking from page to page until she found the shot she was looking for.

The Als go hiking in Freycinet!

Alistair and Alexandra, wearing his and hers raincoats. Joanna grabbed the laptop and searched for images of Japaras. Yes, Alistair and Alexandra both had Japaras.

Was that his backup plan, the one he had sown at the very beginning, when he mentioned seeing someone dressed in a Japara? If it all goes wrong, frame the ex-wife? He'd already planted the seed in the police station when they'd asked him about enemies. She hadn't seen a person a hundred metres away. She was certain of it, almost certain. Perhaps he hadn't either. With suspicions rising and his job on the line, had he decided to plant something else on her, to seal the deal? Several birds with one stone, after all: if Alexandra was convicted of murdering Noah, he'd be the poor innocent ex, he'd get his job back, and – the biggest victory of all – he'd get Chloe.

She raced outside to the tool shed. What had he done last night? Dug something up from Noah's grave to plant on Alexandra? The barbecue was in the shed. He must have put that back since cooking the Noah-infused sausages. The shovel was clean as a whistle. Too clean?

She checked the washing machine. Empty. The dryer had finished its cycle. His jeans and T-shirt – the outfit he had on yesterday – were dry inside it. She looked at all his shoes. None of them had dirt or mud on them.

Back inside, she read the Lonniebaby blog, which was now filled with page after page of facts and discussions about the case. The blogger seemed to know everything: about the many flaws in their relationship, that she hadn't coped on the plane, that they'd argued at the side of the road, that the dirt was because he'd buried the baby. The last comment, from 'Bobblypops', read: 'I think they accidentally overdosed him to stop him crying.'

Before Joanna could ask herself why, she had sent an email.

To: justicefornoah@hotmail.com
From: anonymoussympathiser@gmail.com

It was the fault of airport security.

She waited for a response, but after five minutes there wasn't one, so she browsed around the site, honing in on the page titled: 'Questions Unanswered'.

What I want to know is why Joanna Robertson needed to buy tampons at the milk bar. She was breastfeeding. You don't get your period when you breastfeed. And no one uses tampons for discharge.
They were driving from their holiday house in Point Lonsdale to his mother's house in Geelong, right? So why was their car facing the wrong way when the baby was taken – i.e. as if they were driving towards Point Lonsdale?
My mate knows the lady who owns the house they rented in Point Lonsdale and she says some garden equipment went missing from the shed. Did the cops ever ask them about this? No.
Alistair Robertson says they stopped twice on the road to Geelong to ring his mother about the fires but why did they both get out of the car?

Two drivers report seeing them on the same spot on the side of the Geelong road but their reports are half an hour apart. Did one or both get the times wrong? Or were the Robertsons at the side of the road for at least half an hour? If the latter, why? It doesn't take over half an hour to work out you have no phone signal.

How come they didn't stop at his mother's house first? Geelong's on the way to Point Lonsdale. Surely they'd pop in there, especially if they were worried about her and the fires, which is why they said they were trying to phone her on the way.

She says she expressed milk when they got to the holiday house in Point Lonsdale so her mother-in-law could babysit that night. But the bottle in the hire car was found to have been diluted! Why??

She was shocked at the depth and accuracy of the content. As well as locals and the general public giving opinions and information, it looked as if someone inside the investigation was leaking info to the blogger.

She felt a tinge of pleasure knowing Alistair had made so many mistakes. She'd been too stunned at the time to point out that it would be very obvious that the breast milk was diluted. Looking back, she realised he always made mistakes: getting caught in the marital bed, for instance. Why had she ever listened to him?

Beep. *What do you mean?* From justicefornoah.

I don't know. She was too scared to answer. What was she doing? She either wanted to confess or she didn't. If she did, she should stop with the anonymous emails and the riddles. Her finger hovered over the keys.

She couldn't. She was scared and weak. She'd been scared and weak since the day she found out he was married.

Who are you? the blogger asked.

Just a miserable nobody. Who are you?

Same.

Why you miserable? Joanna typed.

Because the world sucks.

Why are you so into this case?

I believe the baby's dead now. And Joanna Lindsay is evil. I want to see her punished.

She didn't recoil at these words at all. On the contrary, they made her feel strong. She found herself typing: *I want to meet you.*

Today?

Yes. Where?

In two hours. Geelong beachfront. I'll be at the entrance to the pier, wearing a Find Noah T-shirt.

*

The taxi dropped her off a quarter of an hour early. She sat on the beach and watched the pier, wondering to herself if she was really about to hand herself over. Hand herself over! Such modern times, when you hand yourself over to a blogger.

She stared at waves sliding over sand, clawing a layer back when they retreated. She and Alistair were to clink champagne glasses while looking at the bay. Alistair, her partner, the

199

father of her dead child. The father of her alive child, once.

Mesmerised by the waves, she found herself remembering how he used to sing to Noah at night. *Kookaburra sits on the old gum tree-ee/ Merry merry king of the bush is he-ee.* He used to talk to him as if he could understand. 'This was your grandad,' he said one evening, holding a framed photo over the cot as Noah lay gurgling (yes, gurgling!). 'He was a good man. He would have loved you, my baby Noah, my son. You're my son! Joanna Lindsay,' he yelled to her, 'I have a son!' Alistair ran to the hall, grabbed her and twirled her in the air. 'You gave me a son. You bore me an heir! And now, my beautiful Joanna, I am going to bore into you! I love you, Joanna Lindsay. I love you. I love you. I love you.'

This was crazy! Alistair wouldn't frame anyone. Watching him lie was driving her crazy because his lies mirrored hers. Only he wasn't as bad as her. He wasn't the one who killed Noah. She should be grateful to him for protecting her, for holding it all together. She recalled two of the 'facts' Alistair had listed at the side of the road on that terrible day, ones they'd repeated so many times since. They could both go to jail. Chloe could lose both parents.

Her behaviour now was just as it had been during the affair:

Then: One minute she was ending it, the next fellating Alistair in a lane. One minute she didn't trust him, the next, with her life. One minute she didn't love him, the next more than anything in the world.

Now: She wanted to confess, she didn't want to confess.

She didn't understand how Alistair could lie about this, she understood completely. She thought he was planning to frame his ex-wife, this was ridiculous.

This constant turmoil in her mind! She knocked on her forehead with her fist. Stop!

What did *she* think? What did *she* want to do?

What do you want to do, Joanna Lindsay? Make up your mind!

The tide was coming in. As it lapped at her feet she felt the dizziness of being twirled towards the bed, she heard Alistair saying: 'I love you, Joanna Lindsay. I love you. I love you. I love you.'

Shit shit shit! Call it post-traumatic stress disorder, whatever, she had gone mad. She couldn't betray Alistair. She couldn't meet this blogger.

Joanna tried not to look at the person standing at the edge of the pier as she walked along the promenade. It was only once she was in the taxi, and it had turned around to drive her home, that she spotted the T-shirt. FIND NOAH, was written in thick black at the top. A photo of him was underneath.

And wearing it, Chloe.

*

Joanna put her head down between her knees to hide, just like the old days. When the taxi arrived home, she threw twenty dollars at the driver and ran inside to type an email as if she was brushing a hairy tarantula from her chest.

Sorry I couldn't make it. Just want to say not all people are evil. Why don't you move on from this and look at the good things in life? I'm sure you have good things, people who love you? There's lots to be happy about. Signing off now, Anonymous1.

Sent.

Gmail account deleted.

Breathing too fast. Feeling dizzy. Lying on the sofa . . . Feeling . . .

*

Joanna woke to someone knocking at the door. She looked at the clock. She'd been out for the count for over two hours.

It was Detective Phan and the red-haired police officer who'd hugged her in front of the milk bar that first night.

'The neighbours across the road caught someone sneaking around the back of the house about twenty minutes ago,' Phan said, nodding towards the police car in the street and then at Joanna, kindly. 'It was Chloe. She thought the house was empty, says she just wanted to have a look inside. She's in the car. The bathroom window must have been left open and when we got here, she was climbing in. We could charge her, if you want?'

Joanna peered at car. She couldn't see Chloe's face – she was looking in the opposite direction. 'No. Of course not. Is she okay?'

'She's very drunk. Where's Mr Robertson?'

'Um, Melbourne.'

'And Mrs Robertson?'

'Elizabeth? I don't know. Out. She doesn't have a mobile.'

'Chloe says she didn't know you were in the house. She thought it was empty. She doesn't want to see you or her father and her mother's phone is ringing out. Because of the circumstances, with her little brother, I mean, we can take her home. Would that be all right with you?'

'Of course. Thanks.'

Joanna watched as the vehicle drove off but Chloe didn't change the position of her head.

*

It was after eleven at night when Alistair arrived home looking positively cheerful. 'Do you want the good news or the very good news?' he said, sitting on the bed she'd been lying awake on all these hours.

She sat up and welcomed his kiss, nervous about telling him of Chloe's attempted break-in. 'You choose.'

'Okay, the good first. They want us on *60 Minutes* next week!'

'You're joking? How is that good? You've not agreed, have you?'

'And that book offer: fifty grand advance.'

'I repeat: You're joking? How is that good? We're not doing either of those things, Alistair.'

'Okay, okay, I get where you're coming from. I need to

show you something. We'll talk about that later. The very good news is that the lawyer says it's confirmed there's nothing concrete against us. We're not suspects any more, not even unofficially. They see the gossip about us as typical and unhelpful. And,' Alistair continued with excitement, 'Chloe's been skipping school!'

'That's very good news?' Joanna couldn't believe his tone. She suddenly felt very protective towards Chloe. She didn't want to tell him what had happened that afternoon.

'Well of course not, not right now. But it proves she's not safe with that woman, see? She's out of control.'

'Alistair, she wouldn't be safe with me either. We can't go ahead with the hearing now. It's crazy. Chloe hates me. The court will listen to what she feels, what she has to say. They won't hand her over to someone she detests, let alone someone who's going through what I'm going through. I'm not well – in the head, I mean. I'm really not doing very well. I'm seeing things! What's the doctor got me on – anti-psychotics?'

'Just antidepressants.'

'And isn't there a risk she'd be handed over to someone different altogether with all this chaos, that she might even be taken into care?'

He stiffened and presented the first letter of the alphabet. 'A:'

Oh God, point form. If he brought out a finger for this display, she would bend it backwards until it snapped.

'. . . She doesn't hate you – she doesn't know you. B: She's been screwed up by her mother. C: She's a typical teenager, angry that her parents separated. D: She's unsafe and out of control! E: We are good people. And F: The court will see all the above and discard everything else.'

He hadn't used his fingers, but the point-form had fuelled a fury which made Joanna breathe differently and sway a little. 'Sit down so we can talk about this. I need you to listen to me.' She was proud of her clarity and assertiveness. Well done.

Instead of sitting down so Joanna could talk honestly and confidently, Alistair stood up very straight and adopted a monotone. 'No, what's crazy is you think it's okay for me to lose *both* my children. I'm sleeping in the bedroom tonight. You can have the sofa.'

21

ALEXANDRA

1 March

I wake at 5 a.m. to Chloe crying loudly. She's sitting up in bed when I go into her room, arms open wide for me to hold her. 'Mum! I'm sorry, I'm sorry, Mum!'

I tell her it's okay; that the hangover's probably making things feel worse.

'No, it's not that. I've done something really bad.'

She tells me about the blog. First, she felt sure she could help find Noah – she felt it was her duty, as she explained early on. But as the days wore on she believed him to be dead, and revenge became her motivation. She spent every spare moment trying to get evidence against Joanna, and as opinions and accusations flew in she stopped caring if her blog also implicated her father 'because he doesn't give a shit about me'.

I haven't cuddled Chloe in bed for a while, and I hold her while she sobs. 'It's okay,' I say. 'It's okay, my baby.'

Chloe says she's written a letter for the court arguing that she loves me, loves living with me, and does not want to be with them, or in Scotland. This letter would probably have been enough for us to win if Chloe hadn't taken to truancy, alcohol and crime, and if I hadn't been caught physically abusing her.

I almost faint every time I think about it. I keep hoping for a miracle, knowing the only miracle that will save me is if Alistair and/or Joanna are charged with the murder of their baby. And that would be a much worse thing for Chloe than living away from me for a couple of years. 'Just a couple of years!' I say to Chloe, crying. 'And wherever you are, I'll follow. I'll get a work permit and a house so close to yours you'll be sick to death of me.'

'It can't happen. I will not live with them. I don't care about him any more. I even threw that stupid bear out.'

'No! Where is he?'

'Gone. He has nothing to do with me now. And I hate her. I hate that woman.'

'You don't really think she killed Noah, do you?'

'I don't know. Sometimes the hate makes everything skew-whiff.'

'Don't hate her,' I say. 'Try not to hate her. I hope this doesn't upset you, but I'm glad I'm not with your dad. I'm thankful something happened that made it end. And listen, we're not giving up on Noah, but no more blogging. Okay?'

She's looking at me with such love that I know she means it when she nods.

*

After Chloe goes to school, my lawyer phones to say a space has come up in court for the hearing – in forty-eight hours. It would have been postponed – due to the situation with Noah – but Social Work Boy felt Chloe was not safe with me. If the thumb mark hadn't gone by the time he left (he checked and it had) and if I didn't have the support of my 'hardworking, generous and loving' parents, he'd have taken her from me there and then. The lawyer estimates that the chances of me winning might be as low as thirty per cent after what happened yesterday. To add to that, there's nothing concrete to incriminate Alistair and Joanna in Noah's case. The rumours were just that and the police aren't focusing on them any more. Which means in two days, my girl might have to go and live with him and his lover, wherever that may be.

*

As soon as the lawyer hangs up, Alistair phones. He's coming here now. He must have been waiting for Chloe to be at school. He said he wants to bring me some of the things that I stored at his mother's house but that'll just be an excuse. I'm worried. He'll have a plan. He always has a plan. I said okay without thinking. I should have said no, or asked to make it another day and organised for Mum and Dad to be here, but I didn't, I just said okay.

When we first met, I wasn't the kind of person to just say okay. I was tough. I was funny. He said so, in the Carlton bar we met in. 'You're funny! Are you hungry?'

I pace from bedroom one to bedroom two to living room to kitchen to bathroom and even to laundry. I tidy as I pace. I put the kettle on, put fresh coffee in the plunger. I open windows, wipe benches, fluff pillows. I change into jeans. Change into running gear. Change back into jeans. Berate myself.

Since I caught them, I've deserved the moral high ground. You think I'd hold on to it, right? He lied to me for nine months. And if what Phil said is true, he'd been doing the same shit all along. Our marriage was always a lie. He said he was at meetings when he was shagging all over town, leaving juices in our car and on our sheets. Said he worked his biceps and shaved his pubes for me. Said he didn't feel like sex because he was too stressed or too drunk. Or said he did like it, but did it always have to be the same, always in the bedroom, could I not have a bit more imagination? Said he couldn't go to Chloe's school play because he had a conference. Said he loved me. Said he'd always stay with me, no matter what.

It seems impossible that he has grabbed the high ground back so many times.

First: She took my child away from me. Abducted her!

Second: She's a drink driving criminal.

Third: She's a pincher. Maybe she wasn't charged with assault, but the pinch is on file with Social Services now. A child abuser.

Fourth: I am the father of another stolen child. There is no ground higher than that upon which I stand.

How dare he? The ground is mine!

I pour the coffee down the sink, unruffle a pillow, wipe off my lip gloss and put on my Lycra running pants. I do not care what he thinks of me. All I care about is my daughter and my high ground.

I sit on the couch for a few minutes, then get up, turn the radio on, then turn it off, then put the iPod in its dock and search for the Emmylou Harris songs which we used to play together, then slap my own hand for still having Emmylou Harris on my playlist, take the iPod out of its dock, then switch the kettle on. I'm about to reapply lip gloss and change into skirt – no, jeans – when he arrives.

*

The furious buzzing of my insides is numbed when he's standing in front of me. 'Hello, Alistair,' I say, not extending a hand, but opening the door to usher him inside.

He digs for eye contact, loosening his shoulders and speaking in a sad whisper to entice pity: 'Hi Lex.'

'Come in,' I say, refusing to let pity douse the feelings I want to have.

He puts a large box down in the hall. 'Photo albums,' he says.

I squirm at the box, at *our* things. 'Right, thanks.'

He sits at the kitchen bench as I make coffee, clasping his fingers together nervously. After taking a sip he says he's not sure where to start.

I make it easy for him. 'Is there any news?'

'No.' His lip quivers. 'How did everything go so wrong?'

I can't believe what I do when he starts sobbing. I move to his side of the bench and hug him.

'I'm a bad man. It's because I was bad to you. I'm so sorry.'

My top is wet with his tears so I hand him a tissue. 'You have to put all that aside now. Here, blow your nose.'

He doesn't hold back with the nose blowing. And why would he? I've seen him soap his balls and tweeze his nose hairs. It feels like we've never been apart. The familiarity envelopes me. To my horror, I like it.

'I should never have done it, Alexandra. I was a pathetic cliché, indulging a crisis. And she's so ... unbalanced ... I think she always was and I just didn't see it.'

For four years I have argued with him in my head – every day, almost all day. I have so many angry insults ready. I try to muster them.

You are a narcissistic psychopath. Here, look at the profile, mister:

> Glib superficial charm – tick.
> Above average intelligence – tick .
> Considerable poise, calmness, verbal facility –
> tick .
> Promiscuity; impersonal, poorly integrated
> sex life; inconsistent, undependable, and unre-
> liable commitments in life, including marital
> – tick , tick, tick

The long awaited moment has arrived. I can deliver my angry speech.

'I donated some money,' I say instead because all the above is just plain ridiculous, isn't it? The mad rantings of a wronged woman. Hell hath no fury and all that. I'm just the same as all the other bitter bitches who hate their cheating exes. 'I don't know what else I can do.'

Alistair, who I loved with all my heart for many years, blows his nose one last time and holds the tissue in his shaky hand.

I sit on the stool beside him. He turns his legs towards me, knees almost touching mine. 'You're more beautiful than ever.'

'Shut up.' I'm not being coy, I really don't want to hear this shit.

'Being without me suits you.' His knee touches my knee slightly. My reflex twitches my leg out of reach but the brief connection has weakened me, I can feel it. He's so bloody good at this.

'There's nothing you can do.' His phone buzzes and he hesitates, which surprises me for two reasons. First, no matter what was going on, Alistair always answered his phone. And second, his son is missing. What parent would hesitate when it could be the news you're waiting for?

'You should answer.'

He does. 'Bethany, hi . . . No! Really! You're kidding?'

Oh my God, they've found him, I think. They must have. Alistair's over the moon.

'That is wonderful news. Say yes immediately! Thank you

thank you thank you.'

'What?' I ask, smiling with relief, anticipation.

'I'm gonna be on *60 Minutes*.'

'Oh,' I plummet, then lie: 'That's great.'

'The PR woman is amazing. Do you remember her from my MBA course? Bethany McDonald?'

'I do. The stunning one.'

'You think?'

Of course I do. Alistair drooled over the woman for years.

'The police have been incredible too. I can't fault them.'

The notebook I took to the lawyer's is on the bench beside the phone. It reminds me to focus. 'What happens now . . . with Chloe?'

He comes back at me fast. 'Alexandra, why did you steal her from me, for *four* years? Do you know how hard that's been for me?'

He's using an old diversion tactic. Answer a question with a question (Me: 'Where were you tonight?' Him: 'Why are you so paranoid all of a sudden?')

'What happens now, with Chloe?' I ask, more firmly.

'Noah's been missing for fifteen days,' he whimpers.

He's wanting to engage me but I refuse. I use a tactic I learned in law. Don't fill the silence.

It works in that he fills it, but not with the answer I need. 'He's dead, I know it.'

'You don't know that.'

'After seventy-two hours, everyone knows that.'

'Not for sure, Al.' *Alistair*, not Al! Why did I call him that? Al is the name of the man I fell in love with. This is Alistair, the man he turned out to be.

'I can't lose both of them,' he says, and I know what this means. He still wants to take her.

Anger gets me off my stool and sends me around to the other side of the bench. I fold my arms. 'Despite everything, we're still going to court, then?'

He extends his hands out on the bench – open, pleading. 'I've lost my son! He's gone. Chloe's everything to me now. All I want is to do what's right for her. You must know she's losing it? I've fucked everything else up. If I can just do what's right for her. Can't we sort this out, no weapons? Can't we make sure something in the world is okay?'

And he's crying again. And I'm heading back to his side of the bench to hug him again.

'My baby's gone,' he says. 'I hate myself. I hate myself! I'm so sorry for hurting you. I'm so, so sorry. Please tell me you forgive me. Tell me we can sort this out together, tell me we can do this, for Chloe.'

He's not going to steal her from me. We won't go to court. We'll sort it out together! The accusations I rehearsed fade. I tell him I forgive him.

I tell him we can do this.

*

It's elation, the feeling I have. I'm free. I don't have to worry about hiding any more. Chloe won't be taken away from me. I don't have an enemy. No one wants to hurt me. I don't have to convince (or win back) social workers. I won't be crucified in court. I can have a glass of wine when I want. I smile so much during my afternoon shift in the café that I get fifty dollars in tips. I make a note to do that more often.

When I pick up Chloe from school, I tell her she's right, she won't have to leave me, and we jump up and down with happiness. I tell her we're going out. When she asks where, I say wherever you'd like. When she asks if this is so I can take dumb photos for that dumb scrapbook, I take the book from my bag and say, 'Hold one end, like a Chinese cracker.' She does this, and we rip it in half, and laugh.

She feels sentimental, wants to do something we used to do together, so we head to Luna Park and I even go on the Scenic Railway. Nothing scares me. Chloe holds her arms in the air and laughs at how loudly I scream. She buys a blue ice cone and eats it on the ghost train, putting a handful of ice down my back in the dark tunnel and making me jump. We buy fish and chips and eat them on St Kilda beach as roller-bladers whizz by on the promenade, the sun setting over the water. We buy two DVDs and seven packets of lollies on the way home and scoff our way through a movie. She falls asleep halfway through, a smile etched on her face.

I'm elated. Losing Noah has changed Alistair. Somewhere inside is the man I fell in love with. A good man. A grieving man. It's over. I'm safe and I'm happy and I'm falling asleep . . .

The phone. I switch the television off, rub my eyes, shuffle my way to the kitchen, and answer it.

'Hello, Alexandra, this is Joanna Lindsay.' She's speaking in a weird whisper. I see the digital clock on the microwave.

'It's four in the morning,' I say.

'Is it? I'm sorry.'

She's shaky, crying maybe, not sure, don't care, I'm going to hang up.

'Please, don't hang up.'

She's read my thoughts.

'I need to see you, tomorrow morning. It's very important. I want to help you.'

How could she help me? I think to myself. I don't need help any more. She reads my thoughts again.

'It's not something I can say on the phone, I'll explain tomorrow but you have to believe me when I say that you do need my help.'

22

JOANNA

1 March

She woke when Alistair opened the front door to leave. 'Where are you going? Alistair, come here. Alistair!'

'I'm going to Melbourne to see Phil.' He was obviously still furious with her. His face looked different. She recognised the expression, but couldn't place it.

'I'll be back this afternoon. Why don't you go for a walk? You've not been out since it happened, it'll do you good. I've left a hat and glasses on the hall table – not much of a disguise, but it might stop you getting hounded. Maybe you could go to the shops and get some ingredients and cook something.' He walked over, kissed her on the forehead, and then left.

As the car engine started, she recognised the feeling in her stomach. It was related to the expression she'd just seen on Alistair's face. A faint nausea. And then it came to her. That was his cheating face, the one he always had when he phoned his wife from their two-star hotel rooms. Not blinking, lips just managing to suppress an expression: a fearful tremble, or a smile? 'Work's been a nightmare!' he'd tell Alexandra as Joanna lay silent on the bed. 'Has your day been okay? Did Chloe go to dancing?'

God, she was totally paranoid. She should do what he suggested. It was a good, kind idea. She showered, dressed, waved Elizabeth off to whatever pointless Noah-hunting expedition she was going out on today, grabbed the sunglasses and baseball cap Alistair had given her, and stepped outside for the first time *since*.

'Morning, Ms Lindsay,' the security guard on the front veranda said.

'Morning.'

'Ms Lindsay! Ms Lindsay!' One of the two die-hard journalists camped on the pavement said.

She started running.

The greengrocer at the end of the street didn't sell Lilly Pilly berries and recognised her. 'Are you holding up?' the middle-aged man asked.

'Not really,' she said, pulling her cap as far down as it would go.

She began walking into town. She'd only walked one block when she saw her baby's face above the word MISSING.

She ran towards the pole and ripped the poster off, tearing it into pieces and tossing it in a nearby bin. She ran towards Geelong for a few metres, turned back and pulled the ripped sheet out of the bin – her baby's face! She couldn't rip her baby's face to pieces and leave it in a bin! Torn pieces of the missing poster now in her pocket, Joanna ran two kilometres, without looking higher than knee level, all the way into the town centre. She was so out of condition, it was more of a stagger than a run.

The house was still empty when she got back. After getting her breath, she taped the 'Missing' poster back together, flattened it with her hand, and kissed what she could make out of her baby's face. This she put in her hiding place under the mattress. The letters she'd hidden were still there. The police must have left them there. She Googled the jam recipe and set to: washing and boiling the berries, draining the misty pink juice through muslin, adding sugar and lemon, boiling, removing scum, waiting for it to set.

The process didn't calm her as she'd hoped, probably because she was supposed to make this while Noah was jumping on a trampoline in the garden, not pinned to street lights below the word MISSING. She had to stop herself from going outside again to tear down every poster she could find.

She stared out the window and began to obsess about Alistair. It wasn't paranoia. She knew he hadn't gone to see Phil. Kirsty had warned her that she might never trust him. Not a great foundation for a new relationship, she'd said, to know how good he is at lying. At the time Joanna felt annoyed at Kirsty for not giving the poor fellow – the love of her life! – a chance. She and Kirsty drifted apart for a while and began gently repairing the friendship when Joanna announced her pregnancy. But Kirsty still didn't like him, it was obvious. She made sure to visit when Alistair was away at conferences ('That way I get you all to myself!') and couldn't help but make the occasional dig: Do you trust him when he's away? / Do you two laugh a lot? / He doesn't expect you to give up work, does he? / Will he be a hands-on dad, do you think? / Did he put you on a diet? / Are you happy Jo? Really happy?

The first spoonful of the jam was bitter and she was glad that it almost hurt to eat it. She stood at the living room window looking through a small gap in the curtains at the tree, devouring spoonful after spoonful, wincing each time until the jar was empty.

She'd hoped to feel something other than sick, but she didn't. She lay in bed and eventually the nausea gave way to sleep.

*

The doorbell rang at the same time as the phone. She gestured for Detective Phan to come in as she spoke on the phone to Justin someone from *60 Minutes*. 'Just want to say we're thrilled you've agreed to do the interview,' Justin said.

Joanna gritted her teeth. He'd agreed to it already, the arsehole. 'I'm very sorry, I'll have to call you back.'

'Everything all right?' Phan asked.

'Fine, just a Channel 9 thing. Not sure we're up to it.'

'You should think about it. Keeps people aware, you know. In fact, that's why I'm here. I don't know how to say this . . .'

'Just say it.'

'We've sent the volunteers home, closed the hall in Point Lonsdale. It's not that we've stopped the search, it's just that after the initial one, we wait for leads before going at it again. A search isn't a linear thing, I hope you understand. We'll still do everything we can. But that's why it's important for you and Alistair to keep it in the public eye. You should think about the Channel 9 gig.'

She said she would and sent him on his way as fast as she could, furious at Alistair for saying yes behind her back, but relieved that the good people of Point Lonsdale were no longer spending their free time looking for Noah.

When she looked out the window to check he'd gone, she noticed the security guard had gone too, and that one last journalist was packing up his van.

*

When Elizabeth arrived home in the evening, Joanna got up, mortified to have left the kitchen in such a state.

'No, let me clean up,' Elizabeth said. 'I'll get you something proper to eat.'

Half an hour later, a plate of lamb chops and veggies appeared in front of her. Joanna apologised for not being able to eat it.

'That's okay,' Elizabeth said. 'I'm off to bed now. You should get some sleep too.'

*

It was after ten when Alistair arrived home.

'How was Phil?' Joanna asked.

'Hello to you too. Did you go for a walk?'

'Where did you meet him?'

'Town.'

'For lunch *and* dinner?'

'Why are you being so aggressive?'

'*60 Minutes* phoned. They're so pleased you agreed to do the interview.'

'Oh ... Listen ... I'm sorry. But think about it. No innocent parent would refuse. I'll do the talking. You just hold my hand.'

She couldn't even be bothered discussing it. Whatever. 'Just promise me you won't do the book.'

'Can we talk about that later?'

'No. Promise me now.'

'I promise.'

What a worthless thing, an Alistair-promise. 'You didn't meet Phil, did you? Was it Bethany? I've Googled her. She's hot. Do you think she's hot?'

'What? Jesus!'

'Why don't you just answer my question?'

'Why don't you just stop with the paranoia?' Alistair bashed his way around the kitchen, re-heating the plate his mother left for him, then turned the television on. After finishing one mouthful, he sighed. 'Please trust me. I saw Phil.'

Joanna dug her arms into the side of the sofa to maximise her distance from him. There were four feet between them, she calculated. The television in front of them was four feet from her, and four from him. Joanna, Alistair, TV: an equilateral triangle.

She realised why she had been hallucinating about triangles in the bedroom now. The counsellor. The drama triangle.

*

'Have you heard of the drama triangle?' the counsellor had asked, and was surprised when Joanna said no. She set about drawing one on a piece of A4 paper: 'There are three positions, each at one point of the triangle.'

Victim

Rescuer   Persecutor

'In some relationships, each person takes a position. You, for example, might have felt that you were saving Alistair when you got together: from a dull marriage, a difficult wife, a routine life, a sexless relationship. So he might have been the Victim, and you the Rescuer.'

Joanna was tempted to grab the sheet of paper and shove it down the counsellor's throat. Six sessions, she'd had, each less helpful than the last. After each one, she left hating herself more than when she arrived. She always came with a very specific need. The first two: to be told it was okay to have a lover who was married. The third and fourth: to be told it would not hurt anyone as long as she kept it a secret. Five: she wanted to know how to get out. She'd had enough of being a liar. It was no longer fun. She'd tried to end it, and failed, and Joanna had never failed at anything. There must be something obvious she was doing wrong that she could do right. Telling him it was over only led to tears that led to sex that led to loving him more. Changing her telephone number and blocking him on email and Facebook and avoiding their usual haunts only led to him seeking her out or creating a new email or Twitter or Facebook account from which he'd deliver beautiful speeches, which led to her believing he loved her more than anyone could ever love anyone, which led to her not leaving him, which led to the making of a sixth counselling session.

'Just tell me how to leave him!' Joanna begged, but the counsellor ignored her, and held up her diagram.

'What happens is this. Some people, some couples, get caught on this triangle. You change roles, again and again, moving from one point of the triangle to another, but you are never able to get out. Soon after the affair started, you, for example, may have changed from the Rescuer to the Victim. He made you lie. He made you cheat. He turned you into someone you did not recognise or like. You might have been thinking: I was a good person before you. You have ruined me! So you moved to another point on the triangle to be the Victim. And he, the Persecutor.

'Next he might have taken his stand as the Victim. My wife

is unhappy, and now my lover is unhappy. I am unhappy. All I want is to be happy. Poor me. Victim.'

Joanna had paid another thirty-five pounds for this session and she had twenty minutes to go according to the square silver clock behind the velour sofa. The counsellor was not going to help her. She would never come again. She started doing her shopping list in her head.

'Couples on this triangle are dysfunctional,' the woman said, putting the drawing down on the coffee table between them. 'They're stuck, only ever moving from one to two to three, corner to corner to corner.'

The clock ticked loudly. Joanna was supposed to meet him at a bar in town in an hour. She had hoped to go armed with the ammunition to end it, once and for all. They'd been together nine months now. Fifteen minutes to go. She should get eggs at the supermarket too, and try and eat one for breakfast.

'Where are you now, Joanna?'

'What?'

'On the triangle.' The counsellor banged the tip of her pen on the diagram on the coffee table, annoyed that her client was distracted. 'Where do you think you are right now?'

'Um, actually, I need to be somewhere else. Sorry, I have to get going.'

She didn't make another appointment.

Two hours later Joanna found herself with Alistair in the back lane behind a bar in town. After, she promised him: 'Yes,

I will save you from her. We will be together.' She was on a triangle. The Rescuer, at that particular moment, one with cum on her chin.

Alexandra caught them the following week and she forgot all about the triangle.

But it came back when she was delirious.

Sitting on the sofa watching the carefully selected television that did not involve the news and therefore them, she realised he was forcing her to be someone she hated – again.

She wanted to tell the truth, she wanted this lie to end. Victim.

'You're a good person,' he'd say. 'It'll all be over soon.' Rescuer.

They'd assume new positions any moment. She knew that now. She'd be watching to see when it happened.

She felt like ringing her counsellor and thanking her for the diagram.

She felt like wringing her counsellor's neck for not telling her how to get off the diagram.

She *was* going mad. She needed more than antidepressants. The line that connected her to him stuck to her like a shadow, stretching, holding her, then banging her off to her next position.

Alistair was at his end of the couch watching – you guessed it – *60 Minutes*. He'd manage it, you know. His ability to look normal astonished her. He'd made mistakes right enough, but had played his part to perfection, searching the streets for days, yelling at the police to try harder, tweeting and Facebooking and creating a website and even a fund for donations, latching himself to that Bethany. He was so good at it that Joanna wondered if he was human. She looked back on his behaviour during the affair – lying had come to him with similar ease. It didn't trouble him. Since the incident, he had cried in her arms sometimes at night. He sobbed in the bath too – she heard him. But not enough. He didn't need tranquillisers. He didn't hear cries. He wasn't suffering from post-traumatic stress. He didn't want to confess or kill himself. He wasn't tortured enough.

Joanna went to the toilet and sat with her head in her hands. As with the affair, this had started with one lie. Someone has taken my baby. She sat on the toilet and tried to take Alistair's advice – that she could do this, that this was only one lie. Just as she'd done when she told Kirsty that Alistair Robertson was just a friend. Only one lie.

But it wasn't. Now, as then, one lie turned to two.

I just popped into the shop for a minute.

Turned to three.

Alistair had to get wipes.

Turned to two-hundred-and-seventy-thousand-nine-hundred-and-forty-fucking-three.

She pulled at her hair as she sat on the loo, hoping her scalp would bleed like it had last time she did this. She pressed her finger against her tender skull and placed the tip of her finger on her tongue, no blood. She'd have to pull harder.

'Noah,' she said out loud. Her intention was to cry. Crying had made her feel better when she had her afternoon in bed with the calendar. She said the word again: 'Noah.'

No tears. Just the memory of an act, an ever-present image, on replay in her mind. Rocking back and forth on the toilet, she tried to suppress this memory, but it was too powerful: *Alistair is asleep. Noah is screaming. I am sitting in my seat, holding Noah in my arms. I am opening the lid to a medicine bottle. I am filling a spoon with medicine. Some spills. I am filling it again, holding it steady. I am opening Noah's mouth with my finger. I am leaning him back. I am pouring the liquid into his mouth. I am killing him.*

The image rocked back and forth with her. She murdered the redemption she was supposed to have, the happy life she was supposed to guide and enjoy. She gave him the wrong medicine. He was allergic to it. She killed him.

She tried to drown out the image with happy ones. Noah always seemed quite calm while she bathed him. She remembered smiling and admiring his active feet. When he settled in for a feed, his little hand touched her breast. At Dubai airport, she ached with love for him as he slept in her arms. She thought of the pictures of Chloe in the album, growing up happily with her mummy and daddy. Noah would never grow up. And she'd ripped that life from Chloe.

She used to look at Noah and imagine him when he was older, saying 'mummy' and 'I love you'. She used to imagine him riding a bike and squealing with joy and falling off and cutting his knee. In her daydreams, she'd put a plaster on it

228

and kiss the top of his head. She used to imagine making jam on the veranda of her Aussie holiday house while he bounced on the trampoline.

None of these images stuck now. Just the killing one.

Her desire to go to his grave was becoming unbearable. She wanted to talk to him. She wanted to place something special there. What? He was too little to have a favourite thing. And the blanket was down there with him already. The only thing that came to mind was the Bananas in Pyjamas teddy she bought for him. But he didn't care about that. She'd have to find something else to take to him. Oh, it would feel good to sit under the tree with him, say sorry, goodbye.

Alistair would never let her. She'd never get away with it.

She pulled her hair again and this time she tasted blood on her finger. It soothed her. She pulled her jeans up, opened the toilet door, and headed towards the sofa.

Joanna sat on her side of the sofa again.

The news came on – dangerous territory – and Alistair immediately switched it off. 'Let's go to bed.'

*

'I have some things to tell you,' he said as he undressed, not pausing long enough for her to ask what. 'I didn't see Phil today. I went to see Lex.'

Aha! She was right. Oh, thank God, she wasn't totally crazy. But *Lex*? He'd never called her this. She knew he used it from old letters she sent him during their uni days, which

Joanna found in the hall cupboard, and which he hadn't thrown out: 'Al, this is the longest summer ever!' blah blah blah. 'When do you arrive at Spencer Street? I'll be the one wearing no knickers. Love Lex (The most interesting person in the room!) xxx'

'Alexandra. I went to see Alexandra.'

'Oh.' Joanna's face was suddenly unbearably hot. She couldn't identify what was erupting inside: rage, perhaps. He went there without telling her. He was calling her Lex. He should have the decency not to use this name to Joanna's face. She wanted to know every detail: where they sat, how long they were together, what she wore, if she looked good, if they were alone, whether they hugged, kissed, shook hands, had coffee, wine, talked about Noah, about her.

'You're cancelling the hearing?'

'No. It's got to be done properly.'

'But you don't want to take her back to the UK now? If we can ever go back.'

'That's the other thing I want to talk to you about. After the hearing, we have to go back.'

'What?'

'I have to get my job back. They've got Hanson doing it, fucking Hanson. The little prick's been after my position for years. I have to get back. We have to get on with our lives. That's what we would have done, I think. No one would think it strange. It's stranger if we don't.'

Joanna couldn't believe Alistair was thinking about work . . .

There's no way she could even think about a lesson plan. How could either of them concentrate on anything, after what they'd done? No, she did not want to go home. She wanted to stay here, near the tree. 'So what did Alexandra say?' she asked.

'Nothing really. I didn't give details. I just wanted to warm her up.'

None of the questions Joanna wanted answered had been answered. Instead he'd added more facts and plans into the mix that filled her with – yes, definitely – rage. This was just another shitstorm to Alistair, just one shitstorm in a lifetime that was filled with them. Her suspicions about him were not crazy, not paranoid. Perhaps he had gone there to plant something on her, just in case. Perhaps he had left something in her house.

'We have to try and feel normal,' he said, taking off his boxer shorts, lying on the bed, and touching himself. 'Maybe sex would help.'

It was the first time he'd brought up the subject since. 'It might relieve some stress.'

Joanna grasped at anything that might drown out the memory. She hated Alistair right now, and probably wouldn't have agreed if she hadn't. She needed to do something with the anger.

She took her pants off, and noticed the triangle line was now attached to the pubic hair she hadn't cared less about shaving since. The line ended at his foreskin. She watched it shorten and disappear as she sat on him.

He wasn't erect.

And she wasn't wet.

But she wriggled for a while, making it hard, and then he disappeared into her. He shut his eyes and she wondered if he was imagining Lex. All he'd ever said about her sexually was that she had more curves than Joanna and that sex was never as good. 'No details!' he'd say. 'It only upsets you.' She could tell from the expression on his face that he was fantasising. Bethany perhaps.

'Ah, honey,' he said, the fantasy and the wriggling obviously working. 'Ah baby . . . Oh this is helping!'

'We made Noah doing this,' Joanna whispered.

'Shh. Ah, yes, yes, that's it . . .'

'I'm opening a bottle.' Her voice was louder this time.

'Don't talk.' He was almost ready, which meant it was time for him to withdraw and wank onto her stomach, or face, or wherever he fancied, as long as it wasn't inside her, as long as he wasn't looking at her. He started doing this almost as soon as the affair changed into a proper relationship, very few variations since.

He wouldn't tell her what to do any more, she'd had enough of that. 'Get back inside me!'

'Shh, shh.' He was going at himself, eyes only on her bottom half which could have been anyone's from that angle.

'I'm leaning Noah's head back.' Joanna grabbed Alistair's face and pulled it towards hers.

He put his hand over her mouth and closed his eyes. She

tore it off angrily.

His features gathered for the climax.

'Open your eyes.' A louder voice this time. But he didn't obey, wouldn't, too close.

Almost a yell this time: 'I'm killing our son, Alistair. I'm killing Noah.'

*

After pushing Joanna away, Alistair turned to his side and fell asleep. Fell a-fucking sleep. She lay on her back and listened to the hiss of her angry breaths. It was part of the same thing: the affair, the incident. All part of the same screwed-up relationship. Right now, she couldn't recall one happy moment with him. She couldn't recall ever feeling confident with him. She couldn't recall making one good decision with him.

Before him, she was an unfathomably happy Act I character, unaware that she was doomed to die by the end of Act II.

She stared at the ceiling and said, 'I want to be me again.' It didn't wake him. She got out of bed, slipped as quietly as she could into her jeans, T-shirt and trainers, took her phone with her into the toilet, locked the door, and dialled her counsellor in Glasgow. 'Anne, it's Joanna Lindsay.'

'Joanna, my God I've been thinking about you. Are you okay? What time is it over there?'

'Can I talk to you? I can send you money over tomorrow.'

'Go ahead. Forget the money. I'll just go into the other room.' It only took her a few seconds. 'Okay, I'm alone. Talk.'

'I need to get off the triangle.'

'Sorry?'

'You know, the triangle. I'm trapped.'

'Where are you?'

'Right now I don't know which one I am. I could be all three.'

'Is there someone you love nearby, Joanna? Does someone know where you are?'

'I paid you thirty-five pounds a session. I sat on your sofa and listened and all I wanted was an answer and that's all I'm asking for now. I'll pay you double, seventy quid, more, I'll give you my house! How do I get off? Tell me. Please! How do I get off it? I'm banging around from corner to corner and I can actually see the lines when I'm with him now and I have to get off it I have to get off it.'

Anne's voice slowed, lowered, flattened: a soft, counselling monotone. 'Joanna, I am listening to you. Where did you say you are again? Is there anyone with you?'

'Oh God! You don't know! No one knows!' Joanna hung up, got what she needed from the cabinet in the bathroom, a torch from the laundry and car keys from the hall table. No one outside. They'd probably all moved on to a fresh search, for an even cuter kid.

*

She knew where the house was, having looked it up on Google maps about a hundred times on her phone in the toilet, deleting her browsing history afterwards. She drove the silver Ford Alistair hired out of Geelong and along the long, straight, dark, Bellarine Highway. It took her thirty minutes to reach the house. She hadn't noticed anything about the house or the area the last time, but now it seemed as eerie and as flat as the highway she'd just travelled there on. A light fog hung over the flat grassy swamp, which a still strip of moonlight cut in half. There were no hills and no high trees around the lake, just flat land that melted into a distant horizon. A railway line ran along the edge of the lake opposite the houses. The steam train, she supposed: the one Alistair and Alexandra had been married on. If the houses on this street were occupied, the occupants were asleep. No lights, anywhere. Dead silence.

She drove past the large two-storey house slowly to check there were no cars in the driveway, then turned back and parked at the front of the property.

All the lights were off. Curtains drawn. She crept down the side of the building and pointed her torch in the kitchen window. A few of the kitchen units were open – empty, as far as she could see. The cooker still had plastic on it and was unplugged. The new Smeg fridge rested on a trolley in the corner. Satisfied that no one was home, she walked from the paving stones at the back door into the garden, torch pointing up in search of the tree.

Shit! Joanna's shin bashed against something. She pointed her torch down – a short fence. She followed the line of light around the fence. It surrounded a rectangular pool. The edge of the pool was only six feet or so from the high garden fence. She stood up, walked to the high fence, and swept her hand along it all the way round the perimeter of the back garden.

The pool was surrounded by recently laid paving stones. A rectangle of wood chippings was at the back, a rockery at the left, a fountain in the centre-back, and a large square compost bin in the right corner. The block was a meticulously landscaped quarter of an acre at most. She couldn't see any freshly dug earth. And there were no trees.

Panting with confusion and fury, she stood on the bottom rung of the wooden fence and shone her torch over it, doing the same from all sides. It looked as though the garden had been subdivided. There was a large block at the back, with a small driveway at the side of Phil's. The block was levelled and flattened, and had a For Sale sign. The grass had grown after the levelling, which meant the land had been cleared a long time ago, well before the incident. She raced back around the side of the house, jumped in the car, and drove all the way to Geelong with no belt on, her foot flat on the accelerator.

*

Alistair looked surprised to wake with a woman straddling him and a key digging into his neck.

'Where did you put him?'

'What? Joanna, shit. Ow! Get off me.'

'Tell me where you put him or I'll yell the truth so your

mum can hear.'

'Get the key off. It hurts.'

'Elizabeth! I killed . . .'

'Shhh. Okay, okay.'

The key was pressed into his flesh so hard it looked like he had a small cave in his neck. She didn't care. 'Where did you bury my baby?'

'You went there?'

'You never answer a question, always another question. I am asking you a simple thing. Where did you put Noah? You said the garden was two acres, that there was a Lilly Pilly tree. You said it was beautiful. Where is he? Is he in the compost bin?'

'No!'

'The rock garden?'

'No. Ouch, God, I don't remember.'

'You don't remember where you buried our son? Is he even in that garden?'

'Yes, yes, he is. Please, you're cutting my skin now.'

'In the woodchip part? Where? The left? The right? The middle?'

'Yes, under the woodchip but I don't know where exactly. I was in shock. I was in a hurry.'

'You really don't remember? I thought you remembered things, Alistair. I thought out of the two of us you were the one who remembered things. Next to the fountain?'

'Yes.'

'You're just saying that because your neck's bleeding.'

'I'm trying to. I can't. It's blank. I'm sorry.'

'So where do I go to talk to him?'

'Talk?'

'Where do I go? Yes, talk, where do I talk to him? Where do I say sorry? Where do I say goodbye to my son?'

'We can't visit him. What do you think you're doing, going there? What if someone saw you?'

'You're the one who remembers everything and you don't remember digging a grave with a tiny trowel and putting my little boy in the ground and throwing earth on top of him, on top of Noah's face and Noah's legs and arms and toes, and then patting it down, patting it down, even though it's your son down there, you patted earth down on top of him. You don't remember where that was? By the rockery? Next to the fountain? You don't remember?'

Alistair grabbed her wrists and pinned her down so quickly she was still feeling anger instead of fear when she realised she'd lost the power. He had one knee on each arm and a hand on her mouth.

'Shhh, don't kick, ow, calm down Joanna, calm down, we're on the same side. I just didn't want to upset you. It was important to you, that it was lovely, and I couldn't bring myself to tell you. That's all. We're on the same side.'

The same side? Against who, Noah? She couldn't say this because his hand was pressing on her mouth so hard that she couldn't bite him either.

'Shh, shh, my love. Shh. Come on. Jo, Jo-Jo, shh . . .'

*

Noah was not under a tree. His place would not bear Noah fruit. No one would remark on the beauty above him, or make jam – or jelly – after picking from him. Joanna would never hear his cry, feel connected, say goodbye. She had clung to this in these horrible weeks, clung, and it was a lie.

She hushed, just as he ordered. She hushed and didn't mention the tree, or the fucked assumptions they made about their roles on that first dinner date: that Alistair is someone you should listen to, that Joanna is forgetful. She didn't mention the drama triangle, or her killing Noah, or the triangle, which was so clear to her now that other people would surely see it. And they would know what she was now: the Persecutor.

She had a plan. Not Alistair-style, involving facts and the like, a Joanna plan, involving doing the right thing.

Alistair kept his phone in his pocket at all times, and under his pillow at night. Joanna understood why he did this during their affair, but often wondered why it continued afterwards. 'Just habit,' he said when she last asked him. She slipped it out from under the pillow and took it to the toilet with her. He had a four-digit pin number. Last time she asked to use his phone, the number was his birthday, 1307, so she tried that, but it didn't work. He'd changed it. 'I change it regularly,' he said when she asked him once. She tried her birthday, Noah's,

Chloe's. Hers. Nup. She gave up and crept out to check his diary, which was on the desk in the study. Sure enough, Alexandra's number and address were written in the back.

She probably shouldn't have phoned Alexandra when she did, but Joanna had lost touch with time. And Alistair was fast asleep, so it was safe. 'It's Joanna Lindsay,' she whispered from the toilet. 'I need to see you, tomorrow morning. It's very important. I want to help you. It's not something I can say on the phone, I'll explain tomorrow but you have to believe me when I say that you do need my help.'

23

JOANNA

2 March

'I'm going to Melbourne today,' Joanna said over breakfast, 'to do some shopping. You're right. I need to get back into the real world.'

Alistair smiled. She found it hard to believe that not so long ago that smile compelled her to take his hand and put it in her pants in public bars.

'I'll drive you. I'd like to try and catch up with Phil for real this time.'

Yeah whatever, she thought, not interested in checking to see if he had his cheating face on.

They both donned caps and sunglasses, but there was no one to hide from here.

Joanna felt nauseous in the passenger seat. She closed her eyes and reminded herself of the plan.

Twenty minutes after leaving, she realised they were on the same road as last time. 'Alistair, please take another route.'

'I'm afraid there is no other route.'

Joanna wanted to open the door and jump out. But she didn't, she had things to do. And perhaps it was important to see where it had all happened, to remind herself of the first lie in this particular episode. She should embrace the road, face the truth, and the consequences, of her actions. She opened her eyes.

A cross.

Some hills to the left. 'They're the You Yangs.' Alistair had noticed where she was looking.

A lorry.

A huge metal sign: Avalon Airport.

And after a while, to the right – the place where she discovered that her son was dead: Nothing Field.

Or was that Nothing Field over there?

There were a lot of Nothing Fields along this highway.

In the distance she could make out patches of blackened earth, scars from the fire that had refused to kill her.

Apparently it took them an hour to get to the West Gate Bridge. Alistair could have told her it took three hours. He could have said ten minutes. To Joanna, that road was a black hole.

Alistair dropped her at a tram stop in North Melbourne. 'Meet back here at two?' he said, kissing her goodbye.

'Sure.'

'Hey, what about you get some lingerie to cheer yourself up? I have a surprise for you after.' And he drove off.

*

Everyone was looking at her at the tram stop. At first she thought her dress might be tucked into her pants or

242

something, but then she remembered she was famous, and pulled her cap down to cover her eyes. It didn't work, they still recognised her. Most people averted their eyes when she caught them staring, but one gave a sympathetic nod and one touched her on the shoulder and said something about Jesus.

When the Number 19 finally arrived, she walked to the back with her head down. She took a seat and pressed her face against the window to avoid being talked to. The tram rambled through the leafy university suburb of Parkville. The name rang a bell. Oh, that was where the old lady who sat behind her on the plane lived. Melbourne became less leafy after the university area: lots of traffic, low-lying strips of shops filled with eateries like falafel places and cafés and the occasional gun shop. Higgledy-piggledy Victorian cottages after that, the flat land widening out for slightly larger cottages and bungalows.

There was no way to avoid walking past all the remaining passengers when the tram reached her stop. To her dismay, they were all looking at her with compassion. She ran when she got off, following the map she'd downloaded on her phone. Alexandra's house was three blocks away.

She stopped at the sign for Portville Street and caught her breath. This was where Alexandra lived. She was about to talk to her, face to face, for the first time. Except for the phone call last night, she'd had no communication with Alexandra at all. She'd written an email. The seventeenth draft read:

Alexandra,

I am so sorry I deceived and hurt you. I'm ashamed and will never for-give myself.

Joanna

She didn't send it. The words were meaningless and pathetic. Her sixteen previous drafts were even worse. What could she say that wouldn't be self-indulgent bullshit – that she didn't know for a month, that she knew they were unhappy, that she had managed to avoid Alexandra's bed for nine months, that she had never lied before, been the other woman before, hated herself before? No, there was nothing she could write that would make her apology meaningful, nothing that would dilute her hideousness.

The houses were mostly weatherboard, all different colours and shapes and sizes. Alexandra's, the fourth on the left, was a cream Californian bungalow with blue trims. It had a white picket fence and a scruffy looking driveway. It looked like a happy house: pretty and comfortable.

Joanna took off her hat and glasses and put them in her bag. She steeled herself and walked up the drive, along the small veranda, past the stained-glass windows, and knocked on the front door. She heard music being switched off, footsteps, the door opening . . . and there she was, dressed in three-quarter length Lycra running trousers, a sleeveless top, and runners. She was slim and toned, no make-up. By 'bigger curves' Alistair obviously just meant 'bigger boobs'. Alexandra's were at least a C cup, pert and perfect. And she looked younger than Joanna did now, even though she was twelve years older. Joanna had avoided looking at herself, but when she caught an accidental glimpse, she saw a haggard, gaunt wreck with red eyes and black sunken sockets. She could see her ribs nowadays. Her hips bones jutted out like elbows. Alexandra, on the other hand, was a healthy weight, fresh-faced, had well cut hair, and no bags under her eyes. She didn't smile or offer a hug. 'Come in.'

It was perhaps the most nerve-wracking meeting she had ever anticipated. Like being sent to the Head Teacher's office for cheating in an exam or being paraded in front of a jury for cold-blooded murder. No, add those two things together, multiply the result by about a thousand, and that's how guilty and small and scared Joanna felt.

Inside had the same feel as outside – unpretentious, comfortable, but trendy. The long wide hall had stripped floorboards and white walls that were covered with a galleria of framed photographs. Joanna spotted a few as she walked behind Alexandra: Chloe on her bike, at the beach with her mum, with Alistair on Tower Bridge. Joanna was shocked to see the photo of Alistair. She was seeing in-context Alistair again. She liked him more here than in his childhood bedroom.

She asked herself what she was feeling, tried to pinpoint it the way Anne Docherty had taught her. Emotional intelligence, it's called, identifying your emotions. Only then can you deal with them. She was feeling jealous, but she didn't understand why. Or more accurately, she couldn't choose one single reason.

Maybe it was because Alexandra was better looking than her, and in better shape. Even when Joanna was happy, pre-affair, she was a league below the gorgeous woman walking down the hall before her. It must have been newness and youth alone that had propelled Joanna to a league above in Alistair's eyes.

Maybe it was because Alexandra was cleverer. A qualified lawyer – her graduation picture was on the wall in front of her now. And Joanna was 'just' a teacher. While she'd argue against the 'just' at dinner parties (Teachers are underrated / Teachers are underpaid / Teachers are the most important people in the universe), she had to admit she only did teaching because whenever she tried to write the Great Scottish Novel she couldn't get further than two pages, both of them terrible.

She might have been jealous because Alexandra was guilt free, waltzing along like someone who hasn't committed adultery and killed a baby.

Or because she had her baby, and that child was happy – the little girl in the photos there, smiling, growing up, living.

Or because Alistair did not, in the end, turn out to love Joanna more. She was not more special; less so, in fact.

The back of the house had been renovated into a large open-plan kitchen/dining/living area, with glass doors leading out to a pretty patio with a barbecue and outdoor furniture, and a grass area, which had a large round trampoline on it.

An aviary filled with colourful chirping budgies was just outside the back door, a hamster cage was in the corner of the dining room, and a cat purred on the window sill. That's right, Chloe was an animal lover.

'I made fresh coffee for you.' Alexandra pulled the kitchen stool out and indicated that Joanna should sit on it. She then walked over to the other side of the bench and leant her hips against the sink. 'But then I threw it out.'

Joanna almost laughed. She definitely smiled.

'I've imagined this a lot.' Alexandra filled two glasses with tap water and put them on the bench. 'You're usually bleeding by now.'

Joanna pulled the glass towards her and looked at Alexandra. 'I'd quite like that.'

The fridge was covered in school notices and happy photographs. As Alexandra tried her best not to fidget, failed, and started filling the dishwasher with breakfast dishes, Joanna knew what she'd always suspected. This was not the house of a neglected child.

Alexandra put powder in the dishwasher, shut the door, crossed her arms, uncrossed them, and took a large gulp of water. 'I'm sorry about Noah, I can't imagine how you're feeling.' She still hadn't offered eye contact.

Joanna hadn't rehearsed what she wanted to say but it didn't bother her now. Alexandra wasn't making her feel uncomfortable. The opposite. Odd, but she hadn't felt so re-laxed for a long time. Perhaps because the lying was about to end. It reminded her of the day after she and Alistair were outed. She couldn't stop smiling. It wasn't a happy smile, but one of freedom. She didn't have to lie any more. 'Have you ever read *Anna Karenina*?' Joanna found herself asking.

'I've seen the film. Not the Keira Knightly one.'

'Sophie Marceau?'

'Is she French?'

'Yeah, that's the best adaptation, but the book, God, I was obsessed with it as a teenager, re-read it year after year, and I bored my students silly with it before Alistair. Since him, I haven't been able to look at it. I didn't wonder why at the time, but now I know it's because of the book's theme: "You can't build happiness on someone else's pain".'

Alexandra turned the kettle on and spooned fresh coffee in the plunger, a sign that Joanna could go on.

'Alistair doesn't get the book, says, "What kind of woman would throw herself under a train for no reason?"'

'It's not the book Alistair doesn't get.'

The comment gave her shivers. How she wished she'd spoken to this woman as soon she heard of her existence. She felt sane for the first time in four years. 'You're not mad and you're not an alcoholic,' Joanna said.

'Oh, I don't know about that.'

'You're a good mother.'

'That's debatable too.'

'What was Alistair like as a dad?'

'He liked the theory of it.'

'So you felt Chloe would be better off without him?'

'I felt she needed me and her grandparents more.'

Joanna stiffened at the thought of her own father. Tucking her in one night, gone the next.

'He didn't tell me about you for a month. By then . . . it's no excuse.'

Alexandra stopped pouring water into the plunger, shocked, and looked at Joanna for the first time. 'I didn't know that.' She paused. 'It is an excuse. One that expired at four weeks.'

Joanna nodded slowly. Alexandra was funny, clever, wise. In different circumstances, she would have a girl-crush on her. She knew it would never be possible, but she wanted her to like her, or at least to connect. 'I wasn't a liar before him. Now that's all I am,' Joanna said.

Alexandra put mugs and milk on the bench.

'Maybe you're not, but I'm definitely mad,' Joanna continued, unperturbed by the lack of response so far. 'I can never make my mind up about anything. One second it's this, the next that . . . Last night I rang my counsellor in Glasgow. She's probably working out how to get me sectioned today. I told her I was trapped on a drama triangle.'

Alexandra raised an eyebrow and poured the coffee. 'Milk?'

Joanna nodded. 'When I'm near Alistair now, it's almost

like I can actually see it.'

'Victim, Rescuer, Persecutor,' Alexandra said.

'You know about that?'

Alexandra came and sat on the stool beside Joanna. She sipped her coffee in silence for a moment. 'If you're here to say sorry, I don't want or need to hear it. I'm okay.'

Joanna knew she wasn't lying. Everything about her, about this house, was okay.

'A small, weak word, sorry, but I am,' Joanna said. 'If I'm honest, mostly for myself. That's not why I'm here though.'

'Why, then?'

'A few things. Before I do anything I wanted to check what it's like here . . . for Chloe, with you.' Joanna knew what she'd just said came across all wrong: inappropriate, obnoxious. She cringed as soon as the words came out.

Alexandra stood up. If there'd been any bonding it had come to an abrupt end. 'Why don't you leave that to the social workers, eh?'

'That's the thing. I don't want the hearing. Now I'm here I know for certain I don't want him to take Chloe away from you.'

Alexandra walked back to the other side of the bench. 'He's not going to. Didn't he tell you he came to see me, said he wants us to work it out together?'

A wave of heat on Joanna's face. Once again, Alistair had given her information that was different from the truth. He'd told her one thing, Alexandra another. She shook her head, annoyed that this should surprise her. 'He told me he came to see you to warm you up. He still wants to take her back to Scotland, Alexandra.'

Alexandra lost her grip on the coffee mug. 'Fuck!' She raced to the sink, grabbed a cloth, and wiped the spilt liquid with a trembling hand. Joanna could almost feel the fury radiating from her. 'I assumed he meant we wouldn't go to court, but he didn't actually say that. God, I'm still such a fool. I should know how he works by now.'

Joanna understood exactly what she meant. Alistair had a knack for making you think you'd agreed on something, when you hadn't at all. 'I want to help,' Joanna said. 'She should be here in Australia, with you.'

'How are you going to help exactly?' The contempt in Alexandra's eyes scared Joanna.

'I . . . It's . . . Did he leave anything here? Have you found anything?'

'Why?'

'Are you sure? Can you have a thorough look?'

'He left a box with photos. You came here because he forgot something?'

'No, but I wonder if he did leave anything . . .'

'I emptied the box, just three photo albums. Nothing else.'

How should she say it? Did he leave Noah's bib in the box? He said he burnt it, but maybe he didn't. Or did he leave something else of Noah's? 'Just . . . have another look, to check. If there's anything odd get rid of it. Also I think everyone should know I'm a bad mother. Chloe should know he's a bad man.'

Alexandra stood with her hands on the sink, biting her lip again, visibly angry. 'I need to go to Chloe's school.' She was furious, and obviously wanted rid of Joanna.

'But I need to explain . . .'

Alexandra was already heading to the front door. 'I'll point you to the tram stop.'

She was a fast walker, or she was trying her hardest to shake off this shadow. Joanna put on her baseball cap and glasses, and practically ran to keep up with her all the way to the school round the corner. The concrete playground was swarming with groups of teenagers. For a brief moment, Joanna drank it in. She missed her old life.

'I don't want her to see you. The tram stop's just over there,' Alexandra said.

Joanna wasn't giving up, and wouldn't leave, not yet. She stood behind the tree and hid, something she became good at during the affair. Alexandra whistled, using her fingers, and Chloe skulked over.

'Checking up on me?' she asked.

'Yes. Are you okay?'

'No.'

'Why don't you go sit with Blake? Look, he's over there reading.'

'Why don't you mind your own business?' She began walking away, then turned back, guilty, and added, 'Sorry,

252

Mum. I'm okay.'

'I love you.' Alexandra blew a worried kiss at her daughter and watched her walk back to her lonely bench.

Alexandra then turned to Joanna and spoke with a don't-mess-with-me voice. The eye contact she'd yearned for was so intense and assertive she now wished Alexandra would stop looking at her. 'Listen to me,' Alexandra said, 'I am going to fight for Chloe and I'm going to win but I'm not going to turn her against her father. As much as I've hated him these years, I've bitten my tongue. I'm not a politician. I don't go for negative campaigns, dirty tactics. It's been almost impossible sometimes. But I don't want her growing up hating him. It'll screw her up. Despite her behaviour in the last two weeks, she's a happy girl. She doesn't want to live with him – with you – and she's mad with him for being a fucking hopeless father, but she loves him. It's really important for her happiness that it stays that way, that he's this fabulously successful father figure who loves her from a distance. So whatever it is you hope to do to help us, please make sure you don't mess any further with my daughter's image of her dad.' She paused and lowered her voice. 'We are not sisters-in-arms. Never contact me again.'

Before Joanna knew what was happening, Alexandra had turned and walked away, leaving Joanna and her stupid plan outside a secondary school in some place called Coburg.

*

A car whizzed by, brushing her handbag. 'Get off the road, ya mad bitch!' the driver yelled, tooting his horn until he disappeared round the corner. Joanna realised she shouldn't be standing in the middle of the road. Other pedestrians were waiting for the tram on the kerb. She clutched at her bag, walked to the kerb, and stared at the tram tracks.

She'd planned to be smiling by now but her lips were so heavy she felt she'd never manage to turn their edges up. Her eyes were fixed on the tracks. After satisfying herself that Alistair had not planted any evidence to frame his ex-wife, and that Chloe was safe and thriving, she'd planned to walk left, to the police station, where she would unload her torture. She even imagined Alexandra might come with her.

She was such a fool.

Joanna stood rigid and looked right, following the straight tracks that led back to her meeting spot with Alistair. She'd ruined Chloe's life once already. She wouldn't do it again. She wouldn't be the one to make a happy little girl with a fabulously successful yet distant father figure a miserable girl with a father who buried her half-brother, who lied to the police, to the world, to her.

Across the road a couple walked along the street, their little girl in between them. Holding a hand each, the couple counted to three and went *Wheee!* She remembered doing this in Queens Park with her parents. She remembered the things her mother told her after he left: that she should forget about him; that he didn't care about her so why should she care about him; that he was a bad man, a selfish man.

Oh, it was of such tedious interest to the counsellor that Joanna fell for Alistair shortly after her mother's death.

A tram was approaching. Joanna and her crime would get on it. They would go to the grave together. Until then she would live with Alistair Robertson and spend her days replaying the moment when she killed her son.

The Number 19 screeched to a halt in front of her. Joanna tossed her baseball cap and sunglasses in the bin, followed the other passengers onto the road in front of a queue of obediently stationary cars and got on, not caring now if people recognised her. She had a part to play, and she must play it, for the rest of her life.

*

A part to play. A role to act. A punishment to serve, person to be. A shop with lacy underwear in the window. Joanna got off the tram and walked towards it.

It was nestled in amongst the traditional Lebanese restaurants, organic cafes and slow-cooking eateries of Sydney Road. As she got closer, she saw it was called Rockabillies: vampire gear.

The tiny shop was empty bar an enthusiastic assistant wearing jeans and a black latex top with red lace. The woman pounced: 'Beautiful day!'

She could feel her lips shuddering at the rows of blood-thirsty sex gear. She spent a month's income on stockings, provocative pants and see-through bras when she and Alistair started dating. *Dating*: that's what she thought they were doing, in fact they were heading to hell. In the first months, she used to shave her pubes sitting on the edge of the bath, checking her work with a small mirror, then exfoliating and moisturising. She used to try on her new purchases in front of the full-length mirror in her bedroom. A couple of times, she took photos of herself to check if there were any stray hairs in the crack area and to hone her poses.

'This would look fabulous on you!' The shop assistant didn't seem to care that Joanna hadn't spoken. 'The Vampire Vixen!' She held up a short black dress with a high collar and absent middle except for the strings that tied it loosely from boob to pube. Joanna thought it was the least sexy thing she'd ever laid eyes on.

She noticed something on one of the racks at the back. Not the garment, but the name of it. 'The Immortal Mistress', she said out loud, eyeing the gaudy latex skirt and skimpy top, complete with fishnet stockings topped with red bows.

'That'd suit you too,' the assistant said, putting the Vixen back on the rack.

It sure would, Joanna thought. Immortal Mistress. It suited her down to the ground. 'I'll take it.'

'We only have a ten. Don't you want to try it on?'

'No.'

*

It was 1.30 p.m. when she got off at the stop in North Melbourne: half an hour to wait. To survive this new life, she would need assistance. And there was nothing wrong with needing a little assistance, long as you're careful not to confuse medicine bottles, long as you don't kill your child. The corner pub was dark and grotty. She chose a glass of house red, and downed three Valium with the first gulp.

'Hot outside?' the barman asked when she'd finished her second glass.

'Not sure.' She hadn't noticed the weather for weeks. Could be hot, could be not. She pushed the glass and nodded to order a third.

'Hey ... do I know you?'

'Don't think so.'

'Yes I do. Definitely. Or do you just come here a lot?'

'First timer!' Joanna downed her drink, banged her glass down for another.

'Ah, you play volleyball!'

She shook her head. Was this ever going to stop?

'You live in Moonee Ponds?'

'No.'

'Where do you live?'

'Edinburgh.'

'Edinburgh ... So your accent ...'

'Is Scottish.'

'Scottish, eh. I know you. I'm going to work this out. Scottish.' He thought hard, scrutinised her face, then it hit him like a very sluggish tsunami. 'Oh shit, mate. Sorry, really sorry.'

'That's okay,' she said, finishing the fourth glass. 'Why should you be sorry?'

'Just, you know, I just am.' The barman was so embarrassed he pretended he had something to do at the other end of the bar.

She only left without ordering another drink to save him the agony of having to talk to her again.

She fell over a crack in the concrete and bumped into a bin on the way to the meeting place. He was waiting in the car at the side of the road, tapping at his iPhone. She popped a mint in her mouth, took a deep breath, and walked as steadily as she could towards him.

'Hey, darlin',' he said, putting his phone in his pocket and kissing her on the lips. 'You have a good time?'

'It was fine,' she said. 'You?'

'Yep, but it's going to get better!' Alistair's surprise was a hotel on St Kilda beach. 'We so need to get out of Geelong,' he said as they drove along Beaconsfield Parade. 'Just us. Nothing else. We should really try and clear our heads and spend some time together, just for one night.'

'Did you catch up with Phil?' Joanna asked.

'Left a message but he never got back. Haven't seen Phil for seven years, can you believe that? My best mate and he hasn't been in touch since the accident happened. Y'think he'd at least phone me back.'

Accident. So that was the word to describe the moment she killed Noah. 'What did you do, then?' she asked.

'Waited for you.'

Liar. He must have done something other than wait. What? What did the arsehole do? For the rest of her life Joanna would have questions that she'd never even bother asking. That would be part of her punishment, she supposed.

*

It was a far cry from the hotels they used to meet in during the affair, when Alistair would sneak in a back entrance, Joanna entering the foyer a few minutes later. This one was five star, for a start, not the two-at-most they used to book online, using a false name and address, paying half each, in cash. Their room was on the fifth floor and had a view over the beach and across to the city's skyscrapers. Alistair emptied his pockets onto the desk. She used to find this so cute. Now she had an overwhelming urge to check through the scrunched receipts to find out what he'd been buying and doing. He went into the bathroom for a loud piss, leaving the door open, which he never used to do, so even if she could be bothered, which she couldn't, she wouldn't get away with snooping through his receipts. He came back into the room, opened the bottle of champagne he'd ordered in the bar in the foyer and poured her a glass. 'We shouldn't feel guilty trying to be happy,' he said, handing her the flute of bubbly. 'Being miserable and guilty doesn't bring him back. Noah wouldn't have wanted it.'

She laughed. What a fuckwit.

Alistair handed her the flute of bubbly, fear on his face. Only crazy women laughed like that.

'You think Noah wants me to get pissed and shag you?'

Alistair put his drink down and looked at her lovingly. 'I think Noah would want you to forgive yourself.'

'Do you forgive me, Alistair?'

'Of course.'

Ha, caught out. If he forgave her, that meant he thought it was her fault, all her fault.

'See, I don't think Noah would want me to forgive myself at all. I think he'd want to be alive.' She drank the champagne and poured another.

Alistair sat on the bed and put his head in his hands. 'Joanna, come back,' he said. 'Where have you gone? I can't take this any more. Please come back.'

Joanna gulped her glass down, refilled it, and drank another. If only she could be more like this dickwad. He was okay. He was coping. Right now, she envied him. Somehow he even managed to make her feel guilty about how he was feeling. As if she didn't have enough to feel guilty about. 'I'm going to get drunk.'

He lifted his head, optimistic – 'Good idea' – and poured her the third glass in twenty minutes. Four reds at the pub, three bubblies here. She was on her way to being proper wellied. 'Did you get some lingerie?'

Joanna took the Rockabillies bag out of her handbag and threw it on the bed.

'Ooh, stand in front of me!'

Joanna used to like doing as he asked, standing, stripping, touching herself, moving this way, that, while he worshipped her body.

She stumbled and fell to the floor as she took her shoe off. Neither of them giggled. She sat on the floor and ripped the rest of her clothing off in a hurry then staggered to a wobbly but upright position in front of him. The windows were open. The sun highlighted her luminous pale skin, bruised here and there from banging into pool fences and bins. She looked down and giggled at how unsexy she was. If only she'd always been this way. She wouldn't be here now.

'You're gorgeous, Joanna.' His expression did not match his words. 'How about I order some food?'

Joanna looked down and examined her thin pale frame. Her inner thighs were concave and a fold of skin had appeared on the inner edges at the top. Her breasts had burst like balloons: tiny, floppy, weak, empty. Fine pink spider legs spiralled out from each nipple. She touched the top of her pubic hair with her finger, tracing the fire-like stretch marks round and round, following the light brown line that first appeared during pregnancy all the way up to her belly button. She put one foot on a chair and examined herself in the mirror. Hard to tell, but different, definitely.

She stood in front of the mirror and smiled. Her body was

beautiful. There were signs all over it saying: 'Noah was here.'

'Why don't you put your outfit on?' Alistair sounded a little afraid of her. She liked that.

'Whatever you say, Alistair.'

She shut the bathroom door and sat on the edge of the bath. Right, where was she at again? Living this life – as it is now, with no prospect of change. How would she do that? When her father left she coped by burying herself in books and making lists of the positive things in her life (her mother was happy and healthy and beautiful, their home was lovely, Kirsty was always there for her, and always fun). When she and Mike split up she threw herself into gardening and made the list of positive things again (her mother was beautiful, her job was fun, Kirsty was always there).

And now, she would do the same, for Chloe. She had to live with Alistair for the rest of her life. And it would be better if she didn't hate his guts. Shaving at the side of the bath, she listed the things she used to like or love about him. What were they again? Um. He was successful. She liked that, didn't she? Confident, that had seemed nice. He was sporty, a bit, got on a bike every now and then. Well he did when they met, although often the bike ride was just the lie he told his wife. He twirled her in the hallway once and repeated 'I love you.' He bought her great birthday presents – once, a trip to Amsterdam, where they walked along canals, smoked in a coffee shop, giggled, walked, made love, smoked, ate an enormous Indonesian banquet in a weird bright room, smoked, made love, smoked, ate chips with mayonnaise, made love. And he was a beautiful writer, used to send her love letters every night – well, emails. She could remember one, almost by heart.

My darling,

There is no end to us. We are for ever.

Last night I was walking to the station and I spotted you with some friends in Hanjo's. I watched you through the window. Do you realise how people gravitate towards you? You were surrounded, and it's not because you're the most beautiful person in the room (which you are), or because you're the cleverest person in the room (which you are), it's because you are the most interesting person in the room. I can listen to you all day. I intend to do this for the rest of my life. Meet me tonight, Joanna. I need to hold you in my arms.

There is no end to us.

I am forever your

Alistair

This letter had made her giddy. She drank it in, over and over. On the train to work the words floated around before her eyes, coating her in a bliss-induced nausea, making her smile. She printed it out when she got home from work and held it to her chest in bed. Alistair was the best thing that had ever happened to her. Alistair was the greatest man on earth. He loved her. He thought she was interesting.

If he wasn't feeling those things right now, he might again.

And she could live with a man who felt that way, even if it did seem a bit odd in retrospect that he had 'spotted' her in a bar at night. Banish that thought, Joanna. He was not following you. He'd been at a meeting and had merely spotted her.

And banish the memory of the letter she found in the attic, which Alexandra sent him all those years ago. 'Al, this is the longest summer ever! When do you arrive at Spencer Street? I'll be the one wearing no knickers! Love Lex (The most interesting person in the room!) xxx'

So what if he'd used the same phrase with Alexandra? Joanna had used similar phrases with Mike and Alistair, and she'd meant them at the time – You're my best friend, You're my soul mate, I love you, for example. Anyway, perhaps Lex and Joanna were the most interesting people in the rooms to which he referred. It wasn't definitely a total crock of shit.

Oh fuck, she'd nicked herself with the razor.

She covered the bleeding spot with a small piece of toilet paper the way Alistair did when this happened to his face. She took the Immortal Mistress outfit out of her bag and put on the skirt. She had to keep her legs open a little to stop it from falling down. It hung on her hips precariously. A few minutes later, she opened the bathroom door, placing one hand on the frame to avoid falling over.

He was watching television and eating from a tray filled with room-service sandwiches.

'Hello!' Eyes up, down, up. No, not turned on. 'That's . . . is that a bit big? What size is it? Come, have a sandwich.'

As Joanna nibbled the pastrami sandwich on the bed, she wondered if this is how he had behaved with Alexandra: one moment she was his queen, sipping champagne on a steam train. She was perfect, pretty, his: all the way up there on a pedestal. Then, boom, toppled.

Of course this is how it had been for Alexandra. Why would it be any different for Joanna?

'What did you do while you waited for me today?' she asked.

'Nothing.'

'So from, what, 10 a.m. to 2 p.m. you did nothing?'

'Yeah, well, I had a coffee and I read the paper. Why?'

'And that took you four hours?'

'Why are you being like this? I didn't ask you how you spent your time. How did you spend your time?'

Joanna moved over to the dresser and started looking at the scrunched receipts from Alistair's pockets.

'What are you doing?'

'Just having a look.'

'Fine, read them.' A threat. Okay then, but I won't be happy.

'Forget it.' Joanna threw the receipts on the floor. She wasn't sure if she'd done this because she couldn't be arsed reading them or because she didn't want Alistair to leave. Oh God, yes, she was sure which one it was – the latter, she didn't want the fucker to leave. She was just the same as Alexandra was when he left her: unhappy, insecure, confused, needy, upset, pathetic, unattractive, and full of vicious fucking rage.

The arrival of another bottle of champagne from room

service halted the argument. When the door closed again, Joanna skulled another glass and stared out of the window.

She was old-Alexandra, but worse. Added to the mad alcoholic paranoia was the role she had to play. She couldn't pack her bags and run. She had to stay and suffer. This would be her punishment, holding this in, keeping silent, all on her own.

She drank another glass.

It was 4 p.m. In the old days, they'd have had sex once by now and be working towards round two. She'd be doing things his boring wife never did, like swallowing. Although that was probably a lie too. Alexandra probably downed bucket loads.

Alistair finished his last sandwich, turned the television off, and undressed. She noticed he'd put on weight: small love handles on his back; a bulge in the pelvic area which made his dick look smaller, or actually disappear into it a bit.

'Joanna,' he walked over and hugged her. His sticky nakedness made her sick. 'Hey, baby, no more of this, okay? I love you. I want to laugh with you again. I want to make love to you again.' He loosened the embrace so he could look at her. 'I want to marry you.'

The first thing that struck Joanna was that a proposal should not be made by a naked standing man unless you have just had sex with him, and even then it should be outlawed. It seemed the worst possible thing to do, worse than proposing underwater or in Japanese when your prospective fiancée doesn't swim/understand Japanese.

They'd talked about it before. Marriage obviously didn't mean much to him, she'd said to him. What we have is too good for marriage, he'd said to her.

She knew why he was asking now. He needed to own her, to watch over her, to make sure she never left him, broke down, ruined him, told the truth. This would be his part to play, she supposed, for the rest of his life.

Fair enough, Joanna thought. She needed someone to do those things. 'Do you still love me?' she asked.

He stood up straight, serious. 'You're my soul mate.'

'None of that shit. Just convince me you still love me.'

'I do,' he said. 'I still love you.'

'That's not convincing.'

'You're part of me. I wouldn't exist without you.'

'That's bollocks too. Do you still find me attractive?'

'Of course. Look at you, how could I not?'

'In what way?'

'You have the most beautiful smile. I miss it. It's your lips, your lips are my favourite part. Just the right size and shape and it looks like you have lipstick on when you don't and when you smile they take on this totally different, perfect shape. And those eyes . . .'

'Am I interesting?' She wasn't finding him so.

'You're definitely that!'

'I'll marry you on one condition.'

'Oh yeah? What's that?'

'I'll marry you if we stay here. For Chloe. We leave Chloe

with Alexandra, and you see her on weekends or work out some arrangement.'

'You're kidding, right?'

'No.'

He let go of her and headed to the bathroom, turning on the tap for a bath. 'I'm not leaving Chloe with that woman.'

Joanna followed him in. 'You said you had a good talk with her.'

He poured bubbles into the bath. 'She's nuts, I've told you that.' He pointed the bubble-bath container at her like it was a gun. 'She's a fucking alcoholic. What kind of woman kidnaps a child? What kind of person does that?'

'It wasn't kidnap. I don't think she's mad.'

'You don't know her.' He slammed the bubble bath down on the sink and got in the bath.

She was dying to tell him she did know her now, and that she liked her, hell – *admired* her. She stopped herself. 'We're worse.'

Covered in bubbles, Alistair sat up and pointed at her with his fist, the way politicians do. Don't use a finger, it's aggressive. 'We made one terrible mistake. What she did was deliberate and unforgivable.'

'Well I'll only marry you if we stay here.'

His fist retreated. 'Let's not talk about this today.' He ducked his head under the water. Conversation over.

Joanna left the bathroom, and started getting dressed again. She could hear Alistair splashing about. Both her legs wound up in one hole of her pants. She was so drunk. She corrected it and pulled on her dress.

'Joanna, what are you doing?' he yelled.

'I'm leaving.'

'C'mon, Joanna, we've got all afternoon and all night. Don't spoil things.'

She was drunk and fuming, but she would never forget her new mantra. To live the lie. To put an end to other people's suffering, even the arsehole she had to live with till she died. And maybe Alistair would soften. Or maybe they'd lose at the hearing. For now, she had to get the hell out of that hotel room. She put the Immortal Mistress outfit back in its bag and yelled back. 'I just need some air. You have a soak and a rest. I'm going to take this stupid lingerie back.'

*

Joanna hadn't planned on visiting Ms Amery. It just happened. She took a tram as far as Carlton, and headed towards the stop for the Number 19. She walked past the sunbathing students on the flat grass area of Melbourne University. Alexandra had studied law here. Alistair, politics and an MBA. The students looked happy here. Joanna imagined Alistair and Alexandra were happy here too: carefree, confident of a brilliant future, in love.

By the time she got to the main road, she'd tossed the Rockabillies bag in a bin, and typed Ms Amery's address into Google Maps.

Her house was only a five-minute walk. It was a two-storey Victorian terrace with ornate iron balustrades on the balcony and stained-glass windows. Seems she had money, this old lady. Joanna rang the doorbell, not sure why she was there or what she was going to say. She was about to ring again when Ms Amery opened the door wearing gardening gloves and a large straw hat. She looked much younger than she had on the plane, around sixty perhaps. She was slim, but not frail as Joanna had thought. Joanna didn't need to identify herself. 'Joanna! Come in, quick, out of the sun. You don't look well.'

The hallway had checkerboard tiles. They passed two large rooms on the way to the kitchen, both with hardwood floors and stunning fireplaces, one with a grand piano. She had taste as well as money.

Ms Amery took off her gloves and hat, put the old-fashioned kettle on the Aga and cut some slices of brownie from a baking tray. 'Good timing,' she said, putting several pieces on a plate and taking one. 'Eat!' She put a slice in Joanna's hand. 'Have you been drinking? You need to eat.'

Joanna struggled to chew the tiny bite she took. It was alien and unwanted and hurt her throat as it went down.

Books filled the shelves of the whitewashed antique dresser in the corner. Smooth Radio, or its Australian equivalent, played softly from the radio on the enormous country kitchen table.

It wasn't a very Australian garden, from what Joanna could see: winding brick path on a neat lawn, with curved borders bursting with colour. 'Your garden is beautiful.'

'It is! This summer's been hard on it. I'm afraid my bottle brush didn't make it.'

Joanna looked at one of the books from the dresser: *Illywhacker* by Peter Carey. 'You're a bibliophile.'

Ms Amery took the whistling kettle off the Aga and poured water into the pot. 'I used to be an editor. I'm good at details, noticing things others might not. That's my gift. I believe we all have one.'

Joanna put her hand under her chin and stared into the brownie tin. 'Yeah, I had one.'

She was crying, and Ms Amery was moving towards her with arms extended. It was the only hug Joanna had welcomed since. She sobbed on this stranger's chest. She imagined it was her mum holding her: her mum, who was always there when Joanna was upset, who told her she was perfect, and that she didn't need men. She remembered her mum's lingering, difficult death. Joanna had spent every spare minute trying to repay the selfless devotion she'd been given by taking her to the park in the wheelchair, reading books out loud, giving sponge baths.

A bright red rosella with blue and yellow wings flew in through the open door, the memory of her mother disappearing as it brushed her hair and landed on the sink.

Ms Amery laughed. 'Ooh, look who it is. It's Harold.' She moved over to the sink and put her hand out in front of the bird, and to Joanna's surprise he hopped on. She lifted him out the door and he flew away.

'You don't have a phobia, do you?' she asked Joanna.

'No.' Joanna watched the rosella fly once around the garden before settling on a lemon tree. She knew it was silly to wonder if it was the same bird she'd seen the morning after Noah died, but she did. 'I suppose you don't remember much about my baby,' Joanna said.

'My perfect bum's gone – believe me, it was perfect! – but not this.' She tapped her head with her finger. 'I remember everything.'

'I'd love it if you could tell me, please, anything.'

Ms Amery meant it when she said she noticed things. She started at the beginning – when she first spotted him in Joanna's arms at airport security in Glasgow. 'Babies don't all look alike,' she said. 'He had a cute little pear-shaped face, same as yours, exactly. Okay, so his eyes were his father's, but otherwise he was just like his mummy. Even his eyebrows.' She scrutinised Joanna's. 'Great shape. You don't even pluck them, lucky ... I over-plucked in the day. Don't ever do that, don't touch yours! They stop fighting back ... Noah. He was sleeping when you first boarded.'

Joanna didn't remember that.

'When I walked along the aisle to my seat, you were holding him and just staring at him, smiling. I felt a bit sad when I saw you. I never had children. I've never been in love like that.'

'Was I?' Joanna started to cry again.

'Yes! You were. You were a mother in love.'

It was a different cry now, Joanna's body relaxing as she did.

'When he woke you fed him. I could hear his noises from my seat. Gulping!' She made the noise. Squelch squelch squelch. 'I was surprised how loud he was. He was a noisy baby. After he was finished, you put him in the cot on the bulkhead and you sang to him while you checked his nappy.'

'Did I? What did I sing?'

'Because you're gorgeous . . .'

Joanna finished it, 'I'd do anything for you.'

'He slept for about ten minutes then woke again. I admit he did cry a lot after that. You tried everything. I wish I could have made it easier for you. I feel really bad about that.'

'I was hopeless.'

'No. He cried for hours. You were stressed. I would've opened the emergency door and tossed him out. Not really, sorry. But that sound makes everyone, every woman in particular, want to do anything, anything to make it stop. It doesn't have the same effect on men. It's like someone else's bad music to them. That man of yours didn't help much.'

'No?'

'When the baby started crying again before we landed in Melbourne he only lasted about ten minutes before he dosed him up.'

It took a few seconds for Joanna to hear those last four words. Everything that had come before had been so comforting she wasn't prepared to hear something that would change the world.

'He dosed him up?'

'Don't feel bad about that. All the children on that plane were doped to the eyeballs.'

'Alistair gave him medicine when I was asleep?'

'Typical man, asks for all the help he can get immediately.'

'He asked for help?'

'He asked me to hold Noah while he gave it to him.'

'Do you remember if he tasted it?'

'The baby?'

'Did Alistair taste the medicine first?'

'He got the suitcase out of the overhead locker, took the bottle out, filled a spoon, and put it in Noah's mouth while I held him.'

'He didn't taste it?'

'Why?'

'Tell me!'

'He didn't taste it.'

'Are you sure?'

'Alistair was wearing a grey T-shirt with a thin red trim around the neck and arms, and blue Diesel jeans, and white sports socks, and Nike Air runners. His bald patch was about four centimetres in diameter and he was very worried about people seeing it but thought they wouldn't if he tussled what was left enough and he did that a lot. His phone was in his right pocket the entire trip. He finished a small bottle of red wine with every meal, even breakfast. He has a small star-shaped birthmark on the right side of his neck. He didn't taste the medicine. I noticed that he didn't and I noticed that *you did*. Are you okay? Joanna? Joanna. Let me hold on to you. I've got you. I've got you. Joanna . . .'

*

The radio was still on.

'There's been a sighting in the Noah Robertson case. The nine-week-old baby boy was taken from the family's rental car nearly four weeks ago now and the reward raised by celebrities and donations is now at $750,000. Police say they're doing everything they can to identify the man caught on CCTV camera in Bangkok two days ago . . .'

'That's not him,' Joanna said, knowing she hadn't quite got the words out right.

She heard a shh and a click. The radio was no longer on.

Ms Amery wouldn't tell her to shh. She wasn't a shh kind of woman. She'd say something else altogether. Joanna opened her eyes.

The gasp she took was so loud it scared Ms Amery, who was standing beside Alistair.

Joanna sat up.

'Are you okay?' Ms Amery asked. 'I hope you don't mind. I found Alistair's number on your phone.'

Joanna looked out the window: pretty garden, rosella still on the lemon tree. She was on the sofa in Ms Amery's kitchen.

'Hey, missus, you fainted,' Alistair said.

She was tempted to use the little breath she had to protest against the 'missus' but decided to conserve her energy for things less petty.

'Must be the heat.' Joanna sat up and took a sip of the water Ms Amery was offering. 'I'm so sorry. I must have scared you.'

'And all that bubbly! Shall we get you home, missus?'

Oh God, he'd said it twice, in the only two sentences he'd said since she woke. He'd never called her that before. Was this because she had now morphed into his once-downtrodden ex-wife? He now owned her? Her brain swayed. Thankfully her skull didn't give it away by moving with it. 'Yeah, sure.'

She hugged Ms Amery and took Alistair's arm to be escorted to the car.

'Take me to Geelong,' she said, staring ahead as he pulled out of the parking spot. She longed to be on the road where Alistair had said, 'I always taste it, Joanna. Do you?' She longed to be on the road where he made her believe she had killed her baby. For now, getting to that road was all she could concentrate on.

She waited in the car as he collected their things and checked out of the hotel, and closed her eyes as they made their way to the West Gate Bridge, repeating these words in her head: *I didn't kill him. I didn't kill my baby.*

Beautiful, soothing words. She bathed in them.

Once they passed over the bridge, and she saw the land opening out to a sea of flat empty land, the words subsided, relief slowly giving way.

Alistair had a round of questions which he recycled, gathering facts no doubt. Just how mad was his partner, this woman he was now bound to for life?

Are you feeling okay?

Would you like some water?

How's that head?

When did you find your phone?

Why did you visit her? What were you talking about?

Are you feeling okay?

Why visit her?

Would you like some water?

What on earth were you two talking about?

Yes, no thanks, okay, don't know, no... she answered, when required, although she may have forgotten to answer the last one because she recognised the spot. The embankment. Nothing Field. Burnt land in the distance.

'Why are you so quiet?' Alistair asked.

She turned and pressed her hands against the window as they zoomed past the embankment. She could almost see Alistair standing on the roof of their hire car, trying to get a signal, and herself, on the ground, pressing a tiny chest, saying, 'One, two, three, four, five... One, two, three, four, five,' over and over.

'Oh come on, talk to me, Joanna,' Alistair said.

The embankment and the mirage had gone. She turned and looked at the flat road ahead. 'Why didn't you tell me?'

A cross, to the left.

'Tell you what?' Alistair was enjoying the drive: seatbelt off, as usual, leaning back, one hand on the wheel.

'You gave Noah another dose.'

He flinched and gripped the wheel more tightly with the one hand he was using to steer with, then tried to cover it up, loosening his grip again, tapping the wheel with his stumpy fingers. 'What are you talking about?'

'Why didn't you tell me you gave Noah another dose of medicine, before we landed in Melbourne, while I was asleep?'

Alistair tensed, straightened his back, upped the speed to a hundred and twenty kph. 'Where's this coming from?'

'Ms Amery remembers.'

'That old lady? You were asking her stuff like that? Jesus! What would she know?' Two hands on the wheel now.

'She knows. You didn't taste it.'

He turned and gave her a stern look. 'We're really going through all this again?' A hundred and twenty-five now.

She held his gaze with a sterner one. 'And you didn't tell me.'

A hundred and thirty. Face away from her and onto the road. Knuckles white, body leaning into wheel, like that first time they drove this way.

'Why didn't you tell me?'

Foot down. A hundred and forty. Slight rocking of the torso and head. 'See, this is why I didn't tell you. I knew you'd be like this. What are you doing talking to some old lady about this?' He stamped on the accelerator. 'FUCKING HELL!'

'Admit you didn't taste it.'

She waited through the long silence, but could almost hear his brain ticking with plans of attack.

His plan was to relax. 'What if I didn't?'

She was still looking at him, determined to get him to look back. 'Then it'd be your fault, Alistair.'

A quick glance, then back at the road. 'Did I ever blame you? Did I ever say it was your fault?'

'But it wasn't my fault!' she yelled. 'It was yours. And all this time you let me believe it was mine. You let me think I killed my son!'

'I never said it was your fault.'

'Oh that is so you, Alistair, so careful with your words. You never said it wasn't. You made me believe it was. You know that's true. You've lied so long you don't know how to tell the truth. You didn't see someone in a Japara that night, did you? You were thinking ahead. If it goes wrong, frame Alexandra.'

'That's ridiculous.'

She didn't know how fast he was driving now. Very.

'The shit I have put up with, Joanna,' he snarled. 'The way you behave like a fucking nutcase. You've been bloody hard work since we got together, you know that? Worse and worse every single day. I've been on Joanna maintenance full fuck-ing time for four fucking years. *I feel this. No, I feel that.* Oh I don't know what I think or feel! And now I'm the bad guy

279

here? It was a mistake. An accident. There's nothing we can do about it. Our son is dead. What does it matter who did it?'

Alistair accompanied each of the words that followed with a stamp on the accelerator, causing Joanna's head to thrust forward and lunge back with the movements of the car. '*WHAT. THE. FUCK. DOES. IT. MATTER!*

She held her neck. The shouting, the whiplash, the speed, it didn't scare her.

A signpost: EXIT TO AVALON AIRPORT, 2KM.

And suddenly it came to her that she knew how to get off the drama triangle.

In one swift movement, she grabbed the wheel.

It was magical, watching the triangle snap at the angles and break into three separate lines. They scattered out from the car, one of them cracking and separating into two on the way.

And so it was four lines, not three, that floated gently to the earth as the car careered towards the thick metal sign for Avalon.

Beautiful!

She smiled.

There would be two more crosses on the road to Geelong.

24

JOANNA

3 March

Joanna saw something.

She thought something: *Oh no. Oh no, no, no.*

She said something. 'Tell me I'm dead.'

Two figures were standing over her. 'You were in an accident,' one of them said.

'You're a very lucky woman,' said another.

'No!' she screamed, arched her back, ripped at the drip in her arm.

The two figures restrained her on the bed. They slowly came into focus: a female nurse, a female doctor.

'It wasn't an accident,' Joanna muttered.

'She's delirious. Poor thing,' the chubby nurse holding her legs said.

'No, no no!' She tried to wriggle free but couldn't lose that doctor's forearm which was weighing down on her chest.

'Calm down. This is scary, I know, but you're okay; everything's okay.'

She stopped wriggling. The drug was moving into her now.

The doctor released her and checked the drip. 'Joanna? Joanna? You've broken your arm and two ribs. The morphine will make you feel better.'

'Listen to me . . .'

'You can just press this button when you need more,' the nurse said.

'No, please!' She tried to sit up, the pain stopping her. She shouted: 'Please, I AM someone you should listen to!'

'Do you know if there's anyone we should call?' one asked the other.

Joanna calmed herself, tried not to yell: 'No, don't ring anyone. Listen. It was no accident. I did it on purpose. I meant it. I meant to kill us both. Why am I alive!'

She began to sob. She was alive. And no one was listening to her.

'Your seatbelt saved you.' The doctor's kind smile was so wrong here, take it away.

'Seatbelt?' She'd meant to take hers off. She'd forgotten.

The doctor took her hand off the morphine button and sat on the edge of the bed, all caring and worried.

'Is he alive? Tell me. Is Alistair dead?'

Placing one of Joanna's hands in hers, the doctor used her other to brush the hair away from her eyes as if she was someone she knew and loved. Joanna wanted to slap her, but she wanted information more.

After a few seconds, when she felt Joanna was sufficiently calm, the doctor nodded with textbook sympathy.

Joanna squeezed the doctor's hand until it made her wince with pain.

'Good.'

Part Three

THE CRY

25

ALEXANDRA

28 July

I'm in a rush. Chloe didn't want to go to school today so after okaying it with her teachers I had to wait for Mum and Dad to arrive. She's upset after being in court yesterday. Confused, too. Don't know why they needed her to testify. Like so much else that's happened, it's so unfair on her.

I'm late: no time to get the tram.

'Supreme Court, in Elizabeth Street,' I say to the taxi driver.

'You going to the Lindsay trial, by any chance?' the taxi driver asks a few blocks later.

'Um, yeah.' Shit, I don't want to talk to this guy about it.

'Do you know her or something?'

'No.'

'You a reporter?'

'No, just interested.' I'm not going to engage. Stuff him.

He pauses, desperate to get something out of me. 'I know a guy who worked with Alistair Robertson, some PR firm in St Kilda Road. Said he was a great man.'

'Right at the next one, yeah?'

'Right you are. You hear about the sighting?'

'And then second left.'

'Yeah, I know where it is. Some guy was in a garage holding a screaming baby – near Darwin. I have an uncle up there. Bloody hot, drinks a lot! Hard to see the man's face on CCTV.'

'Thanks. Here's just fine.'

'Hate to say it but the baby just looks like a baby to me. Just because he was crying doesn't mean he was kidnapped, I mean he'd be – what now? – seven, eight months?'

I hand over a fifty and wait at his window while he counts the change as slowly as he can. 'She's mad as a snake though, eh?'

'Thanks,' I say, and run inside.

*

I join the coffee queue in the court café. A blonde woman with a Scottish accent is in the queue ahead of me. When she turns to leave I recognise her from my Facebook stalking days – Kirsty, Joanna's best friend. She looks tired and drawn and her hair's frizzy – nowhere near as pretty as in the photos she used to post. She smiles and holds my eyes for a moment. I think she must know who I am. She says 'excuse me' then heads off to court with her takeaway skinny cap. The smile I return her is a bit shamefaced. She'll know why later, because I'll be taking the stand. Chloe was much calmer than I am. She knew what she wanted to say, I suppose. I don't have a clue.

Phil had been my courtroom spy yesterday. Last night he'd

told me what Ms Amery, Mrs Wilson and the trucker had said; how confident Chloe had seemed over the video link. In the afternoon an air stewardess had been called. She'd painted an ugly picture of Joanna, apparently, throwing her dirty looks as she relayed what happened on the plane: Joanna had flown off the handle when told the baby was up-setting the passengers, she explained. She'd accosted several passengers, held the baby as if he was 'some unwanted rub-bish', and been aggressive towards Alistair.

I recognise the air hostess from Phil's description (neat red bob, grey roots). She's whispering to her friend as I make my way to the stand, proud of herself after yesterday's fifteen minutes. I wish I hadn't insisted that Phil stay away today. I need him.

'Ms Lindsay came to see you the morning of the car acci-dent?' the defence lawyer begins. I look directly at him, care-ful not to see anyone else – especially Joanna, whose stare I can sense. Her lawyer has the kind of face I'd never tire of slapping: young, dapper, definitely private-schooled, Scotch College or Geelong Grammar, probably.

'She did.'

'Why?'

'She said she wanted to check if Chloe was safe and happy with me.'

'Did she say why?'

'She said she didn't want Alistair to take her. She said she was going to help me.'

'And how would you describe her behaviour that morning?'

'She seemed completely sane to me.' I'm not saying this to hurt her. I'm telling the truth. I accidentally look at her, and notice that she's smiling at me. She gives me a small nod.

The young Matthew Marks steps to his table and flicks some papers, pretending to look for something. 'I'm sorry, I didn't realise; are you a qualified psychiatrist, Mrs Robertson?'

'It's Ms Donohue.' I say.

He lifts his eyes to the judge, who responds as he wishes: 'Strike that last comment please. Ms Donohue is not qualified to assess the defendant's mental health.'

I'm not saying what I'm saying to help the prosecutor make sure that Joanna is punished as severely as possible. I'm saying what I'm saying because it's the truth.

'So how did she behave, then, the morning she came to see you?' the defence lawyer asks.

'She was articulate. She made sense.'

Joanna's smile is as big as the prosecutor's. Unnerving. If the defence lawyer asked me how I think she's coming over now, I would say she's definitely mad. But she wasn't, not that morning.

'So Joanna Lindsay visited you at around 10 a.m. and said she did not want her husband to take Chloe away and that she wanted to help you. Did she mention anything about her relationship with Alistair Robertson?'

I wrack my brain. What did she say again? 'Well, she said something about ringing her counsellor in Glasgow the night before and coming over a bit crazy . . . I think she was understandably stressed.'

I've said what the private-school wanker wants me to say. 'I'd like to refer to a statement given by the counsellor in question, Mrs Anne Docherty from Rutherglen in South Lanarkshire,' he says, reading from a sheet he's lifted from the table, 'who reports that Ms Lindsay called her the night before the alleged murder and sounded – and I quote, "bizarre and incoherent".'

'Well she wasn't like that when I saw her,' I say.

'No, Mrs Robertson, but you're unlikely to say she was mad, aren't you? You're unlikely to want my client to be deemed mentally ill when she stole your husband from you and then killed him, leaving your beloved daughter fatherless. You'll be wanting the full force of the law. You'll be wanting her to be convicted of murder, not manslaughter.'

'Objection!' I'm not sure who just yelled this. I'm sweating, shaking. I want to go home. Joanna looks like I do now: annoyed, upset. I can tell from her body language that she hates her lawyer as much as I do. Before the judge can respond to the objection, Joanna's lawyer has taken his seat, victorious, and closed his folder with a 'No further questions.'

*

The courtroom is deadly silent when I walk from the stand and take a seat at the back. To my surprise, Joanna's friend Kirsty gives me an understanding smile as I pass. There's a pause. Everyone is waiting for the clerk to speak. He does, eventually.

'The court calls Joanna Lindsay to the stand.'

Joanna fidgets with her dress before standing.

'Ms Lindsay, can you please make your way to the stand?' The judge's tone is kind because she obviously believes she's dealing with a mad woman. That's what this whole event has been about – her insanity – and I can't deny she has been coming across as completely bonkers.

'Of course,' Joanna says. The artist at the front begins scratching away at her sketch pad. Joanna is wearing Antichrist clothes. It's almost as if she wants everyone to hate her. Yesterday she wore a black miniskirt and tight white sleeveless top. Today it's a short, shoulderless red dress with a slit at the side and a small rip. The artist laps up this murderous woman in her adulterous dress. Joanna stands and turns to smile for the artist. Then she looks at the judge and says: 'I can do anything I set my mind to.'

Journalists are tweeting openly and onlookers are doing it secretly. I'm curious and sneak a quick look at the #joannalindsay thread as she walks slowly to the stand and takes her oath.

Fiona Mack @Fionamack
Diminished responsibility my arse #joannalindsay

Harry Dean @hdean
The woman's a fucking nutcase. #joannalindsay

Bobblypops @bobblypops
She's smiling. #joannalindsay #joannalindsayisevil

Bobblypops @bobblypops
She looks like the devil #joannalindsay #joannalindsayisevil

ABC News @ABCNews
Follow us for updates of case against #joannalindsay

Bobblypops @bobblypops
Don't know why the woman from the plane yesterday was trying to be nice to her. She shook the baby. #joannalindsay

Jennifer Weston @jenniferwritesbooks
@bobblypops and killed her husband #joannalindsay

Bobblypops @bobblypops
@jenniferwritesbooks Shouldn't reduce the punishment just cos she confessed. #joannalindsay

Fiona Mack @Fionamack
@jenniferwritesbooks @bobblypops and shouldn't reduce if she's mad either. #joannalindsay

Bobblypops @bobblypops
@fionamack Bad, not mad. Bad. #joannalindsay #joannalindsayisevil

Jonathon Mitchell @johnnyonthepress
I was on the plane with her. She was OUT OF CONTROL!
#joannalindsay

Jane McDonald @janexmacker
She was in my breastfeeding group in Edinburgh.
#joannalindsay

Bobblypops @bobblypops
@janexmacker Really? What was she like? #joannalindsay

Jane McDonald @janexmacker
@bobblypops Best word – loopy. #joannalindsay

Bobblypops @bobblypops
I heard she ripped down one of the missing posters in
Geelong. Why would you do that? #joannalindsay

Jonathon Mitchell @johnnyonthepress
@bobblypops Cos you're a nutjob #joannalindsay

Taniadoeshair @taniadoeshair
Still think she killed baby Noah.
Shame www.lonniebabytheevidence.com has been taken
down. #joannalindsay

Jonathon Mitchell @johnnyonthepress
She defo killed the baby as well, guilty as f**k #joannalindsay

NonnaAngela @nonnaangela
She killed baby Noah. Kidnapping my arse. Guilty as f**k
#joannalindsay

Miketheteacher @MikeWilkes
Oh come on people. Leave her alone. She lost her
son.#joannalindsay

Bertiebeans @bertiebeans
RT @nonnaangela She killed baby Noah. Kidnapping my
arse. Guilty as f**k #joannalindsay

Jim Groves @JimmyChews
What's the difference between Noah Robertson and Noah
Robertson jokes? The jokes will get old. #joannalindsay

Bertiebeans @bertiebeans
@JimmyChews Ba-boom. I didn't know there were dingoes
on the Bellarine Peninsula. #joannalindsay

Bobblypops @bobblypops
OMG! Have you seen what she's wearing!! Scarlet black wid-
ow. #joannalindsay #joannalindsayisevil

Bobblypops @bobblypops
You see that? She smirked when she took the oath. Smirked.
#joannalindsay #joannalindsayisevil

The tweets revolt me. I put my phone away just as the prosecutor asks Joanna if she understands why she's here. She's skeletal, eight stone at most. Her hair's tied back severely. She has too much make-up on, including thick black eyeliner. She's wearing the sluttiest dress I've ever seen. She's smiling, or, yeah, smirking. She's read the manual on how to look and behave in court and is doing everything wrong, everything. Yep, definitely a smirk.

She's sitting down.

'Ms Lindsay, you have already confessed to the murder of Alistair Robertson,' the prosecutor states.

Joanna's young male lawyer gets to his feet. 'Objection! Ms Lindsay admits to the manslaughter of Alistair Robertson on the grounds of diminished responsibility. As evidenced in the psychiatric reports submitted to court yesterday, she was not and is not of sound mind.'

Judge: 'Sustained. Rephrase, please, Ms Maddock.'

'Very well, Your Honour. Ms Lindsay, as Mr Marks has just informed us, your defence is that you are not of sound mind, and cannot therefore take full responsibility. How do you feel about telling the world you are mad?'

Matthew Marks is on his feet again, but Joanna shakes her head.

'I know what my lawyer says and what the psychiatrists argue – that I was suffering from post-traumatic stress disorder following… after Noah… after what happened to Noah. They say I was severely depressed, had flashbacks, that I was hallucinating, behaving oddly. Okay, so maybe, but that's all irrelevant. I didn't kill Alistair because of post-traumatic stress disorder. I killed him because I wanted to. Am I hallucinating now? No. I want to take full responsibility for this. I want to be punished,' she says. 'Convict me of murder because that's what I did. Sentence me to life imprisonment because that's what I deserve. It's my fault and my fault alone. It's not Noah's fault because he wouldn't stop crying, or the Emirates staff because they didn't help me and it was not the fault of airport security.'

'Airport security?' the prosecutor says. 'What do you mean?'

'I mean I want to take responsibility. Why is it so hard for everyone to understand that? Don't listen to my clever young lawyer. Don't listen to anyone but me. I killed him. Take me away. Put me away.' She's shaking now. 'God, please!'

There's a shuffling in the court. She's making everyone very uneasy and I don't think it's because she's completely bonkers, which she clearly is, I think it's because her desire to take the blame leaves these venomous onlookers with nowhere to place their poison.

Joanna's lawyer is smiling in his front-row seat. Hallelujah! His client is coming across as a total nutjob, just as he hoped.

'You're saying you knew what you were doing when you killed him?'

'Yes!' Fury takes her tears away. 'Why do I have to say it so many times? How can it be so hard to be convicted of this? I knew he didn't have his seatbelt on. I knew we were going at a hundred and forty kilometres an hour. I wanted to kill us both. I took hold of the steering wheel. I swerved the car into a road sign.'

'But you had your seatbelt on?'

'That's where my cross ended up and I have to bear it. I forgot to take my seatbelt off. I'm forgetful. I'm an idiot.'

People shuffle uncomfortably at her answers.

'And you confessed to the police that you murdered your partner?' the prosecutor says.

'Jesus. Am I speaking Swahili or something? Yes! I've confessed to everyone.'

There's a fresh flurry of texting and tweeting. The artist turns the page and starts a new sketch.

'Why, Joanna? Why did you kill him?' the prosecutor asks.

She hesitates, thinking hard before answering carefully. 'I killed him because I couldn't stand to be with him for another second.'

'I'd like to ask for a short adjournment, Your Honour.' Joanna's lawyer has taken to his feet and donned a look of concern. I don't think he's asking for a break because his client is suffering up there, but because asking for a break adds to his whole mental-case case. 'My client is clearly distressed and in need of a break.'

'One thing I'm definitely not is too distressed to talk!' Joanna yells.

The judge takes a long moment to examine Joanna – and seems to agree that she's not very well: 'The court is adjourned until 2 p.m.'

*

I can't wait around till the afternoon. Chloe needs me. Anyway, it's not doing me or anyone any good being here. It's time for me to let go.

Joanna hasn't been taken away from the courtroom yet. The old lady who spoke yesterday, Ms Amery, has walked up to the front and is talking to her, holding her hand. Joanna has a pleading look in her eye as she says something. I lip read – Joanna says thank you. She then hugs the old lady, who walks past me purposefully.

I have to get out of here. I have to move on. I want to see Chloe and Mum and Dad and Phil.

I want to stop feeling what I've started feeling: sorry for her.

I want to start enjoying what I've stopped feeling: rage.

I've just made it out into the real world when a female voice yells my name.

When she catches up with me she's out of breath. 'Alexandra,' she says again, 'I'm Kirsty McNicol, Joanna's friend. I don't blame you if you don't want to talk to me, but I wondered if you might have time for a coffee?'

I look at my wrist to delay the making of a decision, remember I haven't worn a watch for years, and say, 'Sure.'

We sit in a booth in an old-fashioned Burke Street cafe,

coffees before us. 'Joanna asked me to give you something,' she says, taking a package out of her bag. 'I don't know what it is but I said I would.'

I take it and stop myself from tearing it open. What on earth would she want to give me?

'You have more reasons than anyone to hate her,' Kirsty says, 'but . . .' She starts crying, grabs a napkin from the holder and carefully wipes leaking mascara from under her eyes. 'Oh, nothing. You should hate her. She was an idiot.'

'What were you going to say?'

'She was so good before him!' Her mascara can't be fixed this time. It's dripping from the thick eyelashes of this loyal friend. 'I've known her since we were at nursery together. Such a smiler! We've been inseparable since then, except when she was sneaking around with him. And her mum – she was just the same. A kind soul. I know it's hard to believe but she's not who everyone thinks she is. She's not evil. That fucking man . . . Just like her father. I'm sorry.'

'No, no, it's okay.' I hand her another napkin. She really needs it.

'I'm not just saying she was good, she really was. Before him, I don't think she'd told a single lie. She was fun. Happy. I loved her so much.' She smiles, wipes her eyes. 'I'll let you get home, eh. I really don't know what's in that package, but if you ever want to talk to me, here's my card.' As she withdraws her hand from the table, she knocks over a glass.

'That's me: bull in china, bur in linen,' she says, putting the

300

glass upright again.

'Sorry?'

'Oh nothing; it's from a poem I like.'

That's right, the one Phil's always quoting. His 'Ode to Al'.
'That one about the klutz,' I say.

'No, no. It's a poem about love. He adores her.'

She hands me the card, places a ten-dollar note on the
table for the coffees, and holds her hand out to shake mine.
Once she's out of sight, I look at her card: Kirsty McNicol,
Events Manager, and an address in Islington. I leave it on the
table and head to the tram stop, her last words making me
smile as I imagine Phil.

It's a poem about love. He adores her.

*

Of course, I can't wait till I get home to look in the package.
I get a seat to myself on the Number 19 and I open it as
the tram rattles through the city and into Carlton. Inside is
a Bananas in Pyjamas teddy bear, a handwritten note and a
printed letter.

The note reads:

Alexandra,

*This package was in Alistair's briefcase. I thought Chloe should
have it.*

I wish I could find better words, but I am so sorry, for everything,

Joanna.

The letter has been printed onto a single A4 sheet. I tell myself it's absolutely necessary to read it before giving it to Chloe, just in case he's said something that might upset her.

My darling Chloe,

You are the most important person in the world to me. That will never change. I am your father, for ever, and you are my beloved daughter.

You shine, Chloe. Wherever you are, people gravitate towards you. It's not because you're the most beautiful person in the world (which you are), or because you're the cleverest person in the world (which you are), it's because you are the most important person in my life. I want to watch you and listen to you all day, for the rest of my life.

I have been so upset these last days, after what happened to your baby brother. I don't want you to see me this way. But I will come and see you soon, my darling girl. I will come and see you and I will be the best father I can be, the father I want to be, the father you need.

I want you to do something for me, Chloe. Can you try not to be consumed by what happened to Noah, by not knowing what happened? Instead of being angry and lost, I want you to try and connect with him, feel him – when you're in the garden, or playing with your animals, or holding his favourite Bananas in Pyjamas teddy bear? It's not forgetting. It's not giving up. It's loving. It's living, again, just as the charred grass and the trees will. It's what Noah would want you to do.

I love you, for ever,
Daddy xxx

The letter oozes Alistair – the turn of phrase, the composition, the beautiful bullshit that used to make me fly with happiness. Even the fact that it's typed – edited and re-edited till it's perfect. But there's something about it that doesn't feel right. I can't put my finger on what it is, but I'm uneasy.

I'm reading it again when Chloe arrives home from school.

'How was the court?' she asks. She's been crying. She looks so sad. She *is* consumed and angry and lost. All I can think about is how Alistair's letters made me feel in the early days: jubilant, wonderful. I wish I never found out that they were bullshit.

'Honey,' I say, 'I have something for you. From your daddy.'

26

JOANNA

Two years later

It was time to listen to Noah.

Joanna didn't realise she'd recorded him until she arrived back in Glasgow. 'Arrived' is a pretty word for it – she was deported and placed in a facility for mad folk. *That* was her arrival. During her first week in the hospital she listened to Noah all day, every day. Listening was torture in the hospital, and they took Alistair's phone away.

The counsellor wasn't a total idiot, but Joanna didn't think she needed to see her any more. She went because she had to go. She had to see her and she had to see a criminal justice social worker and she had to see a quack and she had to take the antidepressants.

Last visit, the counsellor announced that Joanna was ready to have the phone back. 'But don't listen to the recording,' she said. 'You shouldn't be encouraging anguish. Or, if you must, limit how often. Dedicate a half an hour a day to private mourning and maybe listen just once then, but not all the time, not over and over like you did at Leverndale.'

'I don't feel anguish any more,' Joanna said.

The counsellor didn't believe her. 'How's that?'

'Have you ever read *Anna Karenina*?' Joanna asked her.

'No.'

'The theme is this: "You can't build happiness on someone else's pain".'

The counsellor nodded for more.

'Alexandra and Phil were married a month ago. Chloe was bridesmaid. There are photos online.'

She nodded again.

Joanna smiled. 'They're happy!'

The counsellor was confused. 'What are you saying?'

'I'm saying I can build a life on that.'

*

Joanna planted two Lilly Pilly trees a while back. The first had grown to six feet, and was in the middle of her quaint stone-walled garden in Pollokshields, Glasgow.

Well, she hadn't really planted the second. But she bought the block of land it now rests on, and asked Ms Amery if she'd plant it for her. Ms Amery didn't ask why, she just did it.

It's twelve feet tall now. The Australian sun, she supposed. She knew this because Phil's Facebook profile was public. He'd posted two shots of the wedding at Healesville animal sanctuary a month ago, and one of the back garden in Point Lonsdale last week.

Phil's Famous Sunday BBQ! is written above the shot. Phil and Alexandra are laughing as he pours his wife some bubbly, the barbecue stacked with sausages and burgers beside them.

Chloe's lying on one of the deck chairs on the woodchip, a cute terrier snuggled on her tummy. The sky's deep blue, and the tree Ms Amery planted is overhanging the back fence. It's bursting with gorgeous pink berries.

Joanna had copied the image and zoomed in on the tree.

And there it was, on one of the branches: a bright red rosella with blue and yellow wings.

*

She decided to have her private mourning session from 5 a.m. till 5.30 a.m. That'd be around lunch time in Australia. It was summer in the UK, the sun would rise here around then.

She had eight mouthfuls of natural yogurt and did twenty minutes of yoga in the living room. She read seventeen pages of a book, more than she managed last time, which was good.

She checked the time: 4.53. The barbecue would be well alight now.

She placed a blanket on the earth underneath the Lilly Pilly tree. She plugged her earphones in, checked the time again.

The recording was a voicemail message from Joanna to Alistair. She wasn't sure, but she figured the call was made a day or so before the trip. 'Just ringing to check what time you'll be home,' Joanna said. 'Gimme a call. Love you.' But she hadn't hung up properly, and after that there were two minutes of Noah. Crying.

As Joanna waited for the phone's clock to reach 5:00 she

recalled what one of the mothers at the breastfeeding group said: 'He's trying to communicate with his beautiful little voice. You just need to listen.'

She was nervous. When he was alive, it made her crazy. She thought he was so unhappy, judging her, yelling at her: *You're doing everything wrong!* But she now believed the mother was right. He was just calling out to her.

She lay down on the ground and looked up at the dark green leaves.

She closed her eyes and focused: *Phil and Alexandra, laughing. Chloe on a chair on the woodchip, under the shade of the Lilly Pilly tree. The rosella.*

She pressed Play.

Also by Helen FitzGerald

The Donor

Two daughters. One impossible choice.

Just after her sixteenth birthday, Will's daughter Georgie
suffers kidney failure. She needs a transplant but her type is
rare. Will, a single dad who's given up everything to raise his
twin daughters, offers to be a donor.

Then his other daughter, Katy, gets sick. She's just as precious,
her kidney type just as rare. Time is critical, and Will
has to make a decision.

Should he try to buy a kidney? Should he save just one child –
if so, which one? Should he sacrifice himself? Or is there
a fourth solution, one so terrible it has never
even crossed his mind?

'Everybody should read everything that Helen FitzGerald has
written. She is dark, clever, highly inventive.'
Lovereading.co.uk 2011 Great Reads Pick

ff

Dead Lovely

What happens when your best friend gets what you've always wanted?

Krissie and Sarah – best friends for years – have always wanted different things from life. Krissie has no desire to settle down, whereas Sarah married a doctor in her early twenties and is dying to start a family. So when Krissie becomes pregnant after a fling and Sarah can't seem to conceive, things get a little tense.

Krissie and Sarah decide to go on holiday along with Sarah's husband in the hope of getting their friendship back on track. But what starts as a much-needed break soon becomes a nightmare of sexual tension, murder and mayhem . . .

'Outrageous, clever, funny, poignant. Helen FitzGerald really is one to watch.' **Mo Hayder**

'A gripping, addictive psycho-thriller.' *Big Issue*

'Gloriously black comedy.' *Herald*

ff

My Last Confession

**A naïve parole officer in her first month on the job. An
extremely good-looking convicted murderer.
What could go wrong?**

These are some of Krissie's tips for fellow parole officers:

Don't smuggle heroin into prison.
Don't drink vodka to relieve stress.
Don't French-kiss a colleague to make your boyfriend jealous.

If only she'd taken her own advice . . .

When she starts the job, Krissie is happy and in love. Then
she meets convicted murderer Jeremy, and begins to believe
he may be innocent. Her growing obsession with his
case threatens to jeopardise everything – her job, her
relationship and her life.

'Thinking woman's noir.' ***Sunday Telegraph***

'Cool, classy, sexy.' ***Daily Mirror***

'Satisfyingly shocking.' ***Big Issue***